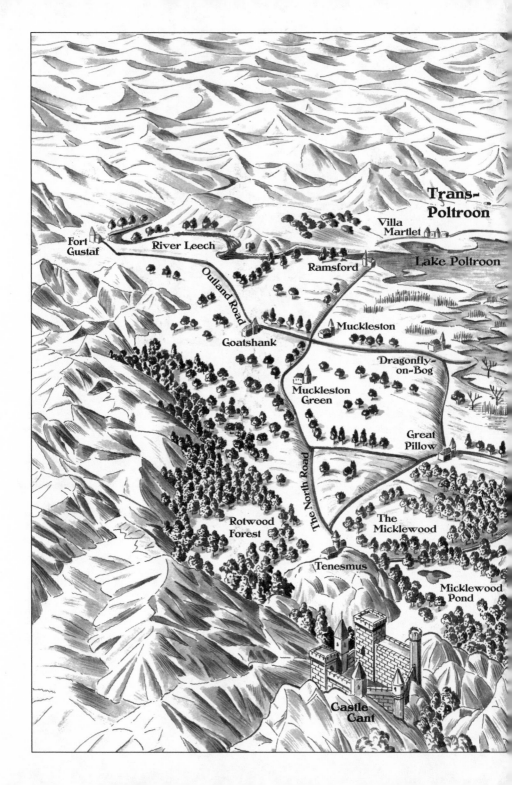

THE SECRET OF CASTLE CANT

*Being an account of the remarkable
adventures of Lucy Wickwright,
maidservant and spy*

K. P. Bath

With artistic embellishments by
David Christiana

LITTLE, BROWN AND COMPANY
New York ❧ Boston

Text copyright © 2004 by K. P. Bath
Illustrations copyright © 2004 by David Christiana

Little, Brown and Company

Time Warner Book Group
1271 Avenue of the Americas, New York, NY 10020
Visit our Web site at www.lb-kids.com

First Edition

Library of Congress Cataloging-in-Publication Data

Bath, K. P. (Kevin P.)
The secret of Castle Cant / by K. P. Bath — 1st ed.
p.   cm
Summary: When twelve-toed orphan Lucy Wickwright is brought to Castle Cant to
be serving girl to the Baron's daughter, the Adorable & Honorable Pauline, she becomes
involved with revolutionaries and uncovers surprising palace intrigues.
ISBN 0-316-10848-0
[1. Orphans — Fiction.   2. Identity — Fiction.   3. Fantasy.]   I. Title.
PZ7.B3225Se 2004
[Fic] — dc22   2004003643

10   9   8   7   6   5   4   3   2   1

Q-FF

Printed in the United States of America

Map and heraldry illustrations by Rodica Prato
Chinese calligraphy by Victor Hsu

The illustrations in this book were done in pencil and ink on
200-lb. soft press Fabriano Uno paper.
The text was set in Centaur, and the display type is Swank.

In memory of Bill and Helen Johnson

A Note from the Author

$\mathscr{I}$f you grew up in a small town, you're probably familiar with the blank or skeptical looks that small-town folk are given when they mention their birthplace. Imagine growing up in a small and little-known *country,* and facing those looks wherever you go. The memoirs of the writer and explorer Lady Glace are filled with such encounters:

> After sherbet had been served, and that thick coffee poured of which I spoke, the Sultan reclined in his cushions and asked, "What part of the world I was pleased to call home?" I told him that I took the world for my home, but that I first drew breath in the Barony of Cant. His Eminence puzzled at this, and called for a globe to be brought him. I was at some pains to convince him that my home-land was real, for he had heard no word of it before, and it was not to be found on his globe, or indeed in any of his maps or atlases at all.*

Few, indeed, have heard of the Barony of Cant, and I've developed a great sympathy for Lady Glace since I began work on this book, a history of recent events in her homeland. Often I've found myself defending the mere reality of the Barony to those who have never heard of it, and who assume, therefore,

---

*Glace, Heseltine Constance. Travels by Camel and Ass. Tenesmus, 1912.

that it can't exist. I've been accused of plotting a hoax, or — worse! — of writing a novel. Publishers are the greatest offenders. Upon reading my manuscript they are apt to get a ghastly twinkle in their eyes, and encourage me to turn Cant into a "magical fairy kingdom" that "appears on no map" — as though I were nothing but a tiresome fabulist.

There is nothing "fairy" about Cant. It is as real as China or Laputa.

Nor is it true that the Barony appears on no map. It is routinely printed on maps — the difficulty is that it's rarely *found* on them. This is due both to the great smallness of the Barony and to its unfortunate geography. Cant sits precisely in the middle of its part of the world, and no sooner do you fold a map of the region than the Barony is simply lost in the crease. A patient student, with a magnifying lens and a not-too-often-folded map, can sometimes discern a tiny "B" or "t" at the latitude and longitude of Cant. But the Barony is admittedly hard to find.

It is also remarkable for its willful, even stubborn isolation from the modern world. In many ways it is a land out of time. Ringed by mountains, isolated for centuries, the Barony sees few visitors except for occasional geographers or intrepid hikers, who are greeted with aloof politeness, tolerated with much muttering, and bidden farewell with gifts and glad smiles.

Cant possesses neither steam irons nor televisions; ball pens and zippers are equally unknown. Travel is by foot or hoof or sail. But it is plain egotism to say — as one sub-assistant editor did, in rejecting my manuscript — that "no such place exists." The Barony may lack flush toilets, child leashes, and other marvels of the more developed nations, but it exists quite well without them. The events described in this book took place in living memory, and the facts may be confirmed in their broad outlines by the patrons of any tavern from the castle to Boondock. I offer this narrative in hope that others will be touched, as I was, by its tale of courage, devotion, and love.

I am grateful to the principals, who gave me the story in their own words, along with their kind permission to share it with the larger world. Thanks are also due my tireless secretary, S. Underfoot.

K. P. Bath

Chapter 1

$\mathscr{S}$pring had come to the Barony of Cant. New grass waved beyond the sheepfolds, and the flocks fairly ran to the shears, eager to be free of their wooly winter coats. The streams sang of melting snow, and high clouds grazed the pastures of the sky. Only an eagle troubled the springtime ease of pasture, brook, and sky. It rode the warm air seeking prey, and when its wings crossed the sun they cast a menacing shadow on the land.

Lucy Wickwright saw the bird, but she had other troubles to contend with this morning. She pushed her glasses up her nose and looked down from her high perch on a tower of Castle Cant.

"The grown-ups aren't going to like this," she sighed.

"Wickwright," said Pauline, "would you quit gawking and make yourself useful?"

Lucy turned around. The Adored & Honorable Pauline Esmeralda Simone-Thierry von Cant was bent over the catapult, a strand of hair dangling in her face. She and Lucy had wheeled the weapon around so that it faced the courtyard, and now Pauline struggled at the winch, her tongue sticking out as she slowly cranked down the throwing arm.

"Mistress," Lucy said, stepping away from the parapet, "I don't think — respectfully — that this is such a very good idea."

Lucy was Pauline's maidservant and had to address her as "mistress," even though she was a year older and nearly a thumb taller than the Baron's daughter. Except for her weekly half-holiday, on Saturday afternoons, Lucy spent the better part of every day caring for Pauline. She dressed her mistress in the morning, served her at table, and tidied her chambers at night. She was also encouraged (in the words of the *Constitution for the Benevolent Employment of Men-at-Arms, Artisans, Husbandmen, & Domestic Servants*) "to satisfy all the Whims & Requests of the Noble Person, excepting such as may give rise to Treasons, Gross Offenses, &c."

Pauline, unfortunately, was terribly prone to Whims.

"The trigger!" she said. "Hurry! My arms are breaking!"

Lucy knelt beside the creaking engine of war and guided the iron catch of the trigger into a ring on the throwing arm. Pauline let go the winch, and the heavy beam caught the trigger with a terrible *clank!* Lucy stepped away as the machine popped and groaned in frustration, like an old man trying to get up from his chair. Pauline brushed her hands on her snowy pinafore.

"So," she said with a satisfied smile, "what do you think *now*?"

Lucy glanced nervously toward the parapet.

"Maybe we could wait till later," she suggested.

"But then no one would *see*," Pauline said. "Come, help me to load it."

The ammunition steamed in a wicker basket at their feet. The girls had crept into the baronial laundry and collected the wet heap of underclothes while Mr. Fuller and his assistants sipped their morning tea. There were long bloomers with frilly gathers, balloonish drawers embroidered with the baronial crest, sleek slips, plain vests, and complex corsets with snapping straps. They had stopped to rest three times as they hauled the basket up the winding steps of the tower.

"This is a madcap caper, Wickwright!" Pauline said, grasping a handle of the basket. "I'm such an imp! This will go down in *history*! On three, then. One! . . ."

Lucy bent over the basket.

"Please to lift with your knees, mistress," she advised.

"Two! . . ."

Lucy gripped the handle.

"Two and a half! . . ."

Lucy held her breath. One never knew how many fractions Pauline might count.

"Two and three quarters! . . . *Three!*"

They upended the soggy contents of the basket into the rope net at the end of the throwing arm. As the mass of underwear slowly settled — like an undercooked pudding turned out of its mold — Lucy again glanced over the parapet. Lord Cant had emerged from the castle and now lumbered across the rocky courtyard called the bailey, his progress attended by guards in crimson frocks and flat bronze helmets. Behind him came a crowd of ministers and nobles who gossiped and traded tablets of chewing gum, their elegant robes sweeping the stones. At the rear straggled a whiskered, unhappy-looking man in a chef's white blouse and hat, who held in his fist the two feet of a clacking, even unhappier-looking hen.

The party reached the prisoner, a well-knit young man who knelt with bowed head on the flints of the courtyard, naked except for a dirty pair of breeches. He had been there since sunrise, guarded by the black-hooded executioner, who stood at attention with his axe. Lucy found her eyes drawn to this prisoner, though she could not say why. Now the bailiff strode from the crowd of spectators and unrolled a parchment. His voice echoed up the castle walls.

"The prisoner . . . *ner, ner* . . . having been found guilty . . . *ty, ty* . . . of the grave and infamous offense . . . *fense, fense* . . . of slandering the noble pastime of chewing gum . . . *um, um* . . . awaits the Just and Benevolent Execution . . . *shun, shun* . . . of the sentence . . . *tence, tence* . . . of Death! . . . *death! death!*"

"Papa's cap is on crooked," Pauline said, peeking over Lucy's shoulder. "I daresay he's just got out of bed."

Lucy imagined she was right. Adolphus, Lord Cant, the Exalted & Merciful Protector of the Barony, blinked sleepily in the morning light. His unwashed hair curled in wayward tendrils from beneath his baronial cap, and he scratched his belly as an underling approached to offer him a paper on a silver platter. He lifted it in a trembling hand.

"Stay thy hand, executioner!" he said, squinting at the script.

His voice was low and wheezy — Lucy could barely hear it from the tower. He coughed feebly, then went on. "We are touched by pity. Our tender heart . . ."

"Too tender!" chanted the ministers and nobles, their words slightly garbled by chewing gum. Lucy heard a bubble pop.

". . . Our tender heart," the Baron went on, "and the precepts of the Wise Teachers, move us to pity. We command that this sentence be lifted, and that the prisoner, for the example of the people and the good of his mortal spirit, be mercifully sentenced to a term of six months at hard labor."

"Hail the Compassionate Protector!" chanted the crowd.

"Poor chicken," Lucy sighed.

"Yet . . . *et, et* . . . the ransom of blood . . . *udd, udd* . . . must be paid! . . . *aid! aid!*" bellowed the bailiff. "Who brings an offering? . . . *ing? ing?* What blood shall answer . . . *ser, ser* . . . for this crime . . . *ime . . . ime?*"

The cook stepped forward and lifted the hen overhead. The startled fowl, having hung upside down all the while, flapped its wings dizzily as it struggled to stay balanced in the cook's upraised fist. Feathers fell as the bird was carried to the Stone of Justice, where the executioner waited, his axe resting on a hairy shoulder.

"Hurrah!" shouted the spectators.

"Now!" Pauline squealed, pulling Lucy away from the parapet. She pressed the lanyard of the trigger into her maidservant's hand. "I'll count down from three!"

"But don't you want to do it?" Lucy asked. Her nose began to drip, as it often did when trouble loomed. She sniffed, hoping her mistress wouldn't notice.

"I'm the mastermind of this caper," said Pauline. "You're the henchman. Masterminds give orders; henchmen obey."

"Yes, mistress."

Lucy heard the chicken flapping and cawing — the cook had laid it on the Stone of Justice. Pauline hurried back to the parapet and leaned out.

"Three! . . . ," she cried. "Two! . . . Just think, Wickwright, you may save a chicken's life. . . . One! . . . Nine-sixteenths! . . . Five-thirteenths! . . . One-twelfth! . . . *Pull!*"

Lucy gave the lanyard a mighty tug. But the catapults of Castle Cant were never meant for heaving soggy underwear over the heads of ministers and nobles, and when the great beam swung Lucy found that wet knickers, slips, drawers, and corsets made the worst missiles imaginable. They tangled in the rope netting of the ammunition basket and the catapult slammed the dripping mass of laundry against the parapet with a great, horrible *squish!*

Had Pauline stood a foot to her left she would have been driven like a peg through the slate roof of the tower. She escaped with a drenching of gray, sudsy water, but only a solitary pair of bloomers was hurled into the sky. Lucy, who had fallen on her backside after pulling the trigger, scrambled to her feet as the catapult's arm swung back, its load of drawstring shorts and lisle stockings peeling free and plopping sadly on the slates around her. Pauline stumbled away from the parapet, wiping dirty bubbles from her eyes.

"You *soaked* me!" she wailed.

Lucy peeked over the wall. The crowd in the bailey gazed up, their attention commanded by the sound of crashing laundry.

The hen had got loose and ran from the pursuing cook. The bloomers unfurled and spiraled down like a maple seed, veering this way and that before landing with a quiet *slurp* on the prisoner's upturned face.

"Oh no," Lucy whispered.

"Seize her! . . . *her!* . . . *her!*" shouted the bailiff.

"Run!" said Pauline.

"Yike!" said Lucy.

She dashed down the parapet walk. Shouted orders echoed from the courtyard, and guardsmen raced to the towers. Lucy hoped her mistress could delay them, for it was a long way to the castle keep, where she might run down the corner tower and disappear in the labyrinth of the north wing. Looking over the parapet, she saw that the guards below were outpacing her.

She ran on, her shoes pounding the slates of the parapet walk, and when she reached the corner tower she stopped, her lungs on fire. To her horror she heard the *patter-flop* of guardsmen's sandals, already well up the spiral stairs. She started back through the arch to the parapet walk, but by now two guardsmen had arrived at the linen-shrouded catapult. One of them offered Pauline a consoling handkerchief.

"There she is!" the other cried.

Lucy flew down the stairs, toward the climbing sandals of her pursuers. They surely thought she had gone mad, running down toward them, and they gave a shout each time a circuit of the stairs brought her into view. For once Lucy was grateful for her outlandish, rubber-soled shoes. They were the only sneakers ever known in the castle, where clothing styles of one hundred and fifty years ago — such as Pauline's pinafore — were considered daringly modern. Down she ran, her feet barely touching the steps, until another turn on the winding stairs would have put her in the guards' clutches.

With a determined *hyuh!* she swung down a dim passage and sprinted to another flight of steps, steep and narrow and less footworn than those of the tower. She scrambled up, on aching legs, to a landing where an oil lamp burned in a bracket on the wall. There she stopped, wheezing hard, her sandal-shod pursuers following noisily up the narrow steps. She turned the lamp's screw until the flame was drowned in oil, then ran blindly on through the darkness. When it seemed her legs could carry her no farther she gained a second landing. A yellow candle burned there, by an oaken door on which a sign warned —

Quiet!

Lucy blew out the candle, opened the door, and entered the familiar, cavernous hall of the Baronial Library. Dusty light fell from the high windows to the floor where, like ancient, molting buzzards in their nests, threadbare scholars sat at tables piled with books. Lucy forced herself to walk calmly, her hands in her pockets. Dr. Azziz, the librarian, glanced up from her tall wheeled chair as Lucy strolled by.

"Good morning, Lucy!" she whispered. "What brings you —"

Her greeting was cut off by a tumult beyond the door — the clang and clatter of guardsmen's helmets striking granite. They had arrived at the darkened first landing, and had tried to put their feet on a step that was not there. Strong oaths barked up the stairs.

"My word!" said the librarian. "What's happening out there?"

"I passed some guardsmen drinking beer, ma'am," Lucy said.

"Outrageous!" said Dr. Azziz. "There are *scholars* working here!" She beckoned her assistant, who was waving a feather duster at a nearby inkstand. "Carlos, take me to the door!"

Lucy walked away as quickly as decorum allowed. She was a scrupulous girl, careful never to lie, and it was true that she had passed drunken guardsmen — many times, in fact. She saw no reason to tell the librarian exactly *when* that had happened, for it would be a long story, and she considered herself to be in a hurry. Already the cursing guardsmen were racing up the last flight of stairs.

At the high canyons of the bookshelves she glanced back to make sure the librarian was not looking, then sprinted silently to the other end of the library. She slipped through the door just as the guards thudded against the one behind her. Kneeling, she took a barrette from her hair and wedged it under the door, kicking it tight with the toe of her sneaker.

A long, windowless corridor stretched before her, hung at great intervals with lamps that seemed to shiver in their thin blankets of light. Lucy groaned. Dr. Azziz might delay the guards for a moment, but they would surely catch her before she made it halfway down the corridor. She ran to the first of the iron-hinged doors — of course it was locked — and heard Dr. Azziz crying in protest as the guardsmen stomped noisily across her library. Lucy ran from door to door, testing each stubbornly bolted latch. Her nose dripped horribly. The guardsmen had begun to throw themselves against the jammed door when, at last, a latch gave way to her hand. Despite her urgent terror she stopped to read the plaque on the door, for Lucy was a well-brought-up girl and would never dream of barging in on an utter stranger. She squinted to make out the words in the dim light.

Baronial Commission on Lexicography,
Orthography, & Grammar
D^R. COSTIVE GUTZ
Sub-assistant Secretary of Synonyms, Antonyms, & Pleonasms

Lucy stepped inside, closing the door quickly but quietly behind her. The door from the library crashed open and the guards dashed down the corridor. She bit her tongue until they had passed the office of Synonyms, Antonyms, & Pleonasms, then fell back against the door and let out her breath.

Chapter 2

*L*ucy found herself in a small, cluttered office. A desk as big as her cot in the servants' garret, and cluttered with books, papers, and half-eaten sandwiches, occupied most of the space between the two ranks of unmatched bookcases, whose shelves sagged under dusty volumes bound in sheepskin. At the narrow window stood a man in a rusty black gown and mortarboard. He faced away from Lucy and spoke in a voice so deep and dank it seemed to rise from the castle's cellars.

"My nephew is festooned with bloomers, Sauersop," he said. "How very strange."

Lucy took a moment to wipe her nose on the sleeve of her t-shirt, then cleared her throat politely.

"Excuse me, sir," she said. "I'm not Sauersop."

The man turned around. His long, yellowish face seemed made of soft wax into which someone had pressed — too deeply — the black stones of his eyes and a dried-out grape-skin of a mouth. His eyebrows — or rather, the bits of skin where another person might have eyebrows — rose in mild reproach.

"You're not Sauersop," he said.

"No, sir," Lucy said. "I'm not."

"It's just as well. I'm not fond of the Master Herald, but I'm obliged to consult him today on a question of heraldic syn-onyms." The man glanced at a cuckoo clock that ticked on the wall over Lucy's shoulder. "I don't expect him until noon. Have you an appointment?"

"I'm afraid I haven't."

The man walked to his desk and sat down. From a tottering stack of papers he took a cardbound notebook, on which *Appointments* was written in an elegant script. After first pressing his finger to a sponge on the desk, he turned page after empty page until he arrived at one inscribed *17 May, XIX Adolphus*. He pursed his lips.

"It appears I can squeeze you in," he said, reaching for his pen.

"Thank you, sir," Lucy said. The man dipped his pen and, after glancing again at the cuckoo clock, wrote:

11:43 a.m.: Little girl.

"I am Professor Gutz," he said, putting his pen into its holder. "You may have gathered from my plaque that I am a doctor, but I am a doctor of words only. I notice that you're breathing rather heavily. Were you seeking a physician?"

"No, sir," Lucy said. "Thank you, sir. I'm just a little winded."

Costive Gutz leaned back in his chair and regarded Lucy closely, his chin resting on his fingertips, as though considering some unfamiliar word he had found in a book. "Before we come to the matter of your visit," he said, "I should like to put a question to you."

Lucy went pale. Had the professor connected her breathlessness with the tumult in the courtyard, and the guardsmen's racing footsteps in the corridor? Her voice came in a high whisper.

"Yes, Professor?"

Gutz leaned forward and aimed the twin shafts of his forefingers at Lucy's chest.

"What, pray tell, is a *Gizmobot*?"

Lucy blushed. The professor had noticed her t-shirt. She was not a vain girl, but she squirmed whenever people drew attention to her clothes, which were poor cast-offs in the fashion of the outside world, which she scrounged from the charity box at the American Mission, in Tenesmus. She wore jeans that barely reached the knobs of her ankles, and worn-out sneakers, and a t-shirt promoting mechanical figures that struck action poses across her belly: THE GIZMOBOTS!

"I believe it's a kind of toy, Professor," she said, crossing her arms nervously under Costive Gutz's gaze.

"I see," said Gutz. "A proper noun, is it? A trademark?"

"Yes, I imagine so."

"Then it's no concern of mine," Gutz said. "It's a matter for the Bureau of Patents and Titles. I can hardly be expected to concern myself with every proper noun that comes across our borders in this day and age. I've accomplished little enough work this morning, as it is, what with all the chaos and riot going on." His eyes narrowed. "Do you know," he said, "that bloomers are falling? My nephew is festooned with bloomers."

Lucy swallowed. In her years as Pauline's maidservant she had become quite expert at evading the troublesome questions of grown-ups, and a time-tested maneuver was simply to ask their questions back at them.

"Bloomers, Dr. Gutz?" she accordingly said.

"I said *bloomers*," said Gutz. "It's scandalous — a sacred and venerable occasion mocked by a malicious prank. Subversive elements are behind it, mark my words. It shows every sign of being the work of the Cause. Did you watch the execution?"

"I . . . I normally stay away from the bailey on Execution Day," Lucy said. (Another useful trick for evading questions was to tell the truth — simply not the truth that was wanted.) "Why was your nephew being punished, Dr. Gutz?" she added (for a grown-up, given the chance to gossip about a relative, might go on all day).

The professor's shriveled mouth turned up in a ghastly smile. He said nothing, but rose from his desk and pulled a musty velvet ribbon that hung near the window. Dimly, from the courtyard, came the sound of running and men's voices.

"They still haven't caught the hen," Gutz said, looking out the window, "but she's run into a corner, foolish thing." He turned to face Lucy. "The word *bailey*, which you used a moment ago," he said severely, "refers to the fortified walls of a castle, not to the space by them enclosed, which is properly called the *ward*. I've made it my life's mission, little girl, to purge the language of such lazy and thoughtless terms."

"Yes, sir," Lucy said, backing up against the door. "I beg your pardon, sir."

"I grant it," Gutz said, smiling. "I fear, however, that you'll not find such a forgiving spirit in the castle guard."

"The . . . the guard, sir?" Lucy asked.

"I said *the guard*," Gutz said. He walked slowly toward Lucy. "Did you really think you could escape them by running into my office?"

"But, respectfully, sir," Lucy said, her hand searching behind her for the latch, "I'm not running from the guard." It was true — she was not, presently, running from the guard. It was Dr. Costive Gutz she now meant to escape. Her hand grasped the cold iron of the latch, but before she could lift it a fist thudded heavily on the door.

"Aie!" she squealed, jumping away. The door swung open, and through it walked a burly man in the white smock of a courier. He was bearded nearly to his eyebrows, and his fingers sprouted thick tufts of black, bristling hairs.

"You rung the bell, boss?" he asked Gutz. Lucy's eyes darted to the velvet ribbon, still swinging back and forth by the window. Gutz sat again at his desk.

"*Rang* the bell, Eberhardt," he said. "Yes, I did. I have reason to suspect that this girl was involved in the late riot in the courtyard. I want you to take her in hand and escort her to the captain of the guard."

"No!" Lucy wailed, but the courier plodded over and locked her wrist in the hairy shackle of his hand. Dr. Gutz folded his hands under his chin, a pleased smile on his face.

"But . . . but . . . ," Lucy pleaded, wincing in Eberhardt's grip, *"why?"*

"When you entered this office, I believed you were my acquaintance, Dr. Sauersop," Gutz said crisply. "I mentioned that my nephew had been draped with bloomers."

"I never meant to eavesdrop," Lucy said in a strained voice. *"Ouch!"*

"Grip the child less tightly, Eberhardt," Gutz instructed.

"Right, boss."

"When I asked if you'd been watching the execution," Gutz went on, "you *implied* — and I stress the word *implied*, for, in fact, you evaded my question — you *implied*, I repeat, that you had *not* been watching."

"I don't like executions," Lucy said truthfully.

"Yet of all the great crowd of persons who are present at those affairs," Gutz said with a triumphant smirk, "you somehow knew that it was the *prisoner* who'd been festooned with bloomers. How, pray tell me, could you have known that my bloomered nephew and the prisoner were the same person, unless you *had* been watching — perhaps from the very tower whence the bloomers fell?"

Lucy groaned. Dr. Gutz was right — she could not have known who his nephew was unless she had watched the execution. She'd been outwitted by a grown-up.

"What's going on in here?"

The man who now spoke was dressed like Gutz in a black

gown, but with a drooping black cap rather than a mortarboard on his head. He stood in the doorway, a smudged monocle hanging from a silver cord around his neck.

"Ah, Sauersop!" Gutz said. "I've just captured the party, or one of the parties, responsible for the recent disturbance of my nephew's execution."

Dr. Sauersop approached Lucy and screwed his monocle into the wrinkled socket of his eye. His gaze fell slowly down, then up again, pausing quizzically at her GIZMOBOTS! shirt.

"She hardly looks like a revolutionist, Gutz," he said. "She's a little girl. Her nose is dripping."

"Nevertheless, I'm convinced she is the culprit, or one of the culprits," Gutz said. "No doubt she is allied with my nephew and those other lunatics who would outlaw the harmless pastime of gum chewing. A mere child, but already a radical. It's shocking. Your parents," he told Lucy, "must be very disappointed in you, girl."

"No, sir," Lucy said miserably. "I'm afraid my parents are dead."

"You poor child," said Sauersop. He took a handkerchief from the sleeve of his robe and offered it to Lucy. "May I extend my sincerest condolences."

"Er, ahem," said Gutz, somewhat taken aback. "Well, certainly that must be considered as a tragedy. I trust you will accept my deepest sympathy, as well."

Lucy accepted Sauersop's handkerchief and wiped her nose.

"Thank you, sir," she said.

"You're entirely welcome."

"However," Gutz continued, "one's personal misfortunes

can never justify criminal acts. I would be derelict in my duties if I did not report my suspicions to the proper authorities."

"You tell her, boss," said Eberhardt.

Dr. Sauersop approached the grammarian.

"In this case, surely, you might overlook an act of tomfoolery," he said quietly. "The poor girl is an orphan, Gutz. Why, when I was her age I —"

"Such wrongheaded compassion," Gutz broke in severely, "would only serve to encourage her scofflaw behavior. High spirits must be beaten down, Sauersop, before they bring us to anarchy." He turned to the courier. "You may take her away, Eberhardt. Inform the captain of the guard that I'll send a full report at my earliest convenience."

Struggling was futile, Lucy knew, but in her wounded pride she made Eberhardt drag her joltingly to the door. As she left Gutz's office the little doors of his clock sprang open with a whirring of gears, and the mechanical bird cawed the arrival of noon:

Cuckoo! Cuckoo! Cuckoo! Cuckoo! Cuckoo! Cuckoo! Cuckoo! Cuckoo! Cuckoo! Cuckoo! Cuckoo! Cuckoo!

Chapter 3

"*H*onestly, Wickwright, you're such a dolt!" Pauline said. She'd come from the banquet given by her father for his sister and brother-in-law, who had arrived that day from their villa on Lake Poltroon. The festival of the Baron's twentieth anniversary drew near, and the castle teemed with such noble visitors. Pauline wore a sparkling dress of emerald satin and a high, pointed hat called a *hennin*, from the peak of which a wispy veil hung nearly to her waist. She set a parcel on one of the laundry tables and climbed up beside it, revealing her pearl-covered slippers. "I don't think 'an *egregious* dolt' is putting it too strongly," she added.

"I suppose not, mistress."

Lucy lifted the hot iron from the stove and began to press a handkerchief. All day, from sunrise, she had toiled in the baronial laundry, her punishment for the crimes of Riot, Mischief, and Insubordination. Now the sky was purple in the high, barred windows, and she worked by flickering torchlight.

"Costive Gutz may be ugly as a raisin," Pauline went on, "but he's bright as a lemon. *I* should never have run into *his* office. He was boasting to everyone at the banquet about how he outwitted you."

"I surely put my foot in my mouth," Lucy admitted. But she was thinking that her mistress would never have *reason* to hide in Gutz's office, because as the Baron's daughter she could never be punished. And she was such a blabbermouth, anyway, that surely she would have given herself away long before Lucy had done. "I trust you enjoyed the banquet, mistress?" she added, hoping to change the subject.

"I did *not*," Pauline pouted. "It was dreadfully dull, except for a show of juggling. Papa was moody because he's given up chewing gum again, and the speeches went on for ages and didn't say a thing. You were lucky to be working. I should have preferred the company of wet clothes to those great bags of wind."

Lucy folded the handkerchief and pressed the crease. *She* preferred to spend Saturdays at her uncle's inn in Tenesmus, as indeed she would have done had not Pauline got it into her head to hurl about laundry the day before. If her mistress believed working was such a treat, Lucy thought, she ought to have volunteered for laundry duty several hours ago. But she kept her thoughts to herself. Pauline, as though curious to see how work was actually *done*, watched Lucy pushing the iron.

"Why does Papa find it so difficult to stop chewing gum, Wickwright?" she asked. "It puts him in *such* a foul temper, and he scarcely eats a crumb. Why do you suppose that is?"

"I don't know, mistress. It certainly has a grip on people."

Lucy had never understood the appeal of gum, which anyway was a luxury beyond her station. Among the nobility, however, many persons chewed it almost without stop — indeed, stopping seemed to be the great difficulty. The housemaids scraped buckets of the stuff daily from the undersides of tables and chairs.

"It's a nasty habit," Pauline declared.

"I agree, mistress."

"But whenever Papa tries to stop chewing, he ends by drinking barrels of wine," Pauline went on. "And wine makes him dreadfully stupid."

"I'm sorry to hear that, mistress," Lucy said sincerely. The Baron had lately been in poor health, and his condition weighed heavily on Pauline, his heiress and only child. Lucy folded the handkerchief twice more, pressed the creases, and tucked it into the back pocket of her jeans.

"Are you stealing that handkerchief, Wickwright?" Pauline asked.

"No, mistress," Lucy said, setting the iron on end. She wiped her brow. "It belongs to Dr. Sauersop. I mean to return it to him."

"That's all right, then," Pauline said. She pushed to the edge of the table the parcel she had carried with her to the laundry. "I've brought you something."

"Why . . . thank you, mistress," Lucy said, walking around the ironing board. One never knew when Pauline might pull a prank, but the parcel did not seem to hold frogs, anyway. It wasn't moving. She pulled the string and unfolded the brown paper. Inside was a cut of roast lamb and the butt of a loaf of white bread.

"Thank you, mistress," Lucy said again, now regretting her disloyal thoughts. During her punishment she had been limited to one rusty dipper of water every four hours, and her mouth watered at the smell of the lamb. She vowed to remember that, while her mistress was certainly an imp, she was still only a young girl, and terribly spoiled by her father and the rest of the court. One could hardly expect her to be as mature as Lucy, who was a year older, and an orphan, and made wise by years of domestic service. She took a remorseful bite of the meat.

"I should think," Pauline said, "that with all his farms and estates and orchards and so on, Papa might find something better than gum to chew upon. Filberts are a thing I enjoy, for example. They can easily be carried about in a purse. Fennel seeds as well. To say nothing of raisins."

"Mn," agreed Lucy, whose mouth was full.

"You know, I said something clever, didn't I, Wickwright?" Pauline asked.

"Mistress?" said Lucy, swallowing.

"'Ugly as a raisin, but bright as a lemon,'" quoted Pauline. "What I said about Costive Gutz. That was very clever, wasn't it?"

"Yes, very clever indeed," Lucy said, happy to show her devotion and gratitude. Normally she ate barley gruel or stewed onions and coarse black bread for supper, and she had not had such a feast since Pauline's last birthday, when all the servants had been treated to a generous sliver of cake.

"I like those things — what do you call them?" Pauline asked.

"Fruits, mistress?"

"No, no — when you say a man is *like* a fruit!"

"Oh! You mean a simile," said Lucy. Pauline considered this for a moment, her pearl-slippered feet swinging under her dress.

"Yes," she eventually agreed, "that's the word. Say, let's play at being poets! One of us will name a thing, and the other has to say what fruit it's like. You go first, and I'll show you how it's done."

"I'm to name a thing, mistress?"

"Yes. That's how 'Poets' is played, I believe I told you."

Lucy thought. She wanted to say something hard, something *very* un-fruitlike, so she might finish her supper while Pauline puzzled over the answer.

"A dog," she finally said, reaching for her crust.

"That's easy," said Pauline. Lucy paused, her mouth open, the bread an inch from her chin.

"Is it?" she asked.

"Certainly," Pauline said. "A dog is like a cocoanut — it's brown and hairy on the outside, and not good to eat."

"But," Lucy said, putting down the bread, "a cocoanut *is* good to eat, mistress."

"It is *not*," said Pauline. "I *hate* cocoanut. And furthermore, a cocoanut gives milk, just like a dog. Do you remember when Cleo had puppies?"

Cleopatra was one of the Baron's foxhounds. Lucy had to grant that Cleopatra *had* given milk when she had puppies, just like a cocoanut.

"I suppose that's so," she admitted.

"That was rather simple, Wickwright," Pauline said. "In

fact, I believe when the cocoanut was first introduced to Cant it was known as the dogfruit to the lower classes."

"Perhaps, mistress." Lucy did not believe the cocoanut was ever called the dogfruit, but she did not like to argue — for when the tide of an argument turned against Pauline the Baron's daughter simply stopped her ears with her fingers and said "La dee da dee da!" until her opponent gave up in despair.

"So I'm ahead, one to nothing," Pauline said, "and it's my turn to name a thing." Her eyes searched the laundry for inspiration, finally coming to rest on Lucy's nose, from which a bead of perspiration dangled. Pauline smiled. "What fruit is like a nose?" she asked.

Lucy thought a moment.

"That's easy as well," she said.

"It is *not!*" said Pauline.

"It is *so,*" insisted Lucy. "A nose is like a crab-apple."

"A *crab-apple*? How is a nose like a crab-apple?"

"Because you may pick it," said Lucy, "but you don't want to eat it!"

"*Ughhh!*" Pauline shouted. "Ooof! *Uck!* That is dis-*gust*-ing!"

Lucy beamed. She chewed another bite of lamb.

"I'm going to *vomit!*" Pauline cried, jumping off the laundry table and clutching her belly. "I'm going to be *sick!* I'm going to *disgorge!* The game is *over!* I *win!*"

"But it's a tie!" Lucy protested. "Respectfully, mistress!"

Pauline spun in circles, bent nearly double, the veil of her hennin floating on the air.

"Yuck! *Blegh!* Ugh! *Arf!*"

"We both made one simile!" Lucy said. "It's a tie!"

Pauline staggered back against the laundry table and lifted a hand to her forehead, palm outward. She gazed devoutly at the high ceiling, her eyelids fluttering.

"Bring me water, Wickwright," she gasped. "I faint!"

"You do *not*," Lucy muttered, but she stomped to the water bucket and carried back the dipper. One could never win a contest with Pauline. The rules always favored her in the games she made up, or else she changed the rules as she went along, or pretended to faint when her opponent scored a point. She sipped the water and handed the dipper back to Lucy.

"I can't allow your answer, Wickwright," she explained. "There are laws against lewd and vulgar speech in this Barony. As my servant, you should set a better example than that."

Lucy bit her tongue and carried the dipper back to the water bucket. Pauline, she thought, was a fine one to talk of vulgarity. She was, in fact, an awful nosepicker; Lucy was always catching her at it and having to avert her eyes, or pretend her sneaker wanted tying, or that a mouse had crossed the floor.

But as she walked back she saw the remains of her supper on the table and remembered her vow of tolerance. Pauline was a good girl, if spoiled, and Lucy must make allowances. The water seemed to have cured her mistress's fainting spell.

"I'm fantastically bored," she now said. "Are you finished here, Wickwright? Let's do something fun."

"It's rather late, mistress," Lucy said. "Perhaps we could read a story before going to bed."

"But it's *Saturday!*" Pauline said. "I sat through that awful banquet and I want to have fun. It's only fair. Come, let's ride Charlemagne." (Charlemagne was her pony.)

"But Mr. Swift is on his half-holiday, mistress," Lucy said. Swift was the Baron's ostler, and like Lucy (when she was not being punished) he was at his liberty from Saturday noon to Sunday morning. "Besides, it's already dark. And you're not dressed for riding."

"His half-*holiday*?" Pauline wailed. "Does nobody *work* in this castle anymore?"

"I'm sorry, mistress." Lucy crumpled the paper from her supper and, opening the stove, tossed it on the coals. A breeze whistled at the high windows of the laundry. The sky had gone black, and a few stars winked between the iron bars.

"Look, Wickwright. Stars!" said Pauline.

"Yes. Summer is coming."

"I've an idea!" Pauline said. "Let's go look through the telescope!"

Lucy wiped her mouth. No doubt Pauline had gorged herself on sweet cakes at the banquet and would never settle down till she had dragged Lucy into *some* kind of adventure. Better to go to the observatory, which required no more work than climbing stairs, than to wait for Pauline's next idea, which might involve hunting mice with pea-shooters or finding something large to set afire.

"Yes," Lucy said, "let's do."

"Do you know the way?" Pauline asked. "One so rarely comes to the laundry. I don't know how you stand it! I'd much rather work in the kitchen."

"Yes, mistress. Follow me."

Lucy took a torch from its bracket and led Pauline past the steaming laundry vats, through the maze of sheets and curtains hanging to dry, and down a narrow passage that ended at a steep fall of stairs. At the bottom was a vast, dark cellar, through which a winding path threaded between enormous heaps of coal. Glimmering cobwebs hung at the dim reaches of the torchlight.

"Mind your skirts, please, mistress," Lucy said. "It's a bit sooty."

After crossing the cellar and climbing several flights of stairs the girls emerged in a long, torchlit corridor. Lucy fitted her torch into a bracket and they proceeded down the passage and up the winding stairs of a tower. These steps continued right to the ceiling, to a door fixed horizontally between two joists and painted with grand scientific titles:

Celestial Observatory of the
Baronial Academy of Natural History
LUIGI LEMONJELLO, A.B.D., CHIEF ASTRONOMER
(Ring the bell)

"*I* want to ring the bell!" said Pauline. She climbed up until the tip of her hennin pressed against the door, then turned the doorbell three times quickly and, after adjusting her grip, twice more. A voice called through the heavy timbers.

"Come up, come up! The sun is behind us!"

Lucy and Pauline looked at one another, baffled by this strange how-do-ye-do, but before either could say a word the door creaked open above their heads.

Chapter 4

The Astronomer's Lair

$\mathscr{T}$here are, in the world, people called *acrophobes*, who suffer from a morbid fear of high places. They avoid treetops and staircases the way a normal person steers away from opera houses, or Pauline from cocoanut pudding. They *hate* heights. But Luigi Lemonjello, the chief astronomer of Cant, was no such person. He *adored* heights with the same passion that other people reserved for flannel pajamas or a well-toasted marsh-mallow. Lemonjello was quite content never to set his foot on the ground, and so he not only worked but lived at the top of the loftiest tower of Castle Cant, and had his door in the floor instead of the wall.

Lucy and Pauline were still puzzling over his strange greet-ing when the astronomer opened that door, and when he saw the girls on the stairs below him he looked as baffled as they were.

"Miss Cant!" he said. "I . . . er . . . well, I mean to say . . ."

"Good evening, Lemonjello," Pauline said. "Are you going to invite me in?"

"Certainly! Certainly! Come in, Miss Cant! I trust His Lordship is well?"

"As well as may be expected, thank you," said Pauline, her dress swishing on the steps as she climbed to the astronomer's chamber. "His breathing seems to improve. You might have seen him at the banquet tonight, had you come."

"Er . . . yes, Miss Cant," Lemonjello said, nervously pulling at the folds of his black robe. "I was invited, of course, but there are all those stairs to go down, and . . . well, the night is so fine. . . ."

Lemonjello wore no shoes, only a pair of white stockings that, not being gartered, had fallen around his thin ankles. He was a man of middle years, and very short and slight, but small as he was he had somehow managed to find a robe that stopped well short of the floor. His black hair sprang from his head in a riot of italic curls, and the lenses of his spectacles were so thick they reduced his eyes to tiny dots. He peered intently at Lucy as she entered the room.

"And how is Ptolemy?" Pauline asked, examining a birdcage that hung from the ceiling. A parrot perched on a stick inside.

"Squawk!" said the bird, fluttering its wings.

"He's quite well, thank you . . . quite hale. . . ." The astronomer had by now so crumpled his robe in his nervous hands that his shins were exposed. "The kettle is on, Miss Cant," he said. "In fact . . . I see it's steaming. May I offer you tea?"

"Yes, please," Pauline said. "It's a thirsty climb up here!"

"Then tea it shall be." Lemonjello let go his robe and took down a teapot from the dresser. "Won't you sit down, Miss Cant? And you, Miss . . . ?"

"Lucy, sir," Lucy said. She looked around the apartment, but saw no place to sit except the astronomer's narrow bed. The room was small and, being round, had no corners in which to put the few pieces of furniture. A large desk piled with star maps and dirty saucers dominated the chamber. On a low table were Lemonjello's slide-rule and astrolabe, along with a tattered book entitled *Parrots: Nature's Mimics*. The wardrobe was piled with more books, and in one of the windows an Æolian harp moaned softly in the breeze. Lucy picked her way through the clutter and sat on the bed, where she was joined a moment later by Pauline.

"And to what do I owe the honor of this visit?" asked the astronomer when the tea had been poured. Unlidding a container labeled *Birdseed*, he took out a small tongs and dropped a lump of gray sugar into each of the cups, then pinched a saucer in each hand and carried the clattering china to his guests.

"We've come to look through the telescope," Pauline told him.

"Oh?" said Lemonjello, glancing at Lucy. "Ah . . . Now I see how it is . . . I think. Well, it's a fine night for stargazing. What bright girls you both must be!"

"I intend to be a space pilot when I grow up," Pauline boasted, though yesterday, before the fiasco with the catapult, she had told Lucy she meant to be a general. Should she ride her pony tomorrow, Lucy knew, she would tell Mr. Swift she meant to be a jockey. Lucy had been full of dreams, too, once upon a time. But why, she wondered, would one dream of growing up to be a mere space pilot, when one was certainly *going* to be the Baroness of Cant?

Pauline chattered on about the planets she would discover and the monsters she would slay, but Lemonjello seemed not to hear. He was looking at Lucy, who glanced away when she caught him staring at her.

"Well," he said abruptly. "Shall we go up?"

"Like rockets!" Pauline said. "That's another simile," she told Lucy. "Two to nothing."

The observation platform was gained by climbing a wooden ladder through a trap door in the ceiling. Pauline went first, followed by Lucy, the astronomer waiting at the foot of the ladder in case of a mishap.

"There is no moon," Lemonjello called up, when the girls had reached the platform. He clambered up the ladder and sniffed the cool night air. "A grand night for stargazing!"

"I should like to look at Mars," Pauline said.

"So should I, Miss Cant," said the astronomer. "But, sadly, Mars is away on the other side of the sun this particular evening, and refuses to show himself. Perhaps we might observe the Ring Nebula, with its angry white dwarf?"

"No," Pauline said flatly. "You showed me that one before, Lemonjello, and it didn't look at all like a dwarf. And besides, I already *have* a dwarf. He juggled at the banquet tonight."

"Ah, yes, the good Marchenoir," said Lemonjello. "How is the poor fellow getting along?"

"Father bade him juggle two live chickens and an *egg*," Pauline said brightly. "It was *most* amusing."

"Indeed. I should have wept, I'm sure. Well, perhaps you would like to look at Saturn? I believe the rings are at a fine inclination tonight."

"Yes, Saturn!" Pauline said. "I want a hat made to look like Saturn!"

While the astronomer arranged the telescope (with much squinting and turning of dials), Lucy walked to the parapet and looked out over the ward. She ached to the roots of her hair from working all day in the laundry, and she hoped her mistress would soon grow tired of looking through the telescope.

"I can see little people!" Pauline exclaimed. Lucy turned around.

"Now, really, Miss Cant," objected Lemonjello. "My telescope is the most powerful in the Barony — indeed, the only one, save those terrestrial glasses used by the guard — but I'm certain that you cannot see —"

"They're juggling chickens in space suits!"

The astronomer clasped his hands behind his back and lifted his eyes. Lucy thought he looked a little cross.

"Miss Cant," he said, "surely a Saturnine chicken would be adapted to that planet's atmosphere. It would have no need of a space suit."

"No," Pauline explained, "the *men* are in space suits."

"Ah. I see. A matter of syntax."

"I'm *freezing!*" Pauline said, her eye still pressed to the telescope. "Please to go down and fetch up my tea, Wickwright."

Lemonjello, who had been gazing at the stars, now looked at Lucy.

"Did you say 'Wickwright,' Miss Cant?" he asked.

Pauline turned her eye from the telescope.

"Yes," she said. "My maidservant, Lucy Wickwright. Wickwright, Mr. Lemonjello."

Lucy pinched the legs of her jeans and made a curtsey.

"How do you do," she said, a little flustered. She was not used to being introduced.

"Ahhhh," the astronomer said.

"My tea?" said Pauline.

"Yes, mistress," Lucy said, going to the ladder.

"Wait!" Lemonjello hurried to the trap door, the loose toes of his socks flapping on the roof slates. "Allow me to go first," he said, "in case you fall."

Lucy thought that if the astronomer was going down anyway, he could as well fetch up Pauline's tea himself. But she was not in the habit of correcting her elders, and when he had reached the floor she followed him down. She found her mistress's tea on the dresser, but when she turned to remount the ladder Lemonjello stood in her way.

"I hope I've not . . . er . . . compromised you," he whispered, "by giving voice to our motto. The sun *is* behind us, but I gather you're under a cloud, eh? When I heard the code rung on the doorbell, I assumed . . . assumed wrongly, it transpires . . . do forgive me . . . that whoever rang was one of us — and alone."

Lucy blinked.

"But, sir, Miss Cant —"

"Yes, of course," Lemonjello interrupted. "*She* would hardly be one of us, would she? Again, I beg your forgiveness for my . . . ah . . . lapse in judgment."

"Think nothing of it," said Lucy, her good manners filling

the blank in her understanding. She had no idea why the astronomer should apologize to her, or what he meant by "the code," or why they stood whispering while her mistress waited for her tea. Lemonjello, after a moment's silence, leaned closer.

"You're *the* Wickwright?" he asked. "The one who . . . er . . . disrupted the execution, yesterday?"

Lucy blushed.

"Yes, sir," she admitted. "But it was really Miss Cant's fault."

"Yes! Yes!" whispered the astronomer, so excitedly that Lucy leaned away from him. "Of course it was! It's . . . it's . . . it's *all* their fault! And the world will know it, some day! Bless you, child. Would that I had the tenth of your courage!"

"But really, sir —" Lucy began.

"We must hurry. She may suspect us," Lemonjello said, glancing up the ladder. "You must do something for me . . . not for me, of course . . . but for our Cause. Will you do it, dear girl?"

The teacup rattled on its saucer. The astronomer's face was inches from Lucy's, his dots of eyes pleading at hers.

"Where is my tea, Wickwright?" Pauline called down.

"I beg you!" said Lemonjello.

"Yes, of course, sir," Lucy said. "If I can do you any favor —"

"Bless you! Bless you!"

So saying, the astronomer hastened to the dresser, where he unlidded a jar labeled *Sugar* and poured a handful of copper farthings on to his palm. He carried the coins back to Lucy and held them out.

"Take this money to Gutz," he whispered. "I *loathe* leaving my tower — in fact, the level ground terrifies me, even more the dungeon — but you seem a fearless sort of girl. One of the guards will pass letters for the prisoners, but it requires a token of gratitude. A bribe, plainly speaking!"

Lucy was more confused than ever — no one had ever called her *fearless* before, and in fact Pauline teased her for being frightened of clowns — but she accepted the coins and put them in her pocket.

"I'm to give this to Professor Gutz?" she asked.

"*Professor* Gutz?" hissed Lemonjello. "That wolf in scholar's robes! No, I'm afraid *Costive* Gutz is . . . is . . . *stubbornly* opposed to our Cause. You're to take it to Arden Gutz, his nephew, in the dungeon. He must pay the guard a farthing for every note he sends."

"Tea!" Pauline called down.

"We've had word from Haslet March," the astronomer said hurriedly, "that Sir Henry Wallow is friendly to our Cause. Wallow is greatly esteemed among the country nobles, and you may imagine the benefit to us should he become our ally! It is *vital* that Arden Gutz be able to write to him. I'd . . . I'd planned to take him the money, but going down stairs is such a strain upon my nerves . . . and you're a brave girl, aren't you?"

"Wickwright!" Pauline cried. "I'm *freezing!*"

Lucy turned to climb the ladder, but Lemonjello held her arm.

"Bless you, child!" he whispered. "The sun is behind us!"

"*Quark!*" squawked the parrot.

Lucy had little opportunity that night to reflect on her curious exchange with the astronomer. Obviously there had been a misunderstanding. She knew nothing about the "Cause" beyond what was whispered by grown-ups in the castle, who themselves held wildly differing opinions. The "Causists" were bohemians or crackpots or revolutionists — depending on who was whispering — or agents of democracy, or theosophy, or free love. They numbered in the thousands and threatened the foundations of the Barony . . . or met in a beer hall that catered to impossible putschists. They flouted law and order, or decried corruption. They were dangerous guerillas, or trembling chickens. The only thing known for certain was that they were violently opposed to chewing gum.

They could not be too bad, Lucy thought, if the mild-mannered Lemonjello had joined them. But it was a matter for grown-ups to worry about and, beyond her taking the astronomer's money to Arden Gutz, none of her business. The last thing Lucy wanted was to become entangled with revolutionists. She had trouble enough looking after Pauline.

Her mistress had grown tired of stargazing and, after finishing her tea, had thanked Lemonjello and wished him a good night. Lucy escorted her back to the castle keep — across the starlit ward, past the Stone of Justice, and through the deserted Great Hall. Pauline had to be got out of her gown and into her nightshirt, and then Lucy had to tend the fire in her bedroom. She yawned as she warmed her mistress's milk, and nearly dozed at her bedside, waiting to take the empty bowl away.

"Good night, Wickwright," said the Baron's daughter, her head settling on the pillow Lucy had fluffed for her.

"Good night, mistress."

Lucy could have fallen asleep in the chair, but Pauline's

hennin had still to be brushed, and her gown laid in its silk wrapper and put away. The bell in the gatehouse had struck midnight before Lucy went to the servants' hall for her candle and climbed the winding steps to the attic.

The younger maidservants slept in a long dormitory under the eaves, their cots arranged in two neat rows along the low walls. Lucy walked softly past the sleepers, shielding her candle with her hand. At the end of the dormitory Mr. Vole, the steward, had ordered a heavy curtain to be hung, to provide a washing-up and dressing room for the girls. Over time this area had got cluttered with household bric-a-brac for which there was no other place — dressmakers' dummies, apple-butter tubs, a rocking horse, and the like — but there remained room for a washstand and an old copper bath. Lucy set her candle on the chipped marble top of the washstand and poured water from a jug, then took off her glasses and scrubbed her face.

She regretted missing the show of juggling. Had it not been for her confinement in the laundry she might have cut short her half-holiday to serve Pauline at the banquet. Banquets were wonderful. The Great Hall blazed with lamps and candles and torches, and there were singers and lutanists, and conjurors who put rabbits in thimbles and pulled pennies from your ear. Lucy enjoyed them so much that she had to take care not to drop a spoon, or lose herself in the dancing lights. How grand Pauline must have felt tonight, sitting at her father's side in her dress like a glittering jewel!

Lucy squeezed the washrag and hung it on a dowel. Beside the pile of bric-a-brac in the dressing room was a long pier glass that had cracked and been put there for the servants' use. Perhaps her tiring work in the laundry was to blame, but when Lucy saw her reflection in the glass — the worn-out sneakers and frayed jeans, her lank, unbrushed hair, the GIZMOBOTS! t-shirt hanging limp as a mop — she promptly burst into tears.

Chapter 5

*L*ucy had not always been a servant. Her parents had been chandlers, before the unhappy incident that took their lives, and her first memory was of the scent of beeswax that perfumed their workshop. As soon as she could stand she had worked alongside her parents, wrapping candles in tissue, brown paper, and string. The Wickwrights took pride in the words painted on their shingle, below *Lon & Hester Wickwright, Chandlers* — words that only the finest artisans of Cant were allowed to display:

By Appointment to the Baronial Court

Once a year, in the mild days of autumn, the Wickwrights and all the suppliers of goods to the court were welcomed to the castle itself, to drink cider and eat roasted mutton and make merry in the gaily decorated ward. The Baron himself opened the festivities, reading a speech full of grand and important words in which he praised the artisans' stalwart industry and inestimable skills. Then, after cries and applause, a representative of the people offered the Baron a Token of Esteem, some especially marvelous example of that person's art, which the Baron lifted overhead to the cheers of the crowd.

In the year of Lucy's seventh birthday a great honor fell to the Wickwrights, for they were chosen to present the Baron with a Token — a great, sculpted column of beeswax, which they had named the Candle of Cant. It stood nearly as tall as Lucy, and towered over her brother Casio, who was only a toddler. Around its base ran the Wolves of Rotwood Forest (emblems of the baronial house), and from its column gazed busts of the twelve Barons Cant.* Lucy was at the Guild Hall when her parents' work was chosen to represent the artisans. Her father had swung her round and round, the crowd laughing and applauding, little Casio running in excited circles under her feet.

On the day of the festival it was decided that Casio should ride in the barrow with the candle. Lucy or Mrs. Wickwright would walk alongside to steady the candle, and Mr. Wickwright would push it to the castle. The day was cool, fortunately, so there was no danger of the wax softening.

---

*Roland, Gullet, Leopold, Ambrose, Gustaf I ("the Fey"), Honoré, Lubin, Pius, Gustaf II ("the Lame"), Elvio, Urbano, and the present Baron, Adolphus, who was pictured both kindly and stern, the two faces arranged symmetrically atop the candle beneath the four-tufted baronial cap.

They were about to set out when a horse and trap rattled down Chandlers Lane and stopped in front of the Wickwrights' house. Behind the driver — who chewed sullenly at a great wad of something in his cheek — there sat a lady in court dress, her face covered by a dark veil. She stepped down from the trap without the driver's aid and, though the shopdoor stood open, rang the bell on the doorpost.

Casio ran behind his mother's skirts. Even Lucy was startled. The lady was so tall she had to stoop under the lintel, and her shoulders strained against the silk of a blood-red gown. Her face, behind the veil, was heavily painted, and in the middle of each tweezered eyebrow a wart bristled with long, unplucked hairs. Mr. Wickwright took off his hat and bowed respectfully.

"Good day, lady," he said. "How may I serve you today?"

The woman cleared her throat gruffly and responded in a high, quavering falsetto.

"You are Wickwright, the chandler?"

"Yes, ma'am," said Lucy's father.

"I am Lady Sweetbread," the woman said. "I come from far away. This is your good wife, I take it, and your little boy?"

"Why, yes, lady," said Mr. Wickwright. The woman glanced at Mrs. Wickwright, then walked over to Lucy and tilted up her chin with a satin-gloved finger.

"And this dark-haired girl?" she asked.

Lucy scowled. She never liked grown-ups playing with her face, though they seemed to think it their natural right to pinch a child's cheek. But what especially annoyed her was the lady's drawing attention to her hair. Lon and Hester Wickwright were renowned for their flaming red curls, a trait they had passed on to Casio. But Lucy was a plain brunette, and this was a sore point in her otherwise happy life. In the midst of her red-haired family she felt like a burnt-down wick surrounded by blazing tapers. She stepped away from Lady Sweetbread, who had leaned so close that Lucy could smell the tang of wine on her breath.

"That is my daughter Lucy," said Mr. Wickwright. "May I ask to what we owe the favor of your presence?" he added nervously. The ceremony began in less than an hour.

"I live far away," the lady said, still staring at Lucy. "You don't know how hard it is to find quality goods in the provinces." She turned to Mr. Wickwright. "Tallow candles, to name an example, are greatly inferior things. They are smoky, and they stink. You must know that."

"Yes, of course," Mr. Wickwright said. "But if it please the lady, we are in a bit of a hurry just now, so . . ."

"I shan't take a moment of your time," the woman said in her high, quavering voice. "I should like to purchase four dozens of your finest beeswax candles. I assure you my coins are not counterfeit."

"Er . . . no, of course not," said Mr. Wickwright, looking around the shop. He had that many candles in stock, but they were piled loose on the shelves, and there was no time to wrap them. "If you could come back tomorrow . . . my daughter will wrap the candles tonight and have them ready . . . you see, we're in a terrible hurry."

"But I'll not be in town tomorrow!" the lady said. She clutched her face in her hands and snuffled through her veil.

"Oh, please help me, good man! Lord Sweetbread will *throttle* me if I don't bring candles!"

Lon Wickwright glanced at the Candle of Cant — it was wrapped in multiple layers of tissue, shearling, and burlap — and tugged nervously at his beard.

"Perhaps you could take a few candles now," he suggested, "and hire a pony cart to deliver the rest."

The woman shook her head.

"I live far away," she sighed. "Black and blue, sir . . . my lord will beat me *black* and *blue!*"

Mr. Wickwright winced. Lucy saw how anxious he was to be off.

"I can wrap the candles now, Father," she offered. "It won't take long. I can catch up to you at the castle."

"The castle?" said Lady Sweetbread. "Why, *I'm* stopping at the castle this afternoon, to visit cousin Orloff! The girl can ride with me in the trap — very likely we'll overtake you on the road." Again she covered her face with her hands. "Oh, Lord Sweetbread will slit my *throat* if I return empty-handed!"

Lon Wickwright was a kind-hearted man and could not bear to see a person weep. He was a practical man as well, with two growing children to feed, and could hardly afford to turn up his nose at a sale of four dozen finest beeswax candles. He picked up the Candle of Cant and bent to kiss Lucy on her cheek.

"Take the lady's money," he told her, "and lock up the house when you've finished."

"Yes, Father."

Lucy kissed her mother and waved goodbye to Casio (who

had lately decided that kisses, except from his mother, were un-manly and poisonous). She watched her father lay the Candle of Cant in the wheelbarrow, hoist up Casio beside it, and set off. With a glance at Lady Sweetbread — who was scratching herself in a very unladylike place — Lucy set to work. Being a nimble-fingered girl with long experience at candle-wrapping, she thought she could easily finish the job and arrive at the cas-tle in time for the ceremony. When she had tied a knot on the fourth bundle of seven candles, the lady, who had looked on silently till then, took a large, mannish watch from her bag and looked at it.

"About an hour's walk to the castle for a man pushing a bar-row, don't you think?" she asked. (Castle Cant stood half a league from the town of Tenesmus, up a narrow road cut into a sheer cliff-face that loomed over a deep fissure bristling with upturned horns of rock.)

Lucy shrugged. "I think so," she said, though in truth she thought so only because the lady suggested it. She had not yet learned the grown-up art of measuring life by hours. Oh, she could read the clock on the Town Hall and tell whether it said 7:25 or 1:15, and she knew that when the little bell rang once it meant half an hour had gone since the big bells rang. But she could never tell, when she began to make a drawing of a house, how many bells would go before she finished. It was finished when she made a curlicue of smoke above the chimney, which was her favorite thing to draw, and which she always saved till the last. Likewise, a walk finished when you got to where you were going, which might be soon or later, depending on whether you skipped right along or picked flowers on the way.

"You seem a useful sort of girl," said Lady Sweetbread. "Handy with a broom, are you?"

"Yes, ma'am," Lucy said. She liked to sweep.

"Hard work is good for the common folk," the lady declared. "It refines the spirit, much as a good book elevates the nobler mind."

Lucy paused in her wrapping.

"But I like to read stories too, ma'am."

"Ah," the lady said, "you know your letters, do you? Well, one can't put smoke back into a bottle, I suppose. But consider your station in life, little girl, and heed my advice: Don't become too caught up in books. They are perilous things to those of inferior birth, and will unfit you for honest labor. A strong back and an humble spirit — those are the virtues to cultivate."

Lady Sweetbread had a queer way of talking, Lucy reflected as she snipped a piece of string. Had the lady read a storybook, she wondered, in which smoke came in bottles, like milk or vinegar? Lucy should like to read that book. She could picture the drawings in her mind, the smoke pouring upward out of the bottle in long wavy lines.

"A strong back and an humble spirit," Lady Sweetbread repeated, measuring Lucy with her eyes. "And sturdy feet. Have you sturdy feet, little one?"

"I suppose so," Lucy said. She had never thought much about them.

"Let us have a look, would you, dear?" the lady asked. Lucy put aside a bundle of candles.

"You want to look at my feet?"

Lady Sweetbread stepped closer.

"Just one of them, dear," she said. "They're both the same, aren't they?"

"Yes, ma'am!"

"Give us a look, then," said Lady Sweetbread, her voice higher and squeakier than ever. Her eyes gleamed behind the veil, as though she was famished and Lucy a plate of dumplings. Lucy thought it an odd thing to ask, but she was in a hurry, and not used to refusing her elders. She stepped on the heel of her slipper and showed her foot. Her mother, had she been there, would have been mortified — Lucy's toenails badly wanted trimming.

Lady Sweetbread squatted on her heels and ran a gloved finger over Lucy's toes — *tickle tickle tickle tickle tickle tickle*. A low chuckle escaped her, though she did not, to Lucy, seem the sort of woman who delighted in playing piggies. She stood up with a grunt, her hands pushing on her knees, and petted Lucy's cheek approvingly.

"Excellent," she said. "Just as I hoped. Now hurry, child, and we'll deliver you to the castle. Your family must be dying."

"Ma'am?" Lucy asked, sliding her foot into her slipper.

"Dying to see you, dear," said Lady Sweetbread. "A figure of speech. An hyperbole. Don't trouble your little head about it. Hop hop! Four dozens of your finest! Mustn't leave Lord Sweetmeat in the dark!"

Lucy tore another piece of tissue and wrapped it round a candle, then looked up at the lady, who was again consulting her watch.

"Excuse me, ma'am. I thought your name was Sweetbread?"

"Why, yes, of course it is."

"But you said 'Lord Sweetmeat' just now."

"Did I say that?" asked Lady Sweetbread. She closed the cover of her watch and put it into her bag. "Why, it was a slip of the tongue, my dear. 'Sweetmeat' is my pet name for Lord Sweetbread. I miss him terribly."

Lucy thought that, rather than missing him, Lady Sweetbread should be glad of a holiday from her husband — who must be very ill tempered, if he was apt to beat his wife black and blue over a few dozen candles. The Wickwrights' cat wandered in from Chandlers Lane, and Lady Sweetbread, shying away from it, abruptly sneezed.

"I must step outside and have a breath of air," she told Lucy in her odd, high voice. "The little beast has played havoc with my nose. Come fetch my driver when you've finished, and he'll help you to carry out the candles."

"Yes, ma'am." Lucy stooped over to pet the cat, then tore another piece of tissue and wrapped it around a candle. She was excited to be going to the castle in a trap. She would pretend to be a visiting princess, from a faraway, exotic land, and that the crowd at the festival had gathered to welcome her.

She was debating whether her royal carriage (the trap) should be drawn by camels or by giraffes when she heard a loud *Hyah!* on Chandlers Lane. Lucy thought Lady Sweetbread must have sneezed again, but when she looked up she saw the driver striking the horse with his whip.

"*Hyah! Hyah!*" he cried, and with a rattling of wheels the trap was in motion. Lady Sweetbread sat behind the driver with her veil thrown up, and appeared to be urging him on.

"Wait!" Lucy said. She dropped the candle she had been

wrapping and ran out to the lane, clutching a scrap of tissue in her hand. The horse was galloping, now, driven to frenzy by the whip, and the trap tipped perilously as it turned up the road to the castle.

"Lady Sweetbread!" Lucy called out, waving her arms. "Your candles!"

But the trap was already out of sight. Lucy looked around, hoping a grown-up would come to her aid, but all the residents of Chandlers Lane had closed shop and gone to the festival. The faint rattle of the trap faded to silence, and Lucy stood bewildered in the lane, not knowing what to do. Far away the castle loomed over the sheer cliff-face, and beyond its gray towers the mountains raised their glittering peaks to the sun. Lucy felt her nose beginning to drip. She wiped it with the scrap of tissue and waited for someone — her parents, a neighbor, even Lady Sweetbread — to come and tell her what to do.

Chapter 6

The Road To Castle Cant

*L*ucy never saw her family again. Lon, Hester, and Casio Wickwright were buried some days later under the tapering larches of the graveyard of Tenesmus, their mortal remains having been discovered among the rocks below Castle Cant. Constable Cronk made an investigation, assisted by the castle guard, but there were no witnesses to the tragedy, and the road to the castle had been so scribbled by carts, barrows, and carriages that nothing could be read there.

Suspicion fell immediately upon the mysterious Lady Sweetbread. The *Baronial Census of Cantlings, Livestock, & Domestic Animals* was consulted, but the name "Sweetbread" occurred only as that of a butcher's cat in the hamlet of Dragonfly-on-Bog. This gave rise to speculation that the crime had been the work of outlanders (as foreigners were called in Cant), and panic seized the townsfolk. Doors were bolted at night and rusty swords were polished and sharpened, for the people of Cant harbored a deep distrust of all things foreign.

The Candle of Cant was never found, and in his final report Constable Cronk deemed that Larceny was the motive of the crime. A candle-mad alien, he surmised — perhaps the agent of some larger, global syndicate — had somehow heard rumor of the Wickwrights' masterpiece. Eluding the border guard, she had entered the Barony and carried out her infamous plot, then escaped with the candle over the mountains. This theory won the endorsement of the people, and for weeks afterward the householders of Tenesmus slept with their candles under lock and key, ears alert for foreign footsteps.

Lucy remembered little of that time, save being pulled this way and that by well-meaning grown-ups, like a toy carriage on a string. She stayed at first with her mother's brother. Hocklin Tooey was an innkeeper who kept a respectable house with a tavern and a small stable. He loved his niece, but he had no experience of rearing a young girl. He held Lucy in his arms, and petted and consoled her as best he could, but there his parenting skills ended. When not taking care of the business of the inn he mostly slumped on a bench by the fire, consumed by his own grief (his sister, after all, had died). Word reached the authorities that Lucy was bathing irregularly and spending hours of each day in the hayloft of the stable, talking to her doll.

A meeting was called of the Women's Benevolent Society. The upshot was that Lucy, for the time being, should be taken to the American Mission, which ran an orphanage in a converted coal barn on Fenway Road. There, at least, she would be properly fed, and made to wash herself, and would have the company of other children and the discipline of chores and grammar lessons to distract her mind.

So a deputation arrived from the Benevolent Society, consisting of Mrs. Fiddle (a neighbor from Chandlers Lane), Mrs. Meddle (secretary to the Society), and Miss Poke (of the American Mission). Uncle Hock held Lucy on his lap while the good women pressed their case. A tavern, said Mrs. Meddle, was no place to bring up a young girl. And surely, reasoned Mrs. Fiddle, Hock Tooey could see that a bachelor, even a loving uncle, could hardly understand the needs of a young girl. Miss Poke smiled brightly at Lucy and talked of life at the orphanage as though it was a grand adventure.

"Why," she said, "on Saturdays, each and every child in our care gets a glass of orange juice! You like orange juice, don't you, Lucy?"

"It's full of vitamin C," Mrs. Meddle added, for the benefit of Uncle Hock.

"The astronauts drink it," put in Mrs. Fiddle. Though only a chandler's wife, she knew something of the wide world.

Lucy hugged her uncle's neck and buried her face in his shirt. She had never tasted orange juice, but she imagined it was sweet and sticky, like Miss Poke herself. She blinked tears from her eyes.

"But I want to stay with you, Uncle Hock," she said. What she wanted really, of course, was to go on living with her mother and father and Casio in their house on Chandlers Lane. But that, as she had patiently explained to her doll, was no longer possible, and they must carry on as best they could in their new circumstances. Now she was being asked to move again, and leave behind the only family left to her.

"I want you to stay too, sweetcheeks," said Uncle Hock, wiping a tear from her face. "But . . . well, perhaps we should listen to the ladies. I want to do what's best for you."

"Your uncle can come see you as often as he likes," said Miss Poke. "It's an easy walk from here. Indeed, several of our children have visitors. And on the Baron's anniversary a clown comes! You want to see the clown, don't you, sweetie?"

It was a curious thing, but while Lucy liked being called "sweetcheeks" by Uncle Hock, she shuddered to be called "sweetie" by Miss Poke. It reminded her, somehow, of Lady Sweetbread's pawing at her face in the workshop.

She sniffled, and while Miss Poke burbled on about the joys of orphanage life her uncle took Lucy's nose in a fold of his shirt and wiped it clean. This brought a high, despairing sigh from Mrs. Meddle. The ladies averted their eyes, and Miss Poke's voice dropped to a faint, uneasy warble. They thought Uncle Hock was a bad uncle, Lucy saw, and they would wheedle and pester him till he allowed them take her away.

"Wouldn't you like to see the clown?" said Miss Poke.

Lucy swallowed the lump in her throat. She had to do what was best for Uncle Hock.

"A clown?" she said, her voice high and thin. And for the first and only time in her life, Lucy told an outright fib — for Uncle Hock's sake. "I lie . . . I mean, I *like* clowns," she told Miss Poke, forcing her mouth to smile.

"There, you see?" said Miss Poke happily.

"Every child loves a clown," put in Mrs. Fiddle, nodding at her own insight.

"I think we may consider the matter settled," said Mrs. Meddle. She was a plump woman, with large, gouty ankles, and it was with some difficulty that she picked up a carpetbag and rose from the stool where she sat. "I had the foresight to bring a bag for the girl's belongings. We can leave at once."

"I'll come see you every day, sweetcheeks," Uncle Hock promised, giving Lucy a squeeze. He looked up at Miss Poke. "It would be all right, wouldn't it, if Lucy visited me sometimes? Perhaps spent the night, if I brought her back early in the morning?"

Miss Poke smiled, but her eyes cringed, as though Hock Tooey had just blown his nose into the fire.

"Well," she said, "I'm sure that's something we can discuss with Reverend Frodd."

Uncle Hock had set up a cot for Lucy in the pantry, his guest-rooms being full at the time of the tragedy. She went there now, carrying the carpetbag, and for the second time in as many weeks she packed her few dresses, her doll (Nancy), her watercolor set, and her hairbrush. Her cat lay on the pillow — that is, her family's cat, Penrod, now employed as a mouser by Uncle Hock — and she was sitting down to give his ears a farewell scratch when she heard a commotion on Baron Gullet Street. She picked up the carpetbag and went through the kitchen to the public room.

The representatives of the Benevolent Society were huddled at a window, and her uncle stood at the open door, nervously wiping his hands on his apron. Lucy looked from the other window. A glittering black carriage had drawn up before her uncle's inn, the Perch & Pillow. A crowd of merchants and curious loafers had gathered round it, for on its doors were

painted the arms of the house of Cant.* Hock Tooey untied
and tossed away his apron as the driver helped out of the carriage its passenger, a man in a wide-sleeved court robe. The
nobleman scowled at the inn's weathered shingle, then strode
solemnly to the door.

"Hocklin Severus Tooey?" he demanded.

"Yes, sir," said Lucy's uncle, bowing awkwardly. "I'm Hock
Tooey."

"I am Cornucoppio Guuzi, Minister of the Public Weal to
His Honor, Lord Cant. I bring a message from His Lordship."

A gasp rose from Mrs. Fiddle, Mrs. Meddle, and Miss Poke.
Lucy went to her uncle and clutched his hand, her heart beating wildly.

"A m-m-message from the Baron?" asked Uncle Hock.

"Attend!" said Minister Guuzi. He produced a folded parchment from his robe, unsealed it, and held it open at arm's length.
He cleared his throat importantly, and read as follows:

*Adolphus, Lord Cant, to His servant, Hocklin Severus Tooey,
Greeting!*

*Report has reached Our ears of the late misfortune that befell
Our loyal subjects, Mr. Wickwright, Mrs. Wickwright, and
Casio Wickwright. We have learned that Our servants, of fond
memory, were, on that infamous day, bound for Our seat, there to
present a Token, by them made, of the affection of those suppliers of
goods to Our household, that yearly foregather, to celebrate a Feast
by Us given.*

---

*Per chevron gules and argent three wolves sable. (That is, three black wolves on a field
of red and silver. See Appendix.)

Our heart is grieved that a girl-child, called Lucy, is left orphaned by this calamity. In keeping with that Mercy, enjoined upon Us by the Wise Teachers, We command that the said child shall enter Our household, and serve as maid to Our very daughter, the Adored & Hon'ble Pauline (replacing that bad servant, lately by Us dismissed, who showed herself unworthy of Our favor, a gossip and a thief of Spoons).

Therefore, let the child Lucy present herself, in clean and suitable dress, to Our house-steward, Mr. Vole, which esteemed gentleman shall instruct her in her Duties. Peace, Hocklin Severus, and farewell! Given this day the 17th October, &c., &c.

Minister Guuzi folded the letter again, its parchment crackling in the stunned silence that followed his announcement. Lucy had withdrawn behind Hock Tooey, though she still clung to his hand. She peeked around him, now, and briefly met the courtier's gaze.

"I have come to deliver the child to Mr. Vole," he said. "Allow me to congratulate you on your good fortune, Hocklin Tooey. This, I take it, is the child in question?"

Hock Tooey, dumbed by the grandeur of his visitor and the staggering import of his news, pulled Lucy in front of him and put his hands on her shoulders. Mrs. Meddle stepped forward and made to Minister Guuzi such a curtsey as her swollen ankles allowed.

"That is Lucy Wickwright, sir," she said. "This is most extraordinary! You see —"

Guuzi cut her short with a glance.

"Who are you, woman?" he asked.

"Why why why," stammered Mrs. Meddle, "forgive me, please! I am Mrs. Meddle, sir, secretary to the Women's Benevolent Society."

"And what, exactly, is your business with me?"

Before Mrs. Meddle could reply, Hock Tooey spoke.

"These kind ladies had arranged to place my niece in the orphanage, at the American Mission. We were just setting off. I'm a bachelor, you see —"

"Yes, your situation is familiar to me," said Guuzi. He turned to Mrs. Meddle. "May I thank you, on the Baron's behalf, for your interest in the welfare of a poor girl. In fact, you've done a great service, if indeed the child is ready to leave. We can depart immediately."

Lucy hardly knew what to think. First she had lost her family and been brought to live with Uncle Hock. No sooner had she got used to *that* idea than she was to be taken away to an orphanage and made to laugh at clowns. Now she was to ride in a grand carriage, with a strange man, and take up lodgings in the castle! Tomorrow, surely, a flying rug would appear and carry her away to the moon.

"But . . . this is all so sudden," said Uncle Hock. "Who will care for Lucy at the castle?"

"Your concern," said Guuzi, "is understandable, and, of course, to be commended. You may trust that Mr. Vole will take a personal interest in the child's well being, as indeed he does for all the domestic staff. She will be put on board wages, be given a bed with the other maids, and will have the benefit of contact with noble persons. I invite you," he added, "to present yourself at the castle — say, a week hence. There you may satisfy yourself that the child is in the best possible care."

"Thrilling! Thrilling!" put in Mrs. Meddle.

There seemed little else to say. The driver was called to carry Lucy's bag, and, after a long embrace and some awkward, tender words, Uncle Hock led her to the carriage and lifted her up. Minister Guuzi climbed in after her and showed Lucy how to put her arm through the strap. Uncle Hock, flanked by Mrs. Fiddle, Mrs. Meddle, and Miss Poke, waved goodbye as the driver whipped the horses into motion.

The carriage jolted and juddered through the streets of Tenesmus. Guuzi stared at Lucy, who looked at her hands. When they had gained the road to the castle the Minister of the Public Weal produced a purse, from which he took a small silver case, wrought with precious stones and gold. He worked the catch with his thumb and offered the open case to Lucy.

"It occurs to me," he said, "that this sudden turn of events, however fortunate, may be a trial to your young nerves. I have found that gum has a calming effect, on such occasions. Please to enjoy a piece with my compliments. It also," he said in a dryer voice, "freshens the breath."

Lucy examined the gum, which she supposed to be a kind of sweet. It was shiny white, like a sugar pastille. She took a piece, put it into her mouth, and began to eat. She chewed and chewed the rubbery stuff, when the sugar had dissolved, until she began to wonder if the minister had played some kind of prank on her. For the gum refused to chew *up*, though she chewed till her jaw ached and the gum had no more flavor than her own tongue. When the carriage had thudded across the drawbridge and come to a halt in the courtyard of the castle, Lucy was *still* chewing the strange sweet, and it remained as un-chewed-*up* as ever.

Cornucoppio Guuzi reached over to open her door. Before the driver could dismount and help her down, Lucy jumped from the carriage and, while no one watched, spat the uneaten gum under the wheels. She looked around the empty courtyard, at the high, forbidding walls of the castle. She doubted somehow that living here was such a piece of good luck as the minister suggested. If this "gum" was what passed for a sweet at Castle Cant, she thought glumly, then the vegetables must be very gruesome indeed.

Chapter 7

A Tea Party

$\mathcal{M}$ost of the maidservants spent only a few years in the service, saving money for their linens and pewter, after which they left the castle to be married. Even a baron could ill afford to dress such a large, ever-changing staff without some economies, so their uniforms were passed from girl to girl, and only when a uniform had been patched upon its patches was it replaced. Lucy had presented a problem, being so much younger and smaller than the other girls. There was simply no uniform to fit her.

Eventually, with much grumbling about the cost, Mr. Vole had been obliged to have one especially made. Lucy wore it proudly, at first. But while Lucy kept growing, her uniform did not, and as time wore on it became an embarrassment. She pleaded with Mr. Vole for a new one, but the steward insisted there was "plenty of good wear" left in the threadbare shift, which by then barely covered Lucy's knees. Only when she publicly burst a seam, to the great merriment of the girls gathered for supper, had Vole allowed Lucy to retire the poor garment.

That had been almost a year ago. Since then Lucy had worn clothes from the Mission, like an orphan of the streets, while Vole put her off with promises that a new uniform would be delivered "perhaps as early as next fiscal quarter."

Meanwhile she was talked about, and teased by the older girls, and squinted at by the likes of Costive Gutz. The towns-people of Tenesmus were used to seeing orphans in outlandish clothes, but to the denizens of the castle she was an object of wonder and fun. When she first presented herself at the guard-house, for example, to deliver Lemonjello's farthings to Arden Gutz, the gaoler on duty had openly snorted.

"No visitors today, lass," he told her, when his fit of chuck-ling had passed. He struggled to keep a straight face. "He he. No, all the prisoners as can work are down at the carriage house, scraping gum from under the seats. You'd think a high and mighty lord could push open the door and spit his gum out," he added, "but no. They leave their droppings behind like rabbits. You'll have to come back tomorrow."

So Lucy had turned away, disappointed. She had somehow looked forward to meeting Mr. Arden Gutz, who had looked so proud and defiant as he knelt by the Stone of Justice — unlike anyone she had known in her years at the castle, which was full of flatterers in flowing robes. She fancied she and

Arden Gutz might share something in common — they both knew the sting of getting into trouble, at least.

She walked back to the ward, the farthings still clinking in her pocket. A grand carnival would mark the Baron's anniversary, and all around the courtyard was the bustle and clatter of preparation. Hammers boomed as workers erected the broad dais where the speeches would be made. A marquee rose over an outdoor kitchen, and gay pennants snapped over the bowling greens, tortoise rides, and other amusements. Tomorrow the long-awaited festival began.

Lucy wandered about, inspecting the arrangements, until the clock struck three. She had left Pauline at her fencing lesson in a corner of the ward, but now her mistress must be got ready, for she was to entertain her cousins at tea. That meant putting her into a bath, and getting her *out* of a bath (for once in, Pauline liked to soak until her fingers pruned), and doing up her hair, and dressing her. Lucy had put away her doll ages ago, but sometime she felt as though she had done nothing but play with a doll since she came to Castle Cant.

She found her mistress turning over stones with the corked point of her fencing foil. The fencing master was gone. Pauline had pushed her mask atop her head, and in her white breeches and quilted white chest-protector she looked very like a straw-stuffed doll.

"Wickwright," she said, "do you know what I should like for tea?"

"No, mistress. What is that?"

"Snails!" said Pauline. "Don't you love them, Wickwright?

There were snails in mushroom caps at the banquet, Saturday, absolutely *bathing* in melted butter, like babies in washtubs. If I were put into prison on a diet of snails and water I should bear it with courage, and write verse on napkins, and become a famous poetess."

Lucy knew that Glenden Galt, the immortal bard of Cant, had composed his epic *Wolves of Rotwood* while imprisoned on a charge of Gross Offenses. But she doubted he had dined on snails while in the dungeon. She was not fond of snails, herself, and could imagine no Offense more Gross than eating one.

"I'm sure Mr. Broom has already made up the menu, mistress," she told Pauline. Mr. Broom was Pauline's cook — the same morose, hapless man who had carried the chicken at Arden Gutz's execution — and Lucy always did her best to shield him from last-minute changes to the menu. "I'll suggest he prepare snails for luncheon tomorrow."

"Do," said Pauline, dislodging another stone with the tip of her foil. "The courtyard is *teeming* with them, after all. You can't turn over a rock without finding a snail. They're like servants! They're simply everywhere! Look at this one, Wickwright — it's *huge!*"

She lifted her foil. A finger-thick black slimy thing writhed at the end of the weapon, wrapping itself slowly round the cork button. Lucy stepped away.

"They've all come out of their shells," said Pauline. "Because of the warm weather, I fancy."

"That's not a snail, mistress," Lucy said. "It's a slug."

Pauline pointed the foil upward, and the slug slid slowly down the blade to the guard.

"Is that a slug?" she asked.

"Yes, mistress. The common garden slug. They don't have shells."

Pauline shifted the foil to her off hand and picked up the slug with her glove.

"In my opinion that's very stupid," she said. "If I were as soft and squishy as *that*, I'd certainly cover myself with a shell." She scratched under her chest-protector with the pommel of her foil. "Are they good to eat, Wickwright?"

"I never heard of anyone eating slugs, mistress."

"One might say," Pauline said, looking closely at the squirming creature, "that the slug is to the snail, as the crab-apple is to the apple."

"I suppose one might," said Lucy. "But we had better get you into your bath."

"Or as the crab-apple is to the crab, for that matter. People eat crabs, don't they, Wickwright?"

"I believe so, in the watery parts of the world. Well, you mustn't keep the Misses Martlet waiting. I'm sure Helen has drawn your bath by now."

"I remember hearing," Pauline said, "that when the slug was first introduced to Cant it was known as the crab-snail to the lower classes. It was a staple food in the olden days, before they began raising sheep. Take a bite, Wickwright!"

Lucy knew Pauline's tricks. She wanted to stay outside and play in her fencing costume, and was trying to distract Lucy by daring her to eat the slug. The bathwater would grow tepid, and Pauline, when finally dragged to the tub, would protest, and Helen, the kitchen girl whose duty it was to fill the baths, would have to carry more hot water up the stairs, and would blame Lucy for it and take revenge by putting something offensive in Lucy's sheets.

"I'm afraid I can't eat slug," Lucy said. "I've become a vegetarian."

"You have not!"

"It's true, mistress." Lucy *had* become a vegetarian — that very moment — and though she intended to renounce her vegetarianism the next time there was meat on the menu in the servants' hall, she would not forsake her principles to take a bite of Pauline's slug. "Perhaps," she suggested, "you should put it back under the rock now."

"No," Pauline said. "I'm going to make a shell for the poor dear, Wickwright, and keep him as a pet. Find a cage for him, and give him something to eat." She turned her foil point downward and dropped the slug into the shallow bowl of the guard, then handed the weapon to Lucy.

"Are you going to give it a name?" Lucy asked, having decided it would be easier to deal with one of her mistress's Whims later than to argue about it now. She began to walk toward the castle keep so that Pauline, if she wanted to answer the question, would have to follow.

After some debate the slug was given the name "Martingale." Lucy had no time to search out a cage for it, so when Pauline went up to her bath she hung the foil by its wrist strap from a peg in the kitchen. Martingale could rest in the guard for the time being. After a few words with Mr. Broom she put on an apron and went to dress her mistress for the tea party.

Pauline was playing hostess to her cousins, the Misses Eugenia and Hazel Martlet, daughters of her father's sister and Sir

Clarence Martlet, the Baronet of Poltroon. Lucy had been all morning readying Pauline's sitting room for the party. Her mistress rarely entertained guests so nearly approaching to her own rank, and she tried to impress her cousins, whenever they visited, with all the pomp and splendor of Castle Cant.* Lucy had filled vases with great geysers of yellow crocuses, and had polished the mirrors, and dusted, and set out sparkling crystal dishes of honey drops and marzipan.

When she had dressed Pauline and installed her in a chair by the tea table she inspected the place-settings a last time, making sure that the forks were shining, the goblets spotless, and the menu cards (written in Mr. Broom's elegant hand) standing upright in their braided wreaths of wildflowers. There were no snails, but the dishes would surely impress Pauline's provincial guests:

Blinis, caviar, œuf dur, ciboule
Sandwich à l'anguille
Salade de pissenlit

At precisely 4:30 the sisters, chaperoned by their nurse, appeared at the sitting-room door. Lucy, serving as footman, announced the guests in the most starched voice she could produce.

"Miss Martlet and Miss Hazel Martlet!"

Pauline rose with a rustling of *crêpe de Chine* and hurried to her visitors with outstretched arms, as though she had not seen

---

The five social classes of Cant being (in order of precedence) Baron (or Baroness), Baronet (or Baronette), Knight (or Dame), Squire (or Squirrel), and Commoner (or, collectively, Folk).

them in years (though of course they had been at the banquet on Saturday). She smiled radiantly.

"Darling cousins!" she cried. "How good of you to come!"

Eugenia Martlet, a young woman of twelve years, seemed less enthused by the occasion than her hostess. She kissed the air in the vicinity of Pauline's right ear, her cheek brushing her cousin's and leaving, Lucy noticed, a faint smudge of face powder.

"Dearest Pauline," she sighed. "One trusts the day finds you well."

"I do splendidly, thank you," said Pauline. "Precious Hazel!"

She bent to kiss her younger cousin, a girl of four who tottered under the weight of her elaborately brocaded costume. Hazel had not quite grown into the dress, and an aroma of cedar hinted at the long years of storage since Eugenia had worn it. Lucy stooped to pick up the girl's doll, which she had let fall when Pauline kissed her.

"Your doll, Miss Hazel."

The girl blinked her round, dark eyes at Lucy and clutched the doll to her chest.

"Dolly threw up in the carriage," she said.

"Oh dear," said Lucy. "I trust she's feeling better?"

The girl nodded. Pauline led Eugenia to the tea table, followed by Hazel and the nurse (Mrs. Healing), who helped Hazel into a chair and tied a napkin round her neck. Before setting out the first course of pancakes, caviar, hard eggs, and onion, Lucy (as instructed by Mr. Vole at the morning staff meeting) invited Mrs. Healing to take refreshment in the kitchen.

"Thank you, child," said the nurse. She was a woman of uncertain years, her clothes, face, and hair all sharing the frumpy, gray-brown color of aging hosiery. "I feel I want a little something. The mountain air no longer agrees with me, I'm afraid, but a drop of the Baron's sherry will put me right. Stay! You needn't guide me," she added (though Lucy had not yet offered to do so). "Oh, I know my way around Castle Cant, dear, perhaps better than yourself. My departed father was head footman to Baron Urbano, you know."

"Indeed, ma'am, I didn't."

Mrs. Healing touched Lucy's arm and spoke in a whisper.

"Do keep an eye on Miss Hazel," she said. "The dear is wont to put candles in her mouth, of late. Unlighted ones, of course, and thank goodness."

"I will, ma'am," Lucy said.

Pauline liked to play at being a grown-up, but at this hobby she fell far behind Miss Martlet, who from the moment they sat down scarcely let her put in a word. That in itself, Lucy knew, was a very grown-up habit, for grown people seemed to think that conversation was a contest, in which whoever managed to talk the most was the winner. Pauline, as hostess, served the tea, and Lucy had nothing to do but listen to Eugenia from the sideboard until a tray wanted carrying to the kitchen. Pauline stifled her yawns, and little Hazel, whose napkin and chin were soon stained with caviar, stared at the painted ceiling. The painting — *The Apotheosis of Gustaf the Lame* — showed that beloved Baron and his family being gathered up into the clouds, and the girl seemed to wish that she, too, could float into its painted heaven.

"There was a frightful row in Boondock just before we came down," said Eugenia during the second course. Lucy marveled that Pauline's cousin had managed to eat any food at all, for the torrent of gossip had not stopped since the tea was poured. "Did you chance to hear about it, Pauline?"

Pauline, who had been making a funny face at Hazel, uncrossed her eyes.

"No," she sighed. "But *do* tell us about it, Eugenia. One so longs to hear these tidbits from the provinces."

"I should think His Lordship your father would want to know about it," said Eugenia. "It was a proper riot, by all accounts. It seems a number of fishers had been lost on the lake when their boat went down in a storm. A tragedy, of course, but all the better families respond wonderfully to these mishaps. A subscription was taken up for a wreath, and almost a dozen noble houses sent representatives to the memorial. Daddy sent his lieutenant, Sir Olive Darning."

At a signal from Pauline, Lucy began to gather up the plates.

"One can imagine how dreary it must have been," Eugenia went on, "with the surviving fishers making tearful speeches, and the widows and orphans getting all moist. Well, finally it came time for a person of the better classes to express our sympathy. Sir Berry du Fesse-Mathieu did the honors — I dare say he is one of the chief men of Trans-Poltroon, after Daddy — and you would think, wouldn't you, that the people would be grateful to hear such an orator?"

"Naturally," Pauline said, probing her nose behind the cover of a napkin.

"Nothing of the sort!" Eugenia cried. "You see, as the memorial wore on, Sir Berry and some of the other nobles had got thirsty, and began to chew gum as a remedy. Unfortunately, Sir Berry neglected to remove his gum before speaking. I may add that Sir Olive believes the crowd rather grumbled when the gum was passed round. Evidently they thought it bad form. But when Sir Berry began chewing during his speech they took it as an insult, and, would you believe, they pelted the poor man with vegetables! I call that being overly sensitive, don't you?"

Gum seemed to have its critics everywhere, Lucy noted. But it was the pelting with vegetables that inspired Pauline's first glimmer of interest. Her face brightened, and she sat upright in her chair.

"I should like to have seen that!" she said.

"What I want to know," Eugenia said, "is what class of person brings vegetables to a memorial? I mean, what? Is it their custom to carry their luncheon about in their pockets? Of course, chewing gum is beyond their means, so perhaps they make do by gnawing upon tubers. I'm sure they were simply jealous. But speaking of frightful events on the lake, Daddy took us sailing last fortnight . . ."

Mrs. Healing was laughing gaily when Lucy carried down the remains of the eel sandwiches. The sherry had put her right, evidently. She burped into her glove as Mr. Broom put the dandelion salads on the tray.

"Lucy, dear," she said. "Please to tell Miss Hazel that the dandelion flower is merely a garnish. It *is* merely a garnish, isn't it, Mr. Broom?"

"A touch of color on the plate," said the cook. "A morsel for the eyes."

"Oh, Mr. Broom, how romantic!" said Mrs. Healing.

"Away you go, Lucy," said Mr. Broom, handing her the tray.

Eugenia was still chattering when Lucy brought in the salads, and had now got on to the subject of heraldry. This was a popular topic in Cant, where the humblest country squire hung a coat of arms over his peat fire and tormented his guests with obscure terms like *a fess engrailed* and *a canton of the last*. Cantlings of the noble classes took great pride in their ability to *blazon* coats of arms (or "describe them in baffling phrases"), and Eugenia was no exception.

"One finds it odd," she said, as Lucy carried round the salads, "that the arms of the house of Cant remain so . . . well, so *elementary*, from the heraldic point of view."

"Dandelion salad," said Lucy, setting a plate before Eugenia. Pauline lifted her teacup, on which the arms of Cant were painted, and squinted at the familiar design.

"Your arms are full of ducks, aren't they?" she asked her cousin. Eugenia took up a knife and fork and began to cut her salad.

"Martins, Pauline," she said after a pause. "Called martlets, in heraldic terms. The symbol traditionally represents a fourth son, but in our case —"

"Oh, I thought they were ducks!" said Pauline. "How stupid of me."

"Dandelion salad," Lucy said, setting down Hazel's plate. She paused to whisper at the girl's ear. "Mrs. Healing says you're not to eat the flower."

"In *our* case," Eugenia continued, "the martlet is a punning reference to the family name, which is more ancient than the grant of arms, of course."

"Naturally," said Pauline. She yawned, but disguised her boredom by filling her gaping mouth with dandelion greens. Lucy retired to the sideboard.

"*My* arms," Eugenia said, "are quartered with those of Cant, because my mother is your father's sister, Pauline. They are blazoned thus: *Arms-quarterly, first and forth gyronny or —*"

"Or what?" said Pauline.

Eugenia frowned.

"Or and sable," she said dryly. "So. *First and forth gyronny or and sable, two martlets purpure, a baton vert three mussel shells or —*"

"Or *what?*" Pauline demanded, a faint giggle — *hee! hee!* — escaping her nose. Lucy sighed and gazed up at *The Apotheosis of Gustaf the Lame.* Pauline knew perfectly well what "or" meant. She was playing stupid only to annoy Eugenia.

"*Or* means the color gold, Pauline," Eugenia explained, putting down her fork. "*Three mussel shells or* indicates three golden mussel shells. The second and third quarters represent the arms of Cant, blazoned thus: *Second and third per chevron gules and argent three wolves sable.*"

"Three wolves able to do *what?*" Pauline said, giggling openly now. Eugenia crumpled her napkin and stood up, her chair sliding on the marble floor.

"Honestly, Pauline, you are such a *little girl,*" she said. "One would think you might at least contain yourself in front of your maid."

Pauline clutched her stomach, helpless with mirth.

"Per chevron — *hee!*" she squealed. "Per chevron gules and argent . . . *hee! hee!* . . . three wolves able to eat all those ducks!"

Eugenia threw down her napkin.

"Oh! You are *impossible!* And to think that one day *you* shall be Lady Cant!" A cold fire gleamed in her eyes. "Though Papa says you have no more claim to the barony than Hazel has!"

Pauline stopped giggling and looked at her cousin.

"Whatever do you mean, Eugenia?"

"People are wont to whisper, that's all," her cousin said coolly. "One need be a first-born child to inherit a title, you know."

"I am the first born, as you know perfectly well," Pauline said. "I'm Papa's only child. And . . . and . . . I remind you to remember your station when you address me! What do you mean by —"

"Dear Pauline! Don't let it trouble you!" Eugenia said. "One mustn't believe every rumor one hears in the Barony, after all." She turned to her sister. "Come, Hazel. Take that thing out of your mouth and . . . *Hazel!*"

"*Martingale!*" cried Pauline.

"Oh *no.*" Lucy sighed.

Hazel Martlet looked up at her sister, then at Pauline and Lucy, with a puzzled expression on her face. She had taken to heart the warning against eating the dandelion flower — it lay on the floor beside her left shoe — but she must have assumed that Martingale was a legitimate part of the salad. She had got the slug halfway into her mouth before her sister cried out. It wiggled there unhappily, now, between two spears of dandelion leaf.

Pauline jumped from her chair, but Hazel had anticipated

her and dashed across the room. Eugenia gave chase, and before Lucy had time even to wonder how the slug had got into the salad, the tea party had fallen into chaos.

Removing a slug from a four-year-old's mouth requires only a level head and a steady hand, but those virtues were sorely lacking in Pauline's sitting-room, even after Mrs. Healing and Mr. Broom — alerted by the sound of riot — had raced up the stairs to join the fray. Teacups shattered, voices rose and battled, and, as always happens in human affairs, opposing parties formed. Lucy and Pauline urged diplomacy, cajoling the girl with honey drops and marzipan, but Hazel had got the idea that Martingale was a kind of special treat, like a coin in a birthday cake, and stoutly refused to let them take it away from her.

The crisis was finally resolved by the party of force. Mr. Broom held Hazel round the middle — face downward and level to the floor, her legs kicking violently — while his allies, Eugenia and Mrs. Healing, prodded the girl's ticklish parts with their fingers. Hazel had no recourse but to shriek, and Martingale fell to Lucy's outstretched apron.

Such a clamor of blame ensued that Mr. Vole was summoned from his pantry to take charge of the investigation. The house-steward was a rigorously dignified man, whose high starched collars scarcely allowed his chin room for speaking. After questioning Lucy and Pauline he led the whole party down to the kitchen, where the evidence spoke for itself. In her rush to get Pauline ready for tea, Lucy had hung her mistress's foil from a peg over one of the kitchen's worktables. The frantic Martingale had thrown himself from the heights and bolted for cover, leaving a moist, damning trail of slime behind him. It ended precisely where Mr. Broom had set out the *salades de pissenlit*, and the conclusion was obvious to everyone. It was all Lucy's fault.

"But —"

"None of your cheek, Lucy!" said Mr. Vole. He turned a grave face to Mrs. Healing. "Please to accept my profoundest apologies. The girl, of course, will be dealt with in due course, and with fitting severity. But with your permission, I'll return with you now and present my apologies personally to Lady Martlet."

"Yes, of course," the nurse said faintly. She had taken a fan from her bag, and waved it at her face. "I only hope my feet will carry me so far. I feel quite shocked."

"Broom!" said Mr. Vole. "Bring the poor woman a glass of sherry!" The cook hurried off, happy to have escaped being caught up in the scandal, and Mr. Vole turned to Lucy. "*You*, Wickwright, I'll deal with when I return — and you may rest assured I've not forgotten your last enormity. Go to my pantry, now, and wait for me."

"But —"

A glance from Mr. Vole cut the protest short. Lucy turned away without so much as a "Yes, sir" and walked glumly past the racks of battered pots, the great lime-encrusted sinks, and the scarred, bloodstained chopping block, where a featherless goose awaited its final end.

Chapter 8

*H*er punishment was cruel. Having got into trouble twice in the space of a week, Lucy was forbidden to attend the carnival. After dressing Pauline she was to spend her day in the maid-servants' garret, "reflecting upon your infamies," as Mr. Vole put it, "and cultivating a fitting remorse."

This sentence posed a problem beyond her missing the carnival, for Lucy still had not delivered Mr. Lemonjello's farthings to Arden Gutz. The astronomer had treated the matter as urgent, so she hated to delay any longer. In the end she could think of no solution but to get up before dawn, the next morning, and steal over to the guardhouse before the rest of the girls were up.

The gaoler protested, of course, when she asked to speak with a prisoner at that uncivilized hour, and she was forced to spend one of the coins on a bribe. A guard was then summoned to escort her. He was a pasty, sleepy-eyed man, and he hummed tunelessly as he led her down a short fall of stairs and along a narrow passage. When they had gone some distance he stopped and turned to her with a mischievous smile.

"Mind your head, little lady!" he said, stooping to pass under a lintel of black granite that blocked the upper part of the passage.

Lucy paused to examine this strange whim of architecture, which hung barely four feet above the floor. The guard waited on the other side, a hand on his knee. The candle he carried threw stark shadows on his face, making a clown's mad grin of his doughy smile.

"That seems a stupid way to make a corridor!" Lucy said. Then, lest she offend the guard in what was, after all, his own domain, she added, "At least, I can't understand it."

Her guide winked, and beckoned with a stubby finger.

"Look here," he said, when she had passed under the stone. "Down yonder is where the prisoners is kept. And back that-away" — he pointed to the stairs from the gatehouse — "is the only way of getting out. Observe, if you please, that there's no lanterns or torches to give you a piece of light. Now then! Suppose one of these rascals manages to break out of his cell — or her cell, supposing it's a rascal on the female plan. They comes high-tailing it down this tunnel, blind as a tater, and what happens?"

Lucy shivered. Her face looked back at her from the polished granite.

"*WHACK!*" said the guard, striking the stone with his palm.

Lucy jumped in her shoes, and somewhere a rat squealed and scrabbled faintly away. The guard chuckled, and petted the lintel fondly.

"They knew how to build a castle, back in the olden days," he said. "Simple, but effective. There's the mark of genius, little lady!"

"Yes, sir," said Lucy. One could always fall back on "Yes, sir" or "Yes, ma'am" when grown-ups said baffling things.

"I could show you a lot of pretty tricks like that," the guard said, continuing down the passageway. "You should see the gadgets left over from the time of Gustaf the Fey. Merciful beetles and snakes! Curdle your blood, they will, and make your hair stand up like a field of corn. I'd be pleased to show you them, should you pay another visit. It's a hobby of mine, see — antiquities and the like."

"Thank you, sir," Lucy said. "I'll remember that."

Water stood in shallow puddles on the floor, for the passage was carved from living rock and its walls dripped cold sweat. When they came to the cells Lucy heard snoring behind the stout doors, and her eyes watered at the smell of slop buckets. The air was so cold that her breath clouded the air, as though winter itself had been imprisoned in the depths of the castle. The guard brought out a ring of keys.

"Your man's down at the end," he said. "Last one on your right."

Lucy impulsively ran ahead of her guide and pounded three times on the wooden door of the cell. She paused, then struck it twice more — the same code that Pauline had rung, unwittingly, on the astronomer's bell. The gloomy dungeon had brought to mind stories she had read, in which cunning agents bore vital messages to wrongly imprisoned men. She waited expectantly by the door.

"Who's there?" came a sleepy whisper. "Is that Lu?"

"Here, little miss! I'll attend to that!" The guard trotted to the cell and stood on tiptoes to speak through a grate in the door. "I've brought you a visitor, Gutz," he said. "Tidy yourself, now!"

Lucy rubbed goose bumps from her arms as her guide unlocked and swung open the door. The prisoner sat up in a blanket in a corner of the cell. A pile of straw covered most of the floor, and by the door stood a bucket covered by a warped pine board. There was scarcely room for the three of them, though the walls rose twenty feet or more to a barred window that let in the first hint of morning twilight. Arden Gutz coughed wetly into his hand.

"Ah, you've brought a fire," he said, glancing at the guard's candle. "I want a bit of warmth."

"None of your cheek, mister," warned the guard. He took a small hourglass from his pocket and gave it to Lucy. "Now see here, missy. You seem an honest sort of girl, but you roused me from my pillow at a terrible hour, and I mean to get some shut-eye while you jaw with this vermin. So give a shout when the sand runs through this glass. I'll be just outside."

He lighted a stub of candle in a niche on the wall and gave a backward, scowling glance at the prisoner before leaving the cell. The door thudded shut, the keys jangled, and the bolt shot fast.

Lucy looked timidly at Arden Gutz, whom she had last seen from the tower as he knelt by the Stone of Justice. He was a striking young man, even with bits of straw stuck in his unkempt dark hair, but he looked terrifically cross. He had sharp black eyes, and a lump on his unshaved throat that rose and fell when he swallowed like a slice of parsnip stuck in his craw. He gazed suspiciously at Lucy but did not at once ask her name or business. A hand emerged from the blanket and pointed to the floor beside him.

"Please to sit down," he said. "I can't offer you a chair, I'm afraid. Mind you don't kick the bucket."

Lucy sat at arm's length from the prisoner. He glanced at the door, then leaned toward her and looked closely at her face.

"It was you who knocked?" he whispered.

"Yes, sir," she said. "My name is Lucy Wickwright."

"I am Arden Gutz," the prisoner said.

"How do you do?"

Gutz pulled the blanket tight under his chin.

"How could I do, but poorly?" he asked. "I shiver in a foul prison while scoundrels walk free in the sun, their noble gobs stuffed with chewing gum. I break rocks and sleep on straw because I dare speak the truth in a warren of lies. I fester, Lucy Wickwright — that's how I do! My soul bleeds!"

A fine hello! Lucy thought. She had to admit, though, that Arden Gutz had every reason to be unhappy. The cold floor was already making her bottom numb.

"I'm sorry to hear that, sir," she said.

"You are very kind. Who sent you to me?"

"It was Mr. Lemonjello," said Lucy. "We were looking at the stars, Saturday last —"

"Wait!"

Gutz stood up, still wrapped in his blanket, and peered through the grate. When he sat down again Lucy noticed that his second and third toes were grown together on both feet. She was not alarmed — such toes were common in the Barony. Lucy was "busy-toed" herself, having six to each foot, but both her father and Casio had been "tongue-toed" like Arden Gutz. He tucked his feet under the blanket and spoke in a murmur.

"The walls have ears," he warned her. "If they had mouths, what stories they could tell!"

"Would they curdle my blood," Lucy asked, "and make my hair stand up like a field of corn?"

"Yes!"

"Then I shouldn't like to hear them."

"Nor should I like to repeat them," said Arden Gutz. "But to what do I owe this honor, Lucy Wickwright? You are a friend of the good Luigi?" Again his voice fell to a whisper, and he clutched her by the wrist. "Are you one of us? So young, and already a soldier of the Cause?"

His eyes had grown bright, and even in the frigid cell his hand was feverish on Lucy's skin. She pulled her wrist from his grasp and reached into her pocket for the astronomer's coins.

"Mr. Lemonjello asked me to give you these," she explained. "But I'm afraid there's been a misunderstanding. You see, I've been in trouble with the castle guard, and somehow it's got about that I'm a scofflaw. Mr. Lemonjello believed I was a member of your Cause, I think. I couldn't explain, because my mistress was calling for her tea."

"A servant, are you?"

"Yes, sir. My mistress is —"

"Why have you no uniform?" Gutz interrupted. "Shouldn't you have?"

"Yes, sir," Lucy said. She hoped Arden Gutz could not see

her blushing in the dim light. "But most girls don't enter the service until they're older, and there's no dress to fit me, presently. I outgrew my first one."

"Bah! How typical of our fine nobles!" said Gutz. "If your mistress would leave off chewing gum for one month she could buy you a dozen uniforms, I'll warrant."

"But she doesn't chew gum," Lucy said. "My mistress is —"

"Did you know," the prisoner asked, "that the domestic staff of this castle have not seen their wages increase since the introduction of chewing gum to Cant? Or that a ha'penny of every shilling produced in this Barony pays for the importation of gum?"

"I'm sure that's very interesting, sir," said Lucy, who supposed it must be interesting to *someone.* "You seem to know a great deal about gum," she added.

"Aye, *too* much," Gutz said, "and so I rot in this dungeon. But I will not rest until everyone knows, Lucy — until everyone sees the blight, the canker, the pox of chewing gum! They cannot keep me forever in this wretched hole. Blast them!" In his anger he brandished his fist at the bolted door, coming very near to striking Lucy on her nose. She scooted away.

"You're here because of chewing gum?" she asked.

"I am imprisoned," said Gutz, "for leveling the lance of my pen at that fiend, Vladimir Orloff, the foul enemy of our glorious Cause. He has silenced me, for now. But spring comes, Lucy! The sun is behind us!"

"Begging your pardon, sir," Lucy said, "but, as I mentioned, there's been a misunderstanding. It's not *our* glorious Cause — that is, it's not *mine.* I don't belong to it, you see." She blew on her cold hands. "Why does chewing gum upset you so?"

"Think, child," said the prisoner. "A corrupt nobility must have its cud, but we have no sapodilla trees in Cant. So the vile stuff must be imported, at great expense —"

"Chewing gum comes from trees?" Lucy asked, astonished.

"It is made entirely of chemicals in most parts of the world," Gutz said. "When I was at Oxford I saw peasant children whose cheeks were always full of the stuff, which is as common there as horehound drops in Cant. But our fine nobles, who look upon iron plows as a dangerous innovation, must have the priceless, the rare, the authentic gum of the sapodilla. Their craving for the cud has drained the Exchequer. Our farmers and merchants are bled by tithes, and a poor servant-girl goes without a proper dress — all because of gum! Why, the sheer tonnage of gum imported . . ."

Lucy struggled to pay attention as Arden Gutz recited the damage done by chewing gum. Considering his fancy words and queer notions, she was not surprised to learn that he had been at Oxford (which she understood to be an ancient, ivy-bearded castle of learning, so full of scholars' sweeping robes that its floors never wanted dusting). Dr. Azziz had been at Oxford, and the librarian, too, could be queer in her thinking. She insisted, for example, that a hammer fell as slowly as a feather when dropped by astronauts on the moon. That was certainly as outlandish as Arden Gutz's belief that Lucy lacked a proper uniform because of chewing gum.*

According to Arden Gutz, the gum trade in Cant was con-

---

*Cantlings took a dim view, generally, of those who traveled to the outlands, and the ideas that such travelers brought back with them were, of course, deemed outlandish.

trolled by one Vladimir Orloff, who held a baronial appointment as Commissioner of Posts. The name sounded somehow familiar to Lucy, but she could not place where or when she had heard it before.

"As Postal Commissioner, he serves as the chief censor of Cant," Gutz told her, "and in that capacity he had me arrested. I've written a manifesto, you see, that boldly proclaims the principles of our Cause. Orloff seized it before I had so much as blotted the ink, and put me up on this charge of Treason. He wields the true power in our Barony, Lucy. Adolphus may wear the baronial cap, but His Lordship is as weak as any chessboard king. Orloff is the queen. He is the scourge of our valiant Cause."

"A queen, sir? But isn't he a man?"

"I spoke metaphorically. He is *like* the queen of a chessboard, because he has greater power than Lord Cant, who answers to the king in a game of chess. Do you see?"

"Yes, sir. Rather like a simile."

Gutz nodded.

"His power lies in his authority over the Post Roads," he said. "Every piece of gum that enters Cant must be brought over them, and Orloff has grown obscenely rich by his fees and imposts and bribe-taking. The nobles are all slaves to the cud, so of course they will not act against him. Thus we have established our Cause, and we will not rest until the yoke of gum is thrown off. Our numbers are few at present, in terms of . . . well, *numbers*. But Henry Wallow is said to be for us, away off in Haslet March. And if the people only learn the folly of their lords, they will rally behind us!"

"Can you not appeal to Lord Cant?" Lucy asked, for it seemed impossible to her that the Commissioner of Posts should have more power than the Baron, who was the Exalted & Merciful Protector of Cant. The prisoner snorted in reply.

"Appeal to Lord Cant?" he said. "Adolphus is the fattest, stupidest fly in Orloff's web. Soon he'll be consumed, and then Orloff's power will be absolute. That's why the manifesto is so urgently needed *now*. When His Lordship is dead it may be too late."

"But then my mistress will become the Baroness," said Lucy. "She won't keep you in prison, I'm sure. She doesn't care for chewing gum. It makes her ears go pop."

Gutz started. He took Lucy's arm in his hand.

"Your mistress?" he asked. "Miss Cant is your mistress? The Baron's daughter?"

"Yes, sir. Pauline von Cant."

Gutz leaned close. His eyes were bright.

"Lucy," he said, "your mistress will become Baroness of Cant before the year is out, if I'm any judge." He picked up the hourglass and held it between them. "Scarcely as much time as this remains to Adolphus, I fear. But think! His daughter cannot rule until her twenty-first birthday, and until then the Privy Council must appoint a regent to rule in her name. And whom do you think that august body, that menagerie, that motley troupe of bubble-blowing harlequins —"

He broke off, overcome with contempt.

"Whom will they appoint, but Vladimir Orloff?" he asked, mastering himself. "They depend on him for their cud! Your mistress will be only a doll in his hands, Lucy. Indeed, her life itself may be in peril. For I shouldn't like to be the mortal girl who stands between Orloff and the baronial cap. There are rumors of blood in his past."

"But we must stop him!" Lucy cried. Gutz clapped his hand over her mouth, and glanced meaningly at the door. Lucy nodded. All his talk of chewing gum and imposts and manifestos had somewhat muddled her head (for she suspected it to be about Politics, a topic that always made her sleepy), but a threat to her mistress! — *that* was something she could understand. "What can we do?" she asked, when Gutz took away his hand. "Can't we tell someone? Can't we tell the guard on Orloff? Can't we get him into trouble?"

"The guard are in Orloff's pocket," said Gutz. "What is needed is to publish my manifesto! That would light a fire in Tenesmus, and give us the numbers we need for action. We might easily retrieve it, too, had we an agent in the castle. But Lemonjello is too timid for spy work, and there is no one else . . ."

His voice trailed off. He threw off his blanket and knelt close to Lucy, and, for the first time since their interview began, something like a smile turned up the corners of his mouth.

"But who would suspect a little girl?" he said. His hair stuck out in wild, romantic curls, and his eyes gleamed. He had not been shaved for some days, Lucy saw, and she leaned away from his black, abrasive whiskers. "Will you do something for me, Lucy?" he asked. "Not for me, of course, but for the Cause?"

Lucy looked at the hourglass. It had already spilled most of its sand.

"What do you want me to do?" she asked.

"You could be our Joan of Arc!" Gutz went on. "Lucy Wickwright, the Maid of Cant, liberator of her people! An historical figure!"

He turned out the hem of his trousers and took a key from a hidden pocket. Lucy had never before met a person with a secret pocket — a device of highwaymen and other such storybook characters — and she trembled as Gutz placed the key in her hand.

"Before my arrest," he explained, "I was given this by a locksmith in Tenesmus who often works in the castle. He is in sympathy with our Cause. It is a skeleton key to every door in the castle — except these cell doors, blast it! Take this key, Lucy. Find Orloff's office, and there you will find my manifesto. Carry it to Tenesmus, to the printer Lu Mingshu. He is one of us. He'll know what to do."

Lucy had the strange feeling that Arden Gutz was unlocking a door to her — admitting her to a storybook, a make-believe world where she could be a dashing spy and rescue Pauline from the villainous Vlad Orloff. But this was real life — and real life, she had discovered, almost never resembled life in storybooks, except in unpleasant matters such as wicked stepmothers and wolves with a taste for young girls. The key lay cold and black on her open palm.

"But, respectfully, sir," she said, "I've been in trouble recently. I shouldn't like to get caught stealing."

"Is it stealing to take back what is rightly yours?" Gutz asked. "Orloff tore the manifesto from my very hands! And think of your mistress, Lucy! Do you care for Miss Cant?"

Lucy swallowed. Pauline's mother, Lady Cant, had died when Pauline was only a baby, and should the Baron die, too, her mistress would be left an orphan. Lucy remembered how pale Lord Cant had looked at the execution, how he had wheezed and gasped with the effort of speaking.

"Do you care for her, Lucy?" Gutz repeated.

"Yes, sir. Of course I do."

The prisoner took her hand and closed her fingers over the skeleton key.

"If you truly care for her," he said, "you will do as I ask. We may yet bring Orloff down before the Baron is in his tomb. But while Orloff remains in power, Miss Cant is in deadly peril!"

The sands had run through the hourglass. Gutz gazed at Lucy.

"Our time is up," he said. "Will you do what I ask?"

"I . . . I shall try, sir," Lucy said. It seemed impossible that she should succeed, but if her mistress was in danger she must try — even if it meant festering, like Arden Gutz, in the frigid confines of the dungeon. Her nose, as though anticipating the dangers she must face, began to drip. The prisoner reached for the blanket and pulled it back over his shoulders. Again a slight smile turned up the corners of his mouth.

"Be brave, little girl," he said, rising to his feet. "The sun is behind us! Guard!"

The guard came, and Lucy scarcely had time to pocket the skeleton key before he had swung open the cell door. Gutz handed him the hourglass, and Lucy followed her escort out of the cell. The guard slammed shut the door and shot the bolt, but they had not gone ten paces down the corridor before Arden Gutz called out behind them.

"Lucy! Wait!"

"Time's up, Gutz!" the guard said, pulling Lucy along.

"Just ten seconds, guard," the prisoner pleaded. "There's a farthing in it for you!"

The guard scowled at Lucy.

"You're not allowed to bring money to the prisoners," he said. "But as you're just a wee snip of a girl, I'll overlook it this once. Be quick, now!"

Lucy ran back to the cell door. She could just reach the grate with her hands, and she pulled herself up to look at Arden Gutz.

"I noticed your shirt," he said. "I meant to tell you, I was a great admirer of the Gizmobots when I was at Oxford. I never missed an episode!"

"An episode?" Lucy asked, her fingers straining on the grate.

"Yes, on the telly! You know about televisions, don't you?"

"Yes, sir." Lucy had learned about televisions from Dr. Azziz. Evidently they were not just another of the librarian's outlandish ideas, like a hammer that fell as slowly as a feather. "I know what televisions are. But pray, what are Gizmobots?"

"Why, don't you know?" Gutz asked. "Mighty Agents of Justice, created by Dr. X to combat Evil and bring forth Good! Plasmatron, Cybertron, and Gravitron, away!"

"That's ten seconds!" called the guard. Lucy fell to the floor, and Arden Gutz dropped a farthing through the grate.

"Be brave, Lucy!" he whispered. "You bear the emblems of justice on your breast!"

Lucy blushed horribly to hear the word *breast* spoken in regard to herself, especially from Arden Gutz's mouth. She caught the coin and hurried back to the guard, who held out his fat hand for it. He led her past the cells and down the dark corridor that led to the gatehouse. Lucy tugged his sleeve when they reached the dangerous, low-hanging lintel.

"Sir?" she asked.

"Aye, missy?"

"You say this is the only way out of the dungeon?"

"Aye, unless you bang down a wall and tunnel your way out." He chuckled. "And if you can manage *that*, with naught but a pile of straw and a slop bucket as your tools, then fortune speed you on your way, little miss, for you're a better man than I am."

"Thank you, sir," Lucy said (for sometimes, when her mind was busy with other things, her good manners ticked on like a clockwork toy). "But," she asked, "if you bring the prisoners *down* this way, wouldn't they know to duck their heads, when it's time to escape?"

Again the guard chuckled.

"You'd think so, now, wouldn't you, little girl? But your noggin gets musty after a pleasant spell of solitary confinement, and not enough gruel to warm your belly. Most of the inmates is cracked as a washerwoman's hands before they ever think of breaking out. Not that many *do* break out, 'cause there's a locked cell door to get through, after all. Still, we've had a few attempts. And they fly down this tunnel like bats out of a bel-fry — only they can't see with their ears, like your bat can do — and before you can say 'merciful snakes and beetles' . . . *WHACK!*" His fat hand struck the polished granite. "Oh, they remember it *then*, to be sure. It's a wonderful spur to the mem-ory, this old piece of stone. Once you've gone to school on *that*, why, you've learnt your lesson. Though you may not remember your name to the end of your mortal life."

He smiled fondly and stooped under the lintel, and Lucy followed him down the corridor. A door creaked somewhere up in the gatehouse, and the guard's candle flickered in the sud-den draught.

"Aye," he concluded, "they knew their business, back in the olden days. Genius, little miss, that's what it was. Sheer genius!"

Chapter 9

*A*s a precaution, Lucy returned by way of the parapet walk. The spies in romances risked their lives with cool heads and gallant hearts, but they never had to face a tongue-lashing from Mr. Vole, which would be Lucy's fate if he caught her crossing the ward when she was supposed to be confined to quarters. Already the courtyard bustled with preparations for the carnival, though the sun remained hidden behind the castle keep.

Arden Gutz wanted her to be the Cantling Joan of Arc, but, if Lucy remembered correctly, Joan's reward for saving France was to be tied to a stake and burned alive — not to mention that she had had to dress like a boy and play at soldiers in the muddy fields thereabouts. Lucy *hated* dressing like a boy, in castoffs from the American Mission, and much preferred a quiet game of croquet on a well-mown lawn. If she must resemble a figure out of French history she would rather it be Marie-Antoinette, with her fancy dresses and jewels and her head neatly severed by a guillotine. It made a prettier picture than hissing and popping over a wood fire like a suckling pig in boy's trousers.

She did not think she liked Arden Gutz. She could not deny he was handsome, but anyone could see he was a vain young man. Lucy would tolerate him, for Pauline's sake, but she refused to swoon over him, as another girl might do. She might even hate him a little. That was a fine romantic notion, like something from the grown-up novels that Dr. Azziz encouraged her to read. She and Arden would become Bosom Enemies, and Cordially Detest one another, but would put aside their Feelings for the Good of the Cause.

When she reached the corner tower she descended to the cellars, from where she could make her way by a stair to the kitchens. Yes, she decided — her best course was to cultivate a passionate dislike of Mr. Arden Gutz. It was annoying enough to be called "little girl" by Costive Gutz, that old lunatic grammarian, but it was positively insulting to be "little-girled" by his nephew, who sat snugly in the dungeon while *she* risked her skin to bring down Orloff and the gum trade. Arden Gutz was not one quarter as handsome as he thought himself, she concluded, and he would have to be twice as handsome as *that* to be one tenth as handsome as a pig on a spit. And she would *rather* kiss a spitted pig, now she thought of it, than allow Arden Gutz to press his lips to her hand, as a gentleman would honor the Maid of Cant, Liberator of Her People.

Having settled that, she quickened her pace. Before serving her sentence in the garret she must take up Pauline's breakfast and dress her, and it would not do to rouse suspicions by arriving late to the kitchen. She navigated the cellars by touch and then climbed a little-used stairway to emerge from a hatch in the floor of a jam pantry. From there she could enter the long corridor that connected the various kitchens and butteries of the keep.

A more experienced spy, before leaving a jam pantry, would have put an ear to the door. Lucy did not. She pushed carelessly through the swinging door and had gone perhaps ten paces down the corridor when, to her horror, she heard Mr. Vole's voice and footsteps coming from a side passage. The stairs from the maidservants' garret came down on the other side of the kitchens, so if Vole found Lucy here it would be obvious to him that she had already been out of quarters.

The starched voice drew nearer. The steward was arguing with another man, whose flopping footsteps indicated he wore a guardsman's sandals. In another second the pair would round the corner and find Lucy standing frozen in the middle of the corridor.

She flung herself through the nearest doorway as the men came round the corner, their hushed voices tangling like grass snakes. The door of the room in which she found herself stood half open, and Lucy flattened herself against the wall behind it. Through the gap by its hinges she saw the house-steward stop outside. She hardly dared breathe. Only when she looked away from him did she notice — too late! — the familiar desk and the threadbare rug on which delinquent maids heard their sentences. She had hidden herself in Mr. Vole's pantry.

"I fail to see how it concerns me," the house-steward said.

"The discipline of household staff when they are outside the castle keep is the guard's affair."

"But the complaint came from within the keep," countered the other man, whose tunic was that of a guard of middle rank. "Professor Gutz, I may add, sits on a Baronial Commission."

Lucy drew in her breath at the mention of Arden Gutz's pompous uncle, then clapped her hand over her mouth. Vole, before answering the guardsman, glanced up and down the corridor as though he had heard a scurrying rat. Lucy trembled, and it took all her discipline not to wipe her nose. At last Vole returned to his argument.

"The *offense*," he said, "occurred on the north flanking tower. In any case, the girl has already served her punishment. She worked in the laundry Saturday last, during her half-holiday. As far as I'm concerned that's the end of the matter."

They were talking about her, Lucy realized. She had no time to marvel at this, however, for Mr. Vole now entered the pantry and walked toward his desk. Lucy slid along the wall, but the half-open door offered little cover, and she expected to meet a terrible fate as soon as the steward sat down. Not only out of quarters, but trespassing!

But the best spies possess luck as well as courage, and it was Lucy's good fortune that saved her now. The guard was a tall, squarely built fellow. He followed Mr. Vole into the pantry, and when the house-steward turned around his view of Lucy was blocked by the imposing man.

"Professor Gutz says the girl entered his office without knocking, and without an appointment," the guardsman said. "So there *was* an offense within the keep, begging your pardon.

Please, sir, the captain wants only a moment of your time. Professor Gutz is convinced there are subversive elements within the staff."

"Costive Gutz!" Vole snorted. "The man can't see two rats nibbling upon the same crumb of cheese, but he imagines they're concocting a plot!"

"That's as may be. But with the festivities underway, and all manner of folk visiting the castle, Captain Retsch doesn't like to take any chances. Please, sir. Just a moment of your time."

"Oh, very well!" Vole said testily. "But I can assure Retsch there is no question of disloyalty on my staff. I haven't served the house of Cant for forty years only to allow revolutionists to go about in maids' uniforms!"

"Professor Gutz claimed the girl was out of uniform," the guardsman said disapprovingly. "This way, if you please." To Lucy's great relief the steward followed him from the room.

When their footsteps had faded to silence she peeled herself from the wall. Her legs shook so frightfully that she could barely stand. She understood how a slug must feel when, having sought refuge in a dandelion salad, it suddenly finds itself caught up in the jaws of a four-year-old. If she meant to be a spy, she must remember in the future to look before she leaps!

Lucy wondered if Arden Gutz had acted wisely in choosing her to retrieve his manifesto. In storybooks, the heroines overcame Insurmountable Odds by virtue of their True Hearts and Pluck. But what if Joan of Arc, on the morning when she was supposed to save France, had been caught out of quarters? What good would Pluck have done then, if she'd had to boil linens all day as punishment, or scrub the kitchen floor? And now Mr. Vole would be watching her more closely than ever, thanks to Costive Gutz!

As she rounded the door to leave the steward's pantry something on his desk caught her eye. On a large sheet of paper Mr. Vole had listed the events of the first day of the festival, and on a matching sheet the related duties of his various staff members. She turned the first paper around, now, and examined a neatly penciled table.

11 O' THE CLOCK: SPEECHES, TRIBUTES, ENCOMIA

SPEAKER	TOPIC
11:00 — SIR ORIEL SAVORY	INTRODUCTORY REMARKS
11:10 — MAYOR GRUNT (TENESMUS)	"TOWN AND CASTLE"
11:20 — SIR CLARENCE MARTLET	"SON OF A NOBLE LINEAGE"
11:30 — (BERTH, FLETCHER, GOOP, HENDERSOE)	(SPONTANEOUS ACCLAMATION)
11:35 — THE REV. MR. PIUS FRODD	"CANT IN THE WORLD"
11:45 — SIR STOMATA CHIASMUS	"ADOLPHUS: CHAMPION OF ORATORY"
11:55 — COMMISSIONER ORLOFF	"ADOLPHUS: FRIEND TO PHILATELY"
NOON — DR. AZZIZ	"A NOBLE MIND"
12:10 (POST-MERIDIAN) — LADY BRIGHTLING	???
12:20 — MINISTER GUUZI	CONCLUDING REMARKS (LUNCHEON TO FOLLOW)

Lady Brightling, whoever she was, had not decided upon a topic. That surely vexed Mr. Vole, who liked things neatly and firmly arranged ahead of time. What struck Lucy, however, was the appearance of Vladimir Orloff on the dais. It meant he must surely be out of his office by eleven o'clock that morning.

If she could only escape the garret, it would be the perfect opportunity to retrieve Arden Gutz's manifesto.

For she knew that, Pluck or no Pluck, she must do what she could to protect her mistress. Pauline, despite her Noble Lineage and many regrettable Whims, was only a little girl, after all — and perhaps soon to be an orphan. Lucy was only a servant, and lofty things like chewing gum and manifestos were surely beyond her. But she knew what it meant to be an orphan — to be pulled this way and that by grown-ups who claimed to be doing what was best for you, but who never thought to ask what you wanted for yourself. So she would do her part for the Cause, even if failure meant shivering in the dungeon the rest of her days. And there was always the possibility that she might succeed, and make Arden Gutz regret ever calling *her* a "little girl."

An idea came to Lucy, inspired by the thought of taking Arden Gutz down a peg or two. (How *could* a person be so vain of his only *slightly* handsome face?) She searched Mr. Vole's desk and found a sharp pencil and a lump of gutta-percha, with which she rubbed out the question marks by Lady Brightling's name. Mr. Vole had written the schedule in block letters, so it was easy to copy his hand.

12:10 (POST-MERIDIAN) — LADY BRIGHTLING   "THE SUN IS BEHIND US."

She put back the pencil and eraser and hurried to the kitchen. It was only a timid attempt at Pluck — hardly more than a girlish prank — but if she meant to be the Maid of Cant, Liberator of Her People, she had to start somewhere.

⌒ 99 ⌒

Chapter 10

*P*auline wanted to preserve a good appetite for the treats of the carnival, so she shared her breakfast with Lucy, who was supposed to be fasting until supper as part of her punishment. Mr. Broom had put an apple on the tray, from last year's harvest, and this Pauline gave to her maid for a makeshift luncheon.

"I do wish you'd stop getting into trouble, Wickwright," Pauline said, studying her reflection in the glass. Lucy had dressed her in blue lisle stockings, a knee-length knife-pleat white skirt with stripes of navy at the hem, and a matching sailor tunic with navy-striped collar. Lucy knelt at her feet with the buttonhook.

"Trouble seems to find me out, mistress," she said. "Please to lift your other foot."

Pauline steadied herself with a hand on Lucy's head, and Lucy slid the footrest under her mistress's unbuttoned boot.

"You should wear a charm," Pauline said. "I'll have Broom set aside a rabbit's foot, the next time rabbit is on the menu."

"I should want a whole leg, I'm afraid."

"Well, your being in trouble is a terrible inconvenience. I'm to be in Mrs. Healing's care all day. I'll have no one to talk to but my dreadful cousins."

"I am sorry, mistress."

"Eugenia makes me *ill*," Pauline went on. She had been in a pettish, moping mood since getting out of bed. Lucy had tried to cheer her, but Pauline acted as if she, rather than Lucy, was the one being punished. "Did you chance to hear what Eugenia said at tea yesterday? She as much as claimed I'm unfit to bear the arms of Cant! Of course, Hazel is a sweet girl, but Eugenia is a great impossible wart."

"Yes, mistress. Foot down, please."

Lucy collapsed the footrest, gathered up the shoehorn and buttonhook, and put them on a shelf of the wardrobe that held Pauline's springtime clothes. There were six large wardrobes in her mistress's dressing room, four of them devoted to seasonal dress and one each to linens and sports wear. When she had locked the wardrobe someone knocked at the dressing room door.

"Come!" said Pauline.

A spotty face peered around the door. It belonged to Delagraisse, the new under-footman. He was a clumsy but earnest boy from Tenesmus, with a tendency to slouch.

"The Misses Martlet are here, Miss Cant," he announced. "I've shown them to the music room."

"Very well," Pauline sighed. "Give them a bon-bon. I'll be along presently."

"Yes, mistress," said Delagraisse. He glanced at Lucy, and swallowed nervously before looking back at Pauline. "A b-b-bon-bon each, do you mean, or one between them?"

Pauline, who was examining her hair in a hand glass, merely rolled her eyes.

"Take them a plate of bon-bons," Lucy told the boy. "Half a dozen, in various colors. Offer Mrs. Healing a glass of sherry. And please to stand straight when you address the Misses Martlet."

Delagraisse nodded, but made no move to close the door. Something troubled him. Lucy went nearer the door and spoke in a low voice, so Pauline would not hear.

"Six bon-bons make half a dozen," she said. Delagraisse smiled gratefully.

"I wasn't exactly sure," he confessed, looking down. The pimples on his forehead reddened. "I get my dozens and pints confused. There are so many of numbers to remember!"

"A pint has twenty ounces," Lucy said helpfully.

Delagraisse nodded eagerly.

"Six bon-bons in a half-dozen, ten in a half-pint. Got it."

Lucy was about to correct him, but servants were not supposed to dawdle while on duty, and Pauline's guests were waiting, so she merely smiled. This was the signal for Delagraisse to go, but the boy clung to the dressing room door, his eyes staring so intently at Lucy, and his lips in such a calfstruck smile, that she feared he might be sick. She took a step back and made a shooing gesture with her fingers.

"Off you go, then," she said.

"I've seen you at the staff meetings," the boy said, slowly pulling the door. "What's your name?"

Lucy glanced over her shoulder. She had done up Pauline's hair in sausage curls that morning, and her mistress stood at the glass, now, tilting her head left and right, making the tight cylinders of hair bounce like springs. Lucy put her hand on the doorknob.

"It's Lucy Wickwright," she said. "Off you go!" She pushed the door, but Delagraisse had got his foot under it. He did not seem very bright, Lucy thought. She doubted he would rise far in the domestic service, for an under-footman was supposed to be quiet and unobtrusive, and . . . well, not *under foot*, loitering about and asking questions like this.

"My name is Blaise Delagraisse," he said.

"Pleased to meet you, Delagraisse. Run along, now!"

Lucy pushed the door again, but Delagraisse only stared at her, and finally she was obliged to kick his ankle. He started back and stood on one foot, rubbing the offended limb, but he did not seem terribly upset. The calfish smile remained.

"Don't forget the bon-bons!" Lucy said, closing the door before Delagraisse could put his foot in it again. Pauline, meanwhile, was hopping from foot to foot at the mirror — trying to jig like a sailor, as nearly as Lucy could tell, though she looked more like an orangutan in a traveling circus. One of her hair ribbons had come loose, and when she stopped to catch her breath Lucy reached up and tightened the bow.

"Have I a suitable parasol, Wickwright?" Pauline asked.

Lucy brought one of white silk with a tasseled fringe and a peak like a circus tent. Pauline rested the wooden shank on her shoulder, twirling it with her fingers as she gazed in the mirror.

"It doesn't suit my costume," she said. "It's not at all nautical. Do you know what 'nautical' means, Wickwright?"

Lucy scrunched her eyebrows, pretending to think. One of the hazards of serving Pauline was that her mistress was convinced she was smarter than Lucy, and was forever explaining things that Lucy understood perfectly well. When a decent interval had passed, Lucy coughed modestly.

"I believe it means *'of, or pertaining to, ships or sailors,'* mistress."

Pauline's mouth turned down slightly, but she said nothing, only twirled the parasol this way and that, intent on her reflection. Lucy watched her in the glass. She was about to remind Pauline that the Misses Martlet were waiting, when her mistress spoke.

"What were you and that boy whispering about?" she asked.

"I was instructing him about the bon-bons, mistress," said Lucy. Pauline was quite careless, normally, about servants and their decorum, and Lucy hoped she had not got it into her head to start being strict.

Pauline closed the parasol and spun around. Her chin trembled.

"Do you have a boyfriend, Lucy Wickwright?" she demanded. "What!"

"Are you 'sweet' on that disgusting boy?" She prodded Lucy's chest and shoulders with the parasol, accenting her words with italic thrusts: "*Sweet* on that dis-*gust*-ing *boy*?"

Lucy had never heard anything more outrageous in her life — not hammers on the moon, not gum-chewing peasants, not even "dogfruit" compared with it. Pauline might as well have accused her of keeping a pet rhinoceros. She stared at her mistress, speechless.

"Well?" said Pauline, stamping her foot.

"That's absurd! Of course not!"

"Good!" said Pauline. "Because I forbid it! You are absolutely, unquestionably, frankly, revoltingly *forbidden* to have a boyfriend!" The parasol fell to the carpet with a rattling of whalebone. Pauline stomped to the window and stood looking over the ward with her back to Lucy, her sausage curls trembling on the collar of her tunic.

Lucy picked up the parasol and folded it properly, too dumbfounded, for the moment, to speak. She smoothed the tassels and brushed off a piece of carpet lint, then held it under her arm and wiped her glasses on her t-shirt. They had somehow got misty.

"Will you be wanting the parasol, mistress?"

"No. I should have to change my costume to suit it."

Lucy returned the parasol to its stand, then stood behind Pauline at the window. The musicians of the court sinfonia were tuning their instruments below, the scraped and tooted notes rising like squawking birds over the gathering crowd. In the distance jugglers tossed their clubs, and a troupe of acrobats warmed up with a round of leapfrog, their maestro crying *Hup! Hup!* as the tumblers vaulted one another's backs. Pauline watched the goings-on with her arms crossed, her mouth fixed in a sullen pout.

"Respectfully, mistress," Lucy ventured to say, "I want nothing to do with boys. They think bon-bons come in pints!"

Pauline toyed with her neckerchief, lowering her gaze to examine the knot. Her sausage curls parted to show the pale skin of her nape.

"I wish you hadn't got into trouble, Wickwright," she said. "I hate being alone all day. And if you go and get a boyfriend, you'll be forever sneaking off and neglecting me. I'll have no one to talk to at all!"

How could Pauline talk of being alone, Lucy wondered, when she would be all day among the mighty and noble, and endlessly amused by jugglers and tumblers and song? Lucy often felt alone in a crowd, but it had never occurred to her that Pauline might feel that way — the Adored & Honorable Pauline! — who was the doted-upon center of attention wherever she went, always asked to recite a poem, or to dance, or to perform upon the zither or theorbo. Lucy reached up and adjusted the bow of one of her mistress's hair ribbons.

"I won't neglect you," she said. "I *certainly* have no intention of finding a boyfriend."

Pauline tugged at her sailor's tunic and adjusted the kerchief again.

"See that you don't," she said. "It's bad enough you're always getting into trouble. And boys are nothing but trouble multiplied, according to Papa. You should be stuck in your quarters forever."

There was another knock at the door.

"Oh, what is it *now*?" Pauline called.

Mr. Vole opened the door, and Lucy blushed guiltily, afraid he might accuse her of vandalizing his schedule. The steward had donned an especially high and stiffly starched collar on this ceremonious day, and had to tilt back his head to give his chin space to talk.

"Miss Cant," he said, "the Misses Martlet await you in the music room."

"Very well," Pauline said. "Give them a bon-bon, Vole. I'll be along pres —"

"They have been given bon-bons, mistress," Mr. Vole interrupted. "Half a pint of them, to be precise, on instructions from your maidservant." He looked crossly at Lucy. "But may I remind my mistress that the festivities commence in ten minutes' time? And that His Lordship awaits you in the bailey?"

Pauline sighed.

"Very *well*," she said. "Come along, Wickwright."

The girls walked to the door. Mr. Vole stepped aside to let Pauline pass, but when Lucy came abreast of him he pinched the sleeve of her t-shirt.

"I needn't remind *you*," he said, "that you are confined to quarters today."

"No, sir," Lucy muttered. She looked up at Pauline, who had stopped on the other side of the threshold. "I hope you have a pleasant day, mistress," she said.

Pauline did not seem to think that a very likely prospect. She sighed again, and rolled her eyes, and spoke in a voice that was somehow both stern and imploring.

"*Do* try to stay out of trouble, Wickwright."

"Yes, mistress," Lucy said. "I'll try."

Chapter 11

A TRUE-LOVERS' KNOT

When Lucy reached the maidservants' garret she found, to her disappointment, that she was not alone in being confined to quarters that day. Jane Cedilla, a girl of thirteen whose job it was to polish the silver, was standing before the pier glass in her nightshirt, having pulled back the curtain of the "dressing room" to take advantage of the light falling from the high dormer windows. Her fingers, blackened by silver polish, clutched the loose folds of her nightshirt at the small of her back. She turned this way and that, examining her reflection, and looked up with a start when Lucy walked in.

"Oh, it's you, Wickwright."

"Good morning," said Lucy.

Jane Cedilla turned back to the glass and pulled the linen nightshirt taut around her midsection. Jane was not stout, exactly, but she was certainly what Lucy would politely call *robust*. Her arms gave evidence of hard labor with the polishing cloth, and her figure suggested that she approached the business of dinner with equal zeal. Lucy sat on the edge of her cot and watched curiously as Jane tugged at the cloth over her chest. Faintly, from the ward, came the sound of trumpets. The festivities had begun.

"Does Miss Cant have a key to Lady Cant's dressing room, Wickwright?" Jane asked.

Lucy very nearly jumped, for keys were much on her mind. Mr. Vole had gone to supervise his staff in the ward, and that gave her a perfect chance to sneak off and use the skeleton key. The only obstacle was Jane Cedilla.

"I suppose Mr. Vole has the key," Lucy said.

"Ugh! I hate that old dried-up mummy," said Jane. She let go her nightshirt. "I want a corset, Wickwright. Can't you get hold of the key somehow? You're always getting into trouble."

"I don't *try* to get into trouble," Lucy said. "What on earth do you want with a corset?"

Jane snorted.

"Of course a little stick like yourself wouldn't understand. A corset," she explained, "trims the figure, and accentuates the bosom. Neither of which you happen to have."

Bosoms were a large topic of conversation among the older girls, along with boys and clothes and face-paint and a host of other things that made Lucy nearly faint from boredom. The older girls suffered terribly from bosoms, and from other buddings and swellings to which they reacted with vanity or mortification. There were whispered hints of grosser ailments, too, that afflicted girls in their teenage years, the very rumor of which made Lucy's hair stand up like a field of corn. She was determined not to become bosomy, herself. To this end she avoided eating sweets, on the theory that they attached themselves unevenly to the body, and resulted in those buds and sproutings that Jane had been trying to discover in the mirror.

"I'm sure I've no use for bosoms," she told Jane Cedilla.

"Nor for a figure, evidently."

"Which spares me from being tied into a corset," Lucy said.

"I *knew* you wouldn't understand," said Jane. She fell down on her cot and folded a pillow under her head. "I'm sure a boy has never given you a second glance, unless he mistook you for a flag-staff and saluted your hair." She gazed at the rafters. "I, on the other hand, have several admirers. Wimp Sweeney, the tinker's boy, brought me a bouquet of wildflowers. He's absolutely smitten."

Lucy yawned extravagantly.

"Oh, don't be jealous, Wickwright," Jane teased. "You can't help being skinny."

"Isn't Wimp Sweeney that cross-eyed boy?" Lucy asked.

"Jealous," said Jane Cedilla.

"Hardly," said Lucy.

"You'll grow up to be an old maid."

"I should like that very much."

"Making a virtue of necessity."

"Hardly."

Jane turned on her side and propped her head on her hand.

"I suppose you have an admirer among the flag corps?" she asked.

"Perhaps I do."

"I doubt it."

"I've had my share of second glances," Lucy said, thinking back — not without a shudder — to Blaise Delagraisse.

"Pish!"

"I have so!"

Lucy realized she ought to ignore Jane, but now that battle was joined it seemed vitally important to prove her wrong.

"Why, just recently . . . ," she said, rifling her memory, "quite recently . . . within the week, in fact . . . a young fellow compared me to Joan of Arc."

"He did not!"

"He certainly did," Lucy said. "And he complimented my figure."

"I don't believe it!"

"Jealous."

"If anyone complimented you," Jane said, "it must have been that blind cobbler who comes around."

"Hardly."

"Who was it, then?"

"Just a fellow I know," Lucy said. She wished Jane would drop it, for she knew she had climbed out on a limb too thin to bear her weight. Arden Gutz had said she might become an historical figure — that *must* be a compliment — and the word *figure* was in there, certainly. So she had not lied, exactly. But why was she quarreling with Jane when she ought to be thinking of a way to escape the garret and retrieve the manifesto? She felt in her pocket for the skeleton key and found the apple that Pauline had given her that morning.

"He must be very ugly," Jane went on. "Is he a hunchback?"

Lucy swung her feet over the edge of her cot and stood up.

"He's nothing compared to Wimp Sweeney," she admitted. "Are you hungry, Jane?"

"I'm starving, of course." Like Lucy, Jane was supposed to be fasting until supper. "Who is he, Wickwright?"

Lucy began to polish the apple with her t-shirt. Jane sat up, tucking her feet under her nightshirt. Her eyes followed the apple.

"Where did you get that?" she asked faintly. "Give me half."

Lucy huffed on the apple, and rubbed it more vigorously on her shirt.

"I'm sure he's a nice boy," Jane said. "I was only teasing."

Lucy polished the fruit until it gleamed like a ruby, then held it out, tantalizingly, to Jane.

"I'm not really hungry, myself," Lucy said. "Would you like it?"

Jane snatched for the apple, but Lucy held it up out of reach.

"Give it here, Wickwright," Jane pleaded. "I'm *starving!*"

"Can you keep a secret, Jane?" Lucy asked.

"I won't tell!"

"Keep a secret for me," said Lucy, "and I may refrain from telling Mr. Vole that you ate an apple on a fast day."

"Give it *here*, Lucy!" Jane begged. "I won't say *anything*."

Lucy moved stealthily across the Great Hall, flitting from tapestry to suit of armor to tapestry, peering anxiously from each hiding place before dashing to the next. Everyone, surely, was at the festival, but after her adventure in the pantry she was taking no chances. Besides, she understood that spy work demanded a great deal of sneaking and peeking and going about on cat feet. Lucy liked adventure books and romances and spy stories, and had read so many of them that, as she crept along, she plainly heard a narrator describing her movements in terse, suspenseful prose.

She had told Jane that she meant to visit her "fellow." (*"Lucy Wickwright!"* Jane had gasped, wiping apple juice from her chin.) It was not strictly a lie, because Lucy *did* mean to visit Arden Gutz, eventually, once she had recovered his manifesto. If Jane chose to believe she was going to visit her fellow *right now,* or that Arden was her "fellow" in the same way that Wimp Sweeney was Jane's . . . well, Lucy was in too great a hurry to fill in the details.

The north wing of the castle was a vast labyrinth of offices in which the business of the Barony was conducted by inky legions of ministers, scribes, and secretaries. Lucy had no idea where, in all that great warren, she might find the office of Vladimir Orloff. She climbed to the first floor and strode down a deserted corridor, reading the doors' brass plaques as she passed them. DEPARTMENT OF WOOLEN EXPORTS — INSPECTORATE OF PILLS AND NAP, said one. Farther on was the COMMISSION ON PROVINCIAL FOLKLORE — OFFICE OF SAGAS, LEGENDS, AND YARNS, and next to it the ACADEMY OF DOGS, CATS, AND HUTCH PETS — DIVISION OF BEDDING AND LITTER.

Lucy climbed from floor to floor, discovering no logic in the placement of the various offices. It seemed absurd to have dogs and cats in the same Academy, while the CONGRESS ON ALPINE RECREATION and the COLLEGE OF MOUNTAINEERING were sepa-

rated by two long flights of stairs. She hurried down the corridors, turning her head this way and that, and failed to notice —
until it was too late — that one of the doors stood open. A
man in a black gown glanced up as she went by.

"I say!" he called after her. "You there!"

Lucy stopped, her heart thumping, and read the plaque on
the office's door.

COLLEGE OF HERALDRY
STORES & FABRICATION

"Hello?" the man said. "Who's there?"

Lucy gulped. She wiped her nose with the back of her hand,
and then wiped her hand on the seat of her pants. She stood
well away from the door.

"It's me," she said in a gruff voice. "Sorry to disturb you."

"Lend a finger, won't you?" the man asked. "Who is it? Let
me see you."

Lucy approached the doorway and peeked in, showing as little of her face as possible. Stores & Fabrication was a manu-
factory for coats of arms, evidently — several specimens hung
from the wall, and on the wooden shelves stood pots of glue,
heaps of pelts, and spools of ribbon on long wooden axles.
The man who had called her bent over the worktable, his face
hidden by a drooping black cap, his hands occupied with a
length of light-blue ribbon. A monocle hung from a silver cord
around his neck.

"Dr. Sauersop?" Lucy asked, no longer disguising her voice.
Sauersop looked up, the peak of his cap falling over one eye.

He frowned, and held his monocle to the other orb. He inspected Lucy from her sneakers to her t-shirt, chuckled softly, then fitted the monocle in place and beckoned with his hand.

"A-ha!" he said. "Our little revolutionist! Miss Wicket, yes? Come in, come in!"

"Lucy Wickwright, sir," said Lucy, making a curtsey.

"Wickwright, of course. How stupid I am." Sauersop motioned to the window, which overlooked the ward. "Planning to throw some laundry on the festivities?" he asked, winking so broadly that his monocle popped from its socket.

"No, sir," Lucy said. She felt in her back pocket for Sauersop's handkerchief. She had forgotten all about it, until now. "I have your handkerchief, sir. Thank you for lending me it. I've washed it out."

"Ah, you are most welcome," Sauersop said, taking the handkerchief. "And I thank you, in turn, for laundering it. That was entirely unnecessary — though gratifying, I assure you."

"What are you making?" Lucy asked. Sauersop replaced his monocle and took up the loose ends of the ribbon.

"I'm attempting to tie a true-lovers' knot," he said. "But I'm handicapped by want of a third hand. Would you be so kind?"

Lucy held her finger where Sauersop indicated while he looped and tied the ribbon, fixing it at each stage of the operation with small pins. When he had finished he curled the loose ends with the blade of a scissors. The knot was tied atop a shield or standard of stiff, painted cowhide, which was fitted with leather loops for hoisting aloft on a stave. It bore the familiar emblems of the house of Cant — *per chevron gules and argent, three wolves sable* — but they were displayed on a lozenge rather than a proper shield. This indicated (in the obscure symbolism of heraldry) that the arms were those of an unmarried woman.

"They are Miss Cant's arms," Lucy said.

Sauersop removed his monocle and cleaned it with his handkerchief.

"Strictly speaking, they are the arms of Lady Cant — or shall be, you understand, when Pauline von Cant assumes the barony. I thought it only prudent, given the state of His Lordship's health, to make ready her processional bearings." He regarded Lucy curiously through the lens of his monocle. "One often sees you about with the Adored Pauline. Are you one of her ladies-in-waiting?"

Lucy shook her head. Pauline had several ladies-in-waiting, all of them daughters of high-ranking nobles, but she rarely saw them apart from ceremonial occasions. Lucy fancied they disapproved of Pauline — out of envy, perhaps, or because of her habit of crawling about in attics and cellars with Lucy — and, for her part, Pauline characterized her noble companions as "colossal gnats." It occurred to Lucy that, apart from herself, Pauline really had no playmates.

"No, sir," she told Sauersop. "I'm her maidservant."

"Ah. I see. Rather young, aren't you?"

"His Lordship was kind enough to grant me the favor of a position, on account of my being orphaned. Can you tell me, sir," Lucy asked, "what is the matter with His Lordship? Is it true the Baron is dying?"

Sauersop hung Pauline's arms on an easel, then went to the window and clasped his hands behind his back. Lucy followed him. The window overlooked the ward, where a great crowd had gathered to hear the speeches in honor of the Baron's anniversary. Lord Cant slumped in a large, high-backed chair upon the dais, and even from this distance Lucy could see the labored effort of his breathing. A page stood at his side, shooing flies with a feather wand.

"The doctors are baffled to diagnose him," Sauersop said at last. "A tapeworm was suspected, but His Lordship grows fatter, rather than thinner. Yet it's not gout. He eats little, but drinks a great deal of wine. He gives no sign of *wanting* to live."

"But, why, sir? Pauline will be left all alone."

"The old wives have a saying in my home village," the herald said. "*The man who guards a secret must perish at his post.* It's a metaphorical way of speaking, you see. Do you know what a metaphor is?"

"Yes, sir. It's when you say someone has a ball of yarn for brains."

"Very good. Well. The guard, in this metaphor, is Lord Cant, and the secret . . . well, if I knew that, it wouldn't be a secret, would it? But it is rumored that His Lordship committed an enormity in his past, which now festers like a canker. Some speak of a scandal — a child, got upon a servant girl, that was exposed in an awful fashion. Others suspect the Baron is the object of blackmail. His subjects grow restless, overburdened with taxes that support a bloated, gum-chewing court. Even the villages are murmuring, and Tenesmus, they say, has become a regular hotbed of unrest since young Gutz was imprisoned. Meanwhile underlings control the Barony, and Lord Cant lies abed with his wine, listening to music boxes. Never become too fond of wine, Miss Wickwright."

"No, sir. I shan't."

"Music boxes you may safely enjoy, in moderation. But, here — why aren't you at the festival? I hope you didn't forego merrymaking simply to return my handkerchief?"

"No, sir. I . . . er . . ." Lucy thought quickly. "Could you direct me to the Department of Embroidery? I believe it's next to the Postal Commissioner's office."

"The Postal Commissioner is one flight up," said Sauersop, taking Lucy by the arm. "But that office is next to Equine Affairs. Perhaps Embroidery is next to the Pustule Commissioner, who is on the fourth floor, if I'm not mistaken. Fond of embroidery, are you?"

"Yes, sir," Lucy said truthfully. Pauline was a great beginner of needlework, Lucy a dogged finisher.

"Well, I thank you again for laundering my handkerchief. You seem an outstanding young girl, whatever Gutz may think. Your mistress should be proud of you."

They had been walking toward the door of the workroom. Lucy stopped, now, and stared up at Sauersop, her face gone suddenly pale. Could Dr. Sauersop have visited the dungeon in the short time since she had been there?

"He said I'm not outstanding?" she asked.

"Er . . . not in so many words. But you mustn't pay any mind to Gutz, dear. He's only an old crank who was never a child himself. I found your little prank rather amusing, frankly."

"Oh, *Costive* Gutz!" Lucy said, flushing.

"Why, yes. Whom did you think I meant?"

Lucy stepped out to the corridor.

"Um, I mistook your meaning," she said. "Thank you for the loan of your handkerchief, sir! Good day!"

"Miss Wickwright!" called Sauersop, before she had gone three steps away. Lucy turned around. Sauersop's kindly face had grown solemn.

"Yes, sir?"

"You're not to speak a word to Miss Cant about her processional arms, or indeed about His Lordship's, ah . . . condition. It is not our place to meddle."

"No, sir," Lucy said.

"Very well. A good day to you."

"Thank you, sir."

At the end of the corridor Lucy looked back to make sure Dr. Sauersop had returned to his workshop. Then, her heart racing, she ran up the stairs to find the office of the Commissioner of Posts.

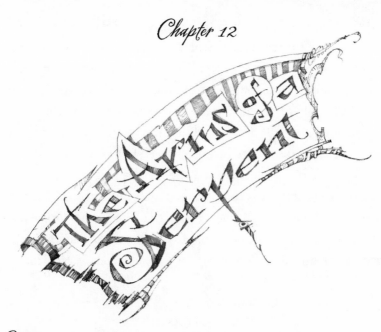

Chapter 12

The Skin of a Serpent

When Lucy lived on Chandlers Lane she was fond of a game called Fetching Squire Felix. In this game, similar to hide-and-go-seek, the child who played Squire Felix had the task of hiding so cunningly from the other children that they spent the better part of an afternoon in finding him. Seekers traveled in pairs, the blindfolded "Knights" led by "Hounds" who were forbidden to speak except by baying, yapping, and tugging at the leash. Lucy loved being Squire Felix, for she could fold her body into such tiny spaces that no one ever thought of looking in them, and she often emerged triumphantly at the tolling of the five o'clock bell to claim from each player the tribute of a clay marble, or fancy feather, or piece of rock.*

---

*That is, lump sugar. When "Squire Felix" was discovered by a "Knight" and "Hound," they (cont.)

As she climbed the stairs to Vladimir Orloff's office, Lucy felt very much as though she played a game of make-believe, though she suspected that getting caught would bring a far worse penalty than a stalk of rhubarb to her backside. She thought grimly of the hair-raising devices of Gustaf the Fey.

The corridor was deserted, but Lucy crept silently on her rubber soles, making sure each door was shut before she passed it. Each time her shoe squeaked she started and froze, expecting a platoon of guards to burst through one of the doors. She passed the DEPARTMENT OF MINES, the OFFICE OF DOMESTIC REVENUES, and the BUREAU OF EQUINE AFFAIRS, and finally, dead in the middle of the corridor, stood at her destination.

COMMISSIONER OF POSTS
VLADIMIR ORLOFF

She almost hoped the skeleton key wouldn't work, but the bolt drew easily, with a faint *shhh* of oiled metal. She lifted the latch and pushed open the heavy door. The hinges were silent as snails. Just inside the door stood a long mirror, and beside it a wooden candle-stand thickly vined with wax. An enormous

---

shared this tribute between them, and enjoyed the further reward of thrashing the "Squire" with a stalk of rhubarb while chanting:

Over to Goatshank we have gone
To fetch the Squire of Muckleston!
Back to Muckleston we've come
To peel his bottom like a plum!
Whack! Whack! Whack! Whack! Whack!

candle had melted down over it, its tendrils reaching nearly to the floor. Lucy shut the door, locked it, and put the key beside the candle's stump.

She paused to wipe her nose, then turned to examine the office. The room was large, its floor covered by a worn, flower-patterned carpet. A pair of leather chairs faced each other by the window. Against the wall to her left rose a vast cupboard, the marble surface of its deeper, bottom part covered with stacks of papers and a pewter tea service. A tall, old-fashioned desk stood against the opposite wall, its many cubbyholes stuffed with official-looking forms, tickets, and receipts. On the wall to Lucy's right hung Orloff's coat of arms: *argent a bordure wavy sable a serpent vert.** It was not pleasant to look at. The serpent rising from its coils seemed ready to strike her with its great fangs.

Lucy had no idea where to look for the manifesto, or, for that matter, what a manifesto was supposed to look like. Did it say "Manifesto" on the cover, like the "Instructions for Use" that came with Pauline's imported toys? She might spend all day searching the cupboard and the great cubbyholed desk, leafing through postal forms and dry books of regulations until her eyes shriveled to walnuts. But again luck was with her. She had gone through only a few papers on top of the desk when she found several sheets of yellow foolscap, held together with a pin, that could only be the manifesto of Arden Gutz.

---

*A green snake on a black-bordered silver field.

Comrades! Cantlings! [it began]

*A foul and perfidious CANKER festers on the land: a
PESTILENCE that lays waste the hopes of working FOLK; a
WORM that battens upon the corpse of RIGHT; a WOLF, in
SHEPHERD'S dress, enslaving the PEOPLE to the folly of
PRINCES & NOBLES, who, neglecting those DUTIES &
CARES to them entrusted by STATUTE & TRADITION,
have given themselves wholly to GREED, CORRUPTION, &
DECADENCE; a PLAGUE more deadly than those from
which our FOREBEARS, in ancient times, fled to this our
HAVEN, our mountain-ringed, inviolate CANT; a POPPY,
whose THRALLS the MIGHTY have become . . .*

Here Lucy stopped reading — not from despair of ever
reaching the end of the first sentence, but at the murmur of
voices in the corridor. Someone was coming. She looked in
panic around the office. The room had no curtains or tapes-
tries or suits of armor to hide behind. She hurried to the cupboard and opened, one by one, the broad doors of the base.
The shelves were stacked with official forms, books of regulations, and reams of foolscap. One was crowded with apothe-
cary bottles and a pestle and mortar, and behind another, atop
a carton of stamps, she discovered a woman's blood-red gown.
The voices drew nearer. She heard the soft shuffle of a guardsman's sandals.

Trembling, she opened the next tier of doors. Here the
shelves sagged under platoons of ink bottles, tins of biscuits,
and ranks of rubber stamps. One door hid a plaster bust of

Gustaf the Fey, who leered so maniacally at Lucy that she nearly cried out. Her nose dripped violently.

The sandals halted outside the office door. A key-ring jangled. Lucy gripped the manifesto in her teeth and scrambled to the marble shelf of the cupboard, being careful not to upset the tea service. As the key penetrated the door-lock she found a cubby, in the topmost tier of doors, where only a few loose papers rested. She grabbed the molding and lifted her feet to the shallow opening. The bolt slid in the office door. By bending double, and pressing her chin against her breastbone and twisting her shoulders, Lucy managed to stuff herself in. The office door opened, and Vladimir Orloff walked in, followed by Sir Tybold Retsch, the Captain of the Guard.

Lucy could see this because, twist and squeeze and scrunch as she might, the cupboard door would not entirely close. A gap remained of about a thumb's breadth, through which she could see the area around the office door. As chance would have it, the mirror beside the door reflected one of the armchairs, into which Orloff now fell with a grunt of impatience.

"Be quick, Retsch," he said, scowling at his watch. "I've a speech to deliver in ten minutes."

Lucy could not see Tybold Retsch, but she was well familiar with his leathery face. When her mistress's Whims made trouble outside the baronial residence it was Captain Retsch, rather than Mr. Vole, who determined Lucy's punishment.

"Sir Stomata will be happy to gather wool until we get back," the captain said. "I think the Commissioner will agree that my news is urgent."

"Well, out with it, Retsch," said Orloff, tucking away his

watch. His face was strangely familiar to Lucy, although to her knowledge she had never laid eyes on him before. He was a tall, broad-shouldered man, and his eyebrows sprouted unruly bristles at their midpoints that probed the air like an insect's hairy feelers.

"Very well," said Retsch. "This morning, not three hours ago, a pigeon arrived from our man in Whey. He was taking a pint at the inn there when a large, armed party arrived from Haslet March. Twenty-four mounts, and an equal number of bowmen."

"Henry Wallow," said Orloff. Lucy recognized the name. Wallow was the nobleman from Haslet March whom Arden Gutz hoped to recruit to his Cause.

"Exactly. Their arms were shrouded, but our man oiled the tongue of one of the bowmen, who was rather too fond of ale for his master's good. Sir Henry is making for Castle Cant."

"Well, what of that?" Orloff asked. "I trust your men can repel a force of forty-eight yokels under the command of a hog farmer!" He snorted. "Wallow must be an even greater fool than I'd imagined. No doubt he's got wind of the Baron's condition, and thinks he can force some concession from the Privy Council before I've . . . before the regent has found his legs. It's just as well. Perhaps his coming will convince His Lordship to settle the matter of his daughter's guardian before it's too late. I'll see to that. You, Retsch, tell your men to sharpen their swords."

It was just as Arden Gutz had said. Orloff meant to become Pauline's regent, and to rule the Barony in her name. But why was Wallow on the move? Lucy wondered. He was supposed to be in sympathy with the Cause, but Arden could not have contacted the nobleman in the few hours since Lucy had given him Lemonjello's farthings.

Orloff put his hands on the arms of his chair, as though to rise, but the captain of the guard coughed meaningly.

"You misunderstand me," Retsch said. "Sir Henry's force is not an offensive one. Nor is he intent on so trifling a matter as tax concessions. I have every reason to believe he intends to challenge the succession. Our man learned that Wallow's force is serving as guard to another member of the party — an old woman, and a commoner. The drunken bowman didn't know her identity, but I think we may safely guess it. They have found Clara Swain."

Orloff shot from his chair.

"Damn His Lordship's soft heart!" he cried.

"Commissioner, please!" the captain reprimanded.

"The Baron tricked us, Retsch," Orloff said, "and thought himself very clever. I warned the fool, when I discovered his treachery, that a tender heart is no virtue in a prince. Let the child live if you must, I told him, but an old woman's tongue will wag, be it from the ends of the earth. She should have been eliminated, Retsch. I should have done it when I had the chance."

Lucy listened closely. She did not understand Orloff's words, but to Arden, perhaps, they would mean a great deal. She was determined to make a good report to him.

"These tidings are grave, surely," said Tybold Retsch, "but they are hardly fatal. Wallow has learned that His Lordship sired an heir before his marriage to Esmeralda. But what of that? The babe was still in swaddling bands when Clara Swain last saw it. And I needn't remind you that *we* have the child, Commissioner. We need only prevent — Hush! Did you hear something?"

Orloff had been pacing the office. He stopped now, visible to Lucy through the opening of the cupboard door. The bristles of his eyebrows quivered, as though feeling the air.

"I heard nothing," he said.

Lucy held her breath.

"Perhaps it was a rat," said Retsch.

Lucy closed her eyes, expecting at any moment to be dragged from the cupboard and carried away in irons. Her glance had fallen to the candle-stand, where she saw that the vining wax had not entirely covered the great stump of the candle upon it. There were figures there, behind the beeswax creepers — a lifted snout, a curling tail, a paw. Lucy remembered, then, where she had seen the Commissioner before, and she squealed aloud in spite of herself. Vladimir Orloff was none other than Lady Sweetbread, and the melted heap of wax, on which the Wolves of Rotwood Forest ran, was all that remained of Lon, Hester, and Casio Wickwright. Lucy had found the Candle of Cant.

Chapter 13

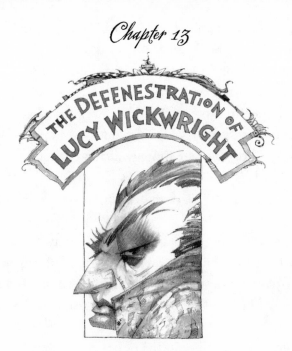

THE DEFENESTRATION OF LUCY WICKWRIGHT

𝒱lad Orloff's antennæ sniffed the air. Lucy shuddered to remember how this horrible man, in the guise of "Lady Sweetbread," had run a gloved finger over her toes, and petted her cheek, and called her "little girl." He had stolen the Candle of Cant, then, and he or his henchman had tossed Lucy's family to the rocks below the castle as though they were nothing but scraps of the burlap that had cushioned the candle. His dark eyes scanned the office, now, and remained a long moment on the cupboard, so intent in their gaze that Lucy feared her beating heart would give her away. Her lungs burned with the effort of not breathing, and cold threads of sweat dripped down her body. The silence was finally broken by a swell of applause from the window. It was a faint sound — for the office faced away from the festivities in the ward — but under its cover Lucy softly let out her breath.

"I heard nothing," Orloff repeated. "But perhaps it was a rat. The castle is full of them." He turned to Retsch. "I must deliver my speech. Now, of all times, we must do nothing to raise suspicions. Send your best scouts to monitor Wallow's progress. We'll discuss our strategy at a later time."

Lucy heard Retsch rise from his chair. Orloff opened the door and glanced down the corridor, then turned again to Retsch.

"I needn't tell you, Captain," he said, "that under no circumstances is the child to leave the castle. Inform the gatekeepers. You may throw her into the dungeon, if need be, but at all events His Lordship's sniveling heiress is *not* to fall into Wallow's hands."

"I could hardly put her in the dungeon without raising suspicions, Commissioner," said Retsch, "but rest assured, she'll not escape the castle on my watch."

Lucy clenched her fists so tightly that her nails dug into her palms. No doubt remained to her, now, of Orloff's depraved and utter wickedness. Throw Pauline into the dungeon! She could barely restrain herself from lunging at the Postal Commissioner's throat. Pauline! The heiress to the Barony of Cant!

At that moment, in her cramped and airless hiding place, Lucy was converted. She became a deadly guerilla in the service of the Cause. She would risk any punishment, overcome any obstacle, to defend her mistress and avenge her family. She would quash the gum trade single-handedly, if necessary, and bring Vlad Orloff down.

She ached for action. But vengeance demands cunning as

well as fury, and Lucy's was soon put to the test. For as Tybold Retsch left the office his eyes chanced to fall on the candle-stand. He stopped, and reached out his hand.

"Commissioner," he said, picking up a small black object, "you've forgotten your key."

Too late Lucy cursed her foolishness — she had left the skeleton key on the candle-stand! Frowning, Orloff took the key from Retsch, turned it in his long, bony fingers, then pushed it into the lock and threw the bolt. His eyes rose to the cupboard, to the door that stood slightly ajar, and a faint smile creased his lips.

Lucy was prepared to fight — Orloff thought nothing of dressing in women's clothes, she reasoned, and a swift sneaker to Retsch's fat belly would drop him like a sack of tadpoles — but the Postal Commissioner only drew back the bolt and held the door wide for Tybold Retsch.

"How forgetful of me," he said. "Thank you, Retsch. It wouldn't do to leave the door unlocked. If there is a rat in here, we don't want him to escape. But come — I'll send up a man with a terrier to sniff it out, after I've finished my speech. We mustn't keep His Lordship waiting."

The door closed, the bolt shot fast, and Lucy was trapped. When she was certain that Orloff and Retsch were well away, she threw open the cupboard door and gulped air. She had held the manifesto in her mouth the whole time, and the pages were soggy now, and torn by her teeth. Her nose had dripped on it, too. She stretched stiff legs from her cocoon and climbed down, then opened the cupboard and wiped the manifesto clean on "Lady Sweetbread's" gown.

A veteran spy would have set about escaping the office at

once, but Lucy was a novice, and an orphaned servant girl besides. She put down the manifesto and went to the Candle of Cant. The beeswax was cool beneath her fingers, and when she pressed her cheek against it she could smell the shop on Chandlers Lane, and hear her father whistling as he dipped the tapers. It had become harder, lately, to conjure her memories of the chandlery. Her parents' faces had blurred, like waxwork busts set too close to a fire, and of Casio little remained but an image from a magic lantern, a shadow-picture thrown by a guttering candle.

If Lucy cried, now, it was not from self-pity, for she was a cheerful girl at heart, and not given to melancholy. If she wept, it was for her family — that nothing should remain of them but wax, and faltering memories, and three white stones that would melt in their turn, consumed by the slow forgetfulness of rain and frost. After a while she dried her eyes and blew her nose on Orloff's gown. She must find a way to escape. She did not know how to pick a lock, and she might throw herself against the heavy door all day without so much as scratching it, but she must find some way out before Orloff returned with his "terrier."

She tested the weight of the candle-stand, rocking it to and fro. It caught the carpet when she tried to drag it across the office, so she laid it down and rolled it, littering the carpet with pale teardrops of wax. Her hands clawed for a grip on the slippery tendrils — the stump of the candle made the stand top-heavy and clumsy to hold — and she staggered as she lifted the impromptu battering ram. She pictured Orloff's features on the bolted door, determined to smash it to splinters.

"The sun is behind us!" she cried, hurling herself toward the door.

It was a case of fury running ahead of cunning. The door budged not the tiniest fraction of an inch, and Lucy, with unstoppable momentum, crashed against its stout timbers at full gallop. The candle-stand fell — nearly crushing her foot — and Lucy followed it to the floor, her skull flashing with fireworks. After a few deep breaths she felt for her glasses (which had fallen off with the impact). When her eyes could focus again she leaned against the office door and gingerly touched the rising knob on her forehead.

"Ouch!" she said quietly.

There came another fanfare at the window. Vladimir Orloff would now be mounting the dais to flatter Lord Cant with a finely worded speech. Pauline would be squirming at Mrs. Healing's side, or tying her kerchief into bunny shapes. Behind them, on rows of hard benches, the nobles and gentle people would be trading gossip, their whispers moist and garbled in their gum-smacking mouths.

Lucy went to the window and looked toward the region of Haslet March, from which Sir Henry Wallow now rode to trouble his ruler, Lord Cant. The outlying districts of Cant — Haslet March, Trans-Poltroon, and La Provence — had risen up against several of its Barons, but there had been no serious challenge to the primacy of the von Cants since the bloody reign of Gustaf I ("the Fey"). Now Pauline was threatened both by Orloff — determined to seize power as her regent — and by an upstart country nobleman who questioned her right to the baronial cap.

Lucy looked down. The castle wall fell sheer to the moat, which made a thin black ribbon at its base. Overhead it rose twenty feet to the windows of the next floor, without the least hint of a toehold in its smooth, well-fitted stones. If Lucy meant to escape by the window the only way to go was down — and the moat looked terribly, terribly small and far away.

She was not a cowardly girl — she had leapt from haylofts and climbed tall trees and swung from a rope into Micklewood Pond — but neither was she foolhardy. How deep *was* the moat? she wondered. She might fall into water no deeper than her knees. Or, leaving her own welfare aside, what if she landed on some poor turtle's back, or trespassed in a family of frogs? Or again, she might jump out too far and miss the moat entirely, and fall *splat!* on the ground, crumpled like a concertina.

But she was between a wolf and a weasel, as they said in Cant, and it was better — as they also said — to fight the weasel than to feed the wolf. First she must find some way to get the manifesto safely to the ground. She searched the cupboard for some heavy, throwable object, eventually choosing one of the postal commission's official stamps. It was hefty and elegantly wrought, its turned wooden handle surmounted by a brass finial in the shape of the baronial cap. Its message, too, seemed to fit the occasion:

RETURN
TO
SENDER

Lucy wrapped the manifesto around the stamp, securing the ends with lengths of twine bitten from a spool. The finished product reminded her of a party cracker, and she hoped it would have a similarly explosive effect on Vlad Orloff's nefarious schemes.

She gave it a good heave at the window. It fell end over end, for a disturbingly long time, and disappeared in a bramble some twenty feet beyond the moat. When Lucy had marked its position she pulled a chair to the window. All that remained was to jump down, retrieve the manifesto, and carry it to the printer at her first opportunity.

But she hesitated. It seemed some kind of preparation should be made for throwing oneself out of a high window into an unknown depth of water. She lifted her feet by turns to the chair and firmly reknotted the laces of her sneakers. Normally this gave her a feeling of confidence, but now, somehow, the effect was wanting.

There was another flourish of brass at the window, and Lucy could stall no longer. Orloff's men might even now be making their way to the office. She climbed the chair to the windowsill, putting her glasses into her pocket. She closed her eyes and imagined standing on a boat-dock on a hot summer's day. She always hesitated to jump into the water at the beginning of summer, but after the first shock it was delightful, and once in the water she scolded herself for having been a chicken. She took a deep breath, and jumped.

Had Glenden Galt still lived (that greatest of Cantling poets) — and had he been provided countless reams of paper, and a bottomless well of ink, and a great flock of goose-quills, and an eternity of solitude in which to write — the immortal Galt, at the height of his powers, might have done justice to the drama of Lucy's fall. No other poet — and certainly no novelist — could hope to describe it. The theme wanted a bard of incomparable range and magnitude. The epic would run to thousands of lines, under a grand, unpronounceable title — perhaps *The Defenestration of Lucy Wickwright* — so that Galt's readers would be obliged to consult the dictionary before reading a single heroic couplet. But their effort would be rewarded, for having once learned that a "defenestration" meant "a throwing [of something] out the window," they would be enthralled by a narrative so gripping in its action, so apt in its figures, and so profound in its sympathy that, by comparison, Milton's account of the Fall of the Rebel Angels would forever after, in their minds, be as the scribblings of the crudest poetaster.

But Galt was dead, and Lucy did not take notes. She fell a very, very, VERY long time, and struck the water in a *whoosh!* of bubbles, her sneakers squelching into the silt at the bottom of the moat. She pulled free her shoes and kicked upward, eyes open in the green, murky flood, swimming frogwise to the sun. A mountain stream fed the moat, and the water was bitterly cold. When she broke the surface Lucy gasped for air and took in a good mouthful of moat-water, which made her gag and cough as she paddled to the bank. The moat, of course, was one great chamber pot to the toads and eels and fishes who lived there, and Lucy's stomach turned when she thought about what she had swallowed.

The bank was steep and slick with mud. She grabbed fistfuls of hanging grass and pulled herself up, then lay gasping on the shore. Something wiggled, and Lucy leapt to her feet, yanking at her sodden t-shirt. A bewildered perch fell out and flopped unhappily at her feet. She threw the fish into the moat, wrung out her hair, and put on her glasses. The manifesto had fallen into a thicket of buckberries, from which she emerged some minutes later with scratched arms and thorn-snagged clothes. Orloff's window watched her like a dark, malevolent eye.

Jane Cedilla lay propped on pillows gathered from the surrounding cots, reading one of the card-bound romances that the older girls traded among themselves. Lucy wanted nothing but to undress and collapse in the warm, dry sheets of her cot, so she had given no thought to her appearance, or to its effect on Jane (who still believed that Lucy had gone to visit her "fellow"). Her hair was matted and lank and did nothing to conceal the purple knot on her forehead. Mud covered her jeans and t-shirt. Black blood beaded her thorn-scratched arms; her glasses were filthy, and she smelled of moat.

Jane glanced up from her book as Lucy walked toward her. She went back to reading, then looked up again, yelped, and erupted from the pilfered pillows, her novel arcing to the floor with a fluttering of leaves. For the first time in her memory Lucy saw something like concern in the eyes of a fellow servant. Jane's mouth hung open, her lips quivered, and the color drained from her face. She jumped from the cot and ran to Lucy, throwing her arms around her and pressing her to the soft folds of her nightshirt.

"Oh, Lucy!" she cried. "What did that awful boy *do* to you?"

Chapter 14

MARKET DAY in Tenesmus

*I*n the morning, Lucy felt that her life had taken a turn. For one thing, Jane Cedilla had decided to become her friend — or at least her protectress. For although Lucy had explained that the lump on her head came from running into a door, Jane persisted in believing that she had been mistreated by a boy. This, strangely, seemed to raise her in the older girl's regard (whereas Lucy would have felt only pity and exasperation toward a girl who stood such nonsense). Before they went down to breakfast Jane cut Lucy's hair in a new style, brushing down a fringe to cover her bruise.

It was Saturday, her half-holiday, when Lucy's only duties were to rouse her mistress from bed, dress her, and carry up a tray of breakfast. Those were not easy tasks on the best days, but this morning they required a monumental effort. Pauline had gorged on candyfloss the night before, and had run riot at the carnival — banging a toy drum, tooting a kazoo, and racing from ring-toss to cocoanut-shy like a hardened gambler. When Lucy arrived she refused to budge. She had to be dragged out of bed, and even then she clutched at the blankets before falling with a *thump!* to the floor. She staggered to the mirror, groaned, and ordered Lucy to bring cucumber slices for her eyes, and chamomile tea. With the extra work it was fully eleven o'clock before Lucy arrived at the castle gate, and there she met a further, and more troubling, delay.

"I'm sorry, miss," the sentry said. "You're not to leave the castle."

Lucy had been about to walk past him. Rain fell beyond the long, arched tunnel of the gateway and dismally dripped from the sharp spikes of the portcullis.

"But I'm going to town," Lucy said. "It's Saturday."

The guardsman was young, probably a new recruit from the provinces. He looked away from Lucy, his hand resting on the hilt of his sword.

"Those are my orders, miss," he said — adding, in a slightly less threatening tone, "It's no weather for a walk."

Lucy put her hands on her hips and scowled, as her mother used to do when she or Casio was being stubborn about a bath. She had tucked an umbrella, sword-wise, into her belt.

"Now, see here," she said. "This is my half-holiday. I've every right to go into town if I please — or all the way to Boondock, for that matter!" *All the way to Boondock* was a Cantling way of saying "to the ends of the earth."

"You're Miss Lucy Wickwright?" the sentry asked.

"I certainly am," said Lucy. "I've a half-holiday every Satur-day. And today is Saturday, if you hadn't noticed."

"I'm sorry, miss," the sentry said again. "I have my orders." His fingers tapped nervously on his sword, and he stared past Lucy at the empty tents and stalls of the carnival.

"What *orders*?" Lucy demanded.

"The orders that you're not to leave the castle," said the guardsman.

"But it's my half-holiday!" said Lucy, her voice rising in ex-asperation. "Who gave such an order?"

The sentry hesitated.

"It came through the chain of command," he said. "I'm sorry, miss. I don't give the orders. I'm only doing my duty."

Lucy fumed. Whenever you asked grown-ups *why* you couldn't do this or that, they always said "Those are the rules" or "Because I said so" or "It's for your own good," which were all different ways of saying "I'm bigger than you, so there!" And this guardsman was hardly a grown-up at all — he looked like a boy playing at soldiers, except with a real sword instead of a broomstick. Before turning back to the ward Lucy drew the umbrella from her belt, which made the sentry flinch and pull his weapon an inch from its scabbard.

"I'm telling my uncle about you," Lucy said, "who, by the way, could tie your tongue to your big toe and string you up like a pretzel. *And* I'm telling Mr. Vole, *and* my mistress, who is Pauline Esmeralda Simone-Thierry von Cant, for your infor-mation, the Baron's daughter! To think that a poor, honest, hardworking, orphaned servant-girl . . . Oh!"

Words failed her, and she spun on her toe and stomped out

of the tunnel in a fury. She had no intention of complaining to Mr. Vole or Pauline — the steward would merely shrug and tell her not to make trouble, while Pauline would concoct some madcap scheme to steal the sentry's helmet, or fill his scabbard with mashed beets — but neither did Lucy intend to waste her half-holiday in the servants' garret. Years of playing hide-and-go-seek with her mistress had taught Lucy all the ins and outs of the castle — and it was to one of the latter that she next hurried her steps. There were ways out of Castle Cant that even its sentries knew nothing about.

Lucy went first to the American Mission, to see if any new second-hand clothes were to be found in the charity box. Usually she found it empty, for she could check it at most once a week, whereas the other orphans were on the spot when new things arrived. Today, for once, her timing was good, and she found a greedy throng of children gathered around the box, which had just been refilled.

Lucy plunged into the melee. There was no question of sorting through the clothes at her leisure, like a lady in a shop. In the crush of bodies around the box she simply had to grab as many items as possible and carry them to the safety of the dining hall, where a great hubbub of bartering was underway. The din was terrific. Small boys held up frilly skirts in circles of anxious girls, who cajoled them with breeches and brass-buttoned blazers.

In a series of trades that involved at least half a dozen children, Lucy replaced her too-short, too-tight jeans with a roomy pair of trousers such as she never knew existed — outlandish olive trousers with big pockets sewn to the sides of the legs, and a leather belt to hold them up. She walked away in her old sneakers (American shoes rarely fit her busy-toed feet), but now they were padded by new (never-worn!) white ankle-stockings, and over her GIZMOBOTS! t-shirt she wore the most marvelous thing of all: a handsome gray jumper (which Miss Poke had called a *sweatshirt*) with pockets to warm her hands and a hood with a drawstring to keep off the rain.

With her head lightened by a haircut and her heart made buoyant by the success of her spy work, Lucy felt she hovered a foot above the muddy lanes of Tenesmus. The passing dogs greeted her with eager tails. The town teemed with folk this market day, and their laughter spilled from the doors of public houses, where they sipped hot cider and dried their boots by comforting coal fires. Carts heaped with vegetables skidded and sloshed on the rutted lanes. In Market Square the townsfolk haggled with their country cousins, examining small potatoes with such profound anxiety that one might think they were adopting a child.

Lucy was eager to see her Uncle Hock and tell him all the fantastic things that had happened since her last visit, but first she had to deliver the manifesto to the printer, Lu Mingshu. How proud Arden Gutz would be of his spy! Lucy imagined his sharp look melting when she told him the news. He would smile, for once, and hold her in a grateful embrace.

The rain had left off, though clouds still scudded overhead. Lucy wandered into Market Square, looking for someone of whom to ask directions to the printer's shop. A few of the orphanage children were there, selling pamphlets and bootlaces and startling the country folk with their outlandish clothes. A crowd had gathered by the steps to the Guild Hall, where an orator held forth on top of an overturned bushel basket. Lucy was not a great one for speeches, but sometimes Pauline asked for the news from Tenesmus when Lucy came back from her holiday. So she paused to listen, standing next to a matron at the back of the crowd.

"And what do they do with your taxes, when they've snatched the last penny from your purse?" the speaker asked scornfully. "Do ye see them here, buying from the hardworking Cantling, who toils at the bellows and plow and loom? Nay! Honest goods of the country ain't smart enough for your noble creatures in yon castle!" The man's arm shot out, and his finger pointed accusingly to where, hidden in clouds, the castle loomed on its cliff top. "Nay! It's all wagonloads of foreign stuff, nowadays, coming down the North Road like a plague on wheels! That's where the money's gone, comrades — right out of the Barony!"

It sounded like a very tedious speech to Lucy, who decided to press on to the printer's shop. She tugged at her neighbor's apron.

"Excuse me, missus —" she began.

"He's more than half right," the woman said, glancing down. "The nobles must have their fancy silks and cottons, as like they're too good to wear woolen things. I still sell a bit of bobbin-lace to the gentry, but not like I used."

"The fine folk must have their cud!" shouted a man near the front of the crowd. The speaker, who had paused to wipe his mouth, nodded grimly at this sentiment.

"Aye, that's what comes of bringing in foreign goods," he said. "They brings their outlandish ways with 'em. Chewing gum . . . bah! They've gone soft in the teeth, up in yon castle, and 'soft in the teeth, soft in the head,' as Grandma says about Grandpa."

This inspired a general chuckle, and the speaker, sensing the crowd was on his side, pressed on. Lucy pricked up her ears at the mention of chewing gum.

"It's all a foreign plot, if ye ask my humble opinion," the speaker said. "The outlanders, see, they wants to take over without a fight. So they brings in this chewing gum, and before ye can say *spit!* the nobles is gone stupid as cows. It saps their strength, and puts nothing in their bellies, till they're as weak as the next pot of tea. That's when the foreigners strike. They lands one of them rocket ships smack inside the castle walls, and takes over without so much as lifting a sword!"

"Rocket ships!" said Lucy's neighbor. "Great stars and bunions! Next it'll be talking fish and magic beans. Well, no good comes from the outlands, that's a fact, and most change is for the worse. You didn't used to see noble folk talking with their mouths full, back in the olden days. What good is gold and riches if you ain't got good manners, I ask you?"

"I don't know, missus," Lucy said.

The woman looked at her. Only now, it seemed, did she notice Lucy's clothes. Her eyes narrowed, and instinctively she felt for the small purse of coins in the pocket of her apron. Pickpockets were not unheard of in Tenesmus.

"You're from the Mission, are you?" she asked, gazing at Lucy's outlandish outfit. "Well, I don't want to buy anything, so you may as well move along. And if you want *my* humble opinion," she added testily, "His Lordship was mad to let gum chewers and outlanders set up shop in the Barony. And you may tell *that* to your masters at the orphanage."

Lucy had not asked the woman's humble opinion, but it seemed the speaker had stirred up the whole crowd, which now buzzed with humble opinions, like a wasps' nest some boy had prodded with a stick.

"Begging your pardon, missus, I'm from the castle, not the Mission," Lucy explained. "I wondered if you might direct me to the premises of Mr. Lu Mingshu?"

The woman started, and clutched her marketing bag to her bosom.

"You say you're from the castle?" she asked.

"Yes, missus. I do for Miss Cant, the Baron's daughter."

The woman's jaw dropped.

"I . . . I . . . I meant no disrespect to His Lordship!" she said. "I . . . I . . ."

"Do you know the way, missus?"

The flustered matron moved away from Lucy.

"Lu Mingshu? Is it the printer you want?" she asked.

"Yes, missus."

"You'll find him in Stork Lane," the woman said, stepping into a puddle of rainwater as she backed away. "Forgive me, darling, I meant no disrespect. Bless His Lordship! Bless him! And isn't Miss Cant the little angel!" The woman's feet splashed through the puddle, and a bystander cursed as she struck him blindly. "I waved at Miss Cant once in a parade. She's adorable! Adorable!"

The woman turned and crashed into a boy carrying a tray of sausages. He managed to keep his feet, but the dogs following him sensed their chance and began to leap up and snap the air. The woman stumbled over one of the mongrels, dropped her bag, and gave Lucy a last, frightened *"Adorable!"* as she snatched it up and disappeared into the crowd.

Well! Lucy thought. She would have to give Arden Gutz a report on the mood of Tenesmus when she saw him next. It was not unusual in town to hear grumblings about the castle, but never before had Lucy heard such sentiments from atop a bushel basket, or from marketing matrons' mouths.

She made her way to Stork Lane, the manifesto crackling in her pocket. The sky began to clear. Lucy walked twice past the printer's shop before seeing it, for it was tucked away in a narrow alley between a smithy and the corn factor's depot. Over the door was a latticework trellis blooming with sweet-smelling flowers, and from it hung the queerest shingle in all Tenesmus.

陸 明 梳

Lu Mingshu, Printer
(formerly Michael Lowell)

Lucy squinted and closed one eye, but she could make no sense of the curious brushstrokes above the printer's name. She stepped over a puddle at the door and entered the shop with a satisfied smile, having brought her first piece of spy work to a successful end.

Chapter 15

the Brush of Lu Mingshu

A heavy scent of ink and incense filled the shop. Behind the counter stood a printing press, flanked by many-drawered cases of type and shelves heaped with paper. An iron stand held spattered jars of ink labeled *celadon, madder, black,* and *indigo.* Rush mats covered the floor, and from the wall to Lucy's left hung tasseled scrolls brushed with curious figures like those on the printer's shingle. A long table, pushed to the wall below them, held a collection of marvels — carved figurines in jade and ivory, porcelain dolls, inlaid boxes with cunning drawers, and a silk purse in the shape of a sow's ear.

Warmed by her walk from the market, Lucy pulled off her jumper and tied its arms round her waist. The shop was deserted, but that was common in Tenesmus, where merchants generally lived above their shops and left a bell on the counter to call them down. Here Lucy found, instead of the usual bell, a small gong hanging by chains from a wooden frame, and beside it a cork mallet. She struck the gong, and presently heard footsteps shuffling overhead.

"Coming!" a voice called out.

A book lay open beside the gong — *Treasures of Old Cathay*, by Lady Glace — and Lucy began to look at the plates. The curious brushstrokes on the printer's shingle, she saw now, must be in the alphabet of Old Cathay. It looked terribly complicated, and she was grateful that she'd had only the twenty-six letters to master when she first learned to read. A cat flew down the stairs, followed by the most outlandish-looking Cantling Lucy had ever seen.

"Ah! Reading a book!" the man cried. "You are a wise girl!"

Lucy could only stare. The printer's face was one she might see a hundred times a day on the streets of Tenesmus (except for the long moustaches like parentheses around his chin), but everything else about him was, as Pauline might have put it, "strange as a pickled clock." His black hair fell over his shoulder in a braid almost as long as his arms. He wore a silken gown on which a fantastical dragon grinned in green and gold embroidery so finely worked that Lucy could have counted its scales. He bowed to Lucy, and she caught the scent of unknown blossoms.

"Welcome, honorable girl," he said.

"How do you do, sir?" said Lucy, making a curtsey. "My name is Lucy Wickwright. Are you Mr. Mingshu?"

"Mr. Lu," said the printer. "I am well, thank you."

"Oh," said Lucy, confused. "I'm looking for Mr. Lu Ming-shu."

"You have found him."

Lucy looked around the shop.

"You are Lu Mingshu?" she asked.

"Yes. I am Mr. Lu."

Perhaps it was the custom of printers, who spent all day setting type from right to left, to use their first names as their last. Lucy supposed it was all right, but it was certainly odd. She made another curtsey.

"Forgive me, sir, but isn't that backward?"

"It is the Chinese way," explained the printer. "The family name comes first. If you lived in China, you would not be Lucy Wickwright, but Wickwright Lucy. Come."

He beckoned Lucy to the end of the counter. There was an inkpot there, with a brush-stand and a small bowl of water. The printer took a sheet of paper from beneath the counter, pushed up his sleeves, and dipped the brush in ink. Holding the brush over the paper, he closed his eyes. He stood motionless a long moment, then wrote Lucy's name in a fluid series of strokes.

"So," he said, opening his eyes again. "Do you know where China is?"

"Yes, sir," said Lucy. There was a big globe in the Baronial Library, and Lucy liked to spin it around, imagining what lay beyond the mountains of Cant. "It's on the other side of the world."

"Very good," said Lu. "Now, here is your name on paper. Lucy first, Wickwright last. You see?"

Lucy Wickwright

"Yes, sir."

The printer walked round the counter, took up the paper, and held it between Lucy and the windows at the front of the shop. When Lu turned the paper around she saw that her name showed through with the light behind it.

Lucy Wickwright

"The world is like this paper," said the printer. "On the other side, what was last becomes first."

Lucy's mind filled with pictures of topsy-turvy lands. She wanted to travel to China and see the clocks running backward, and ladies leading dances, and horses trotting behind their carts. She would wear a gown like Mr. Lu's, with the Gizmobots embroidered in carnelian, plum, and gold. The cat came round the counter and rubbed its whiskered muzzle on her leg.

"Have you been long in Cant, sir?" she asked the printer.

"Yes, quite a long time," he said. "Since the day I was born. That was in the year of the pig."

"But! . . . ," said Lucy, "I thought you were from China!"

"Not China, Chitterling!" said Mr. Lu. He motioned Lucy to a bench by the window. "You know Chitterling? Away over in Haslet March? My parents were swineherds there."

Lucy sat down, speechless. The printer smiled, and patted her knee.

"There was a big brood of Lowells in Chitterling," he went on. "I was Michael Lowell, the runt of the litter. My biggest brother was a swineherd, next brother a swineherd, sister a swineherd, all down the line. I thought, Who needs another swineherd? So I came to Tenesmus, and learned to be a printer. I read all the books about printing. Do you know where printing started?"

Lucy shook her head.

"China!" said Lu. "The wood-block print dates from the Tang Dynasty. Moveable type, Song Dynasty. China first made paper, too. Do you like tea, Lucy Wickwright?"

Lucy nodded.

"You know where tea started?"

"In China?" Lucy guessed.

"In China!" said Lu. "And what kind of pot do you make tea in, Lucy Wickwright?"

"China!" said Lucy, excited now. It only made sense!

"China pot!" said Lu Mingshu. "The more I learned about China, the more Chinese I felt. You are a wise girl, Lucy Wickwright. Do you know where babies come from?"

"China?" Lucy asked. It seemed unlikely, but nothing could surprise her now.

"Chinese babies come from China," Lu granted. "But Cantling babies?"

"Oh, I know. We come from our mothers."

"Just so," said Lu. "A mother pig makes piggies, a mother cat makes kitties. But listen. A mother makes a baby nine months. When the baby grows up, it's time he make himself. So what did I do? I made Lu Mingshu. And Lucy Wickwright — why, that's just a name on paper. Turn the paper over, and look. You're a new girl now!"

"I'm a spy!" Lucy blurted. She felt as she had when she first wore glasses, when the fuzzy, squinting world had suddenly come into focus. Mr. Lu had shown her a new way of seeing. *It all depends on how you look at things!* Lucy had thought of herself as a servant-girl, an unfortunate orphan, because that was how others "wrote" her. She had never thought to turn the paper over. Her spy work was play-acting, an elaborate game of make-believe, in which she pretended to be a daring girl out of a story-book. It had never occurred to her, till now, that she might really be such a girl, or that someone, some day, might write a book about *her.* But it was true — she *was* a spy!

Lu Mingshu raised one eyebrow, a faint smile on his lips.

"You are a spy, Lucy Wickwright?"

"Yes, sir!" Lucy said, fumbling at her pocket. She took out the manifesto and gave it to Lu. "Arden Gutz gave me a key, and I led Jane Cedilla to believe I had a boyfriend, but I really went to Vlad Orloff's office and hid in his cupboard! The captain thought I was a rat, but Orloff locked me in — I'd left the key on the candle-stand — so I tied the manifesto to a stamp and jumped out the window! Orloff has the Candle of Cant! He was Lady Sweetbread all along! I found her gown in the cupboard, and that means he's a murderer! The Baron is dying! Pauline is in danger — the captain said she mustn't leave the castle! We have to help her!"

The printer unfolded the manifesto. When he saw what he

held, he rose from the bench and lowered a paper blind over the window. The cat, which had been warming in a sunbeam, stretched itself and curled to a ball. Lu bolted the door, then sat close to Lucy and had her repeat her story, stopping her often to put questions, or to whistle aloud. He was especially interested in the news of Sir Henry Wallow and Clara Swain, and pressed Lucy to recall the slightest details of Orloff's conversation with Tybold Retsch. When he had heard it all, down to Lucy's being stopped at the gatehouse that morning, he rolled up the manifesto and hid it in his sleeve.

"You are a very wise girl, Lucy Wickwright, and a brave girl, too," he said. "Tell me again, who were your parents? How did you come to serve Miss Cant?"

So Lucy told about her family, and "Lady Sweetbread," and how she had gone to live with Uncle Hock, and was to be taken to the orphanage until Minister Guuzi arrived with the summons to the castle. The printer slipped the sandal from his foot and rubbed the cat's belly with his toe.

"Think again of what you heard from the cupboard," Lu said. "Orloff and Retsch, they said that this child lives? This secret child of the Baron, who might claim the baronial cap?"

"Yes, sir."

"And Retsch said, 'We have the child'?"

"Yes, sir."

"Now think deeply, Lucy Wickwright. Are you certain that Orloff said Miss Cant was not to leave the castle?"

Lucy nodded.

"He said, 'Miss Cant is not to leave the castle'?" Lu persisted. "He said her name?"

Lucy thought.

"No," she said, frowning. "He said 'the girl,' I think. No, wait. It was 'the child.' He said, 'The child is not to leave the castle.' That's it. 'Under no circumstances is the child to leave the castle.' He called her a sniveling heiress!"

Lu stroked his moustaches with his thumb and forefinger.

"Your honorable uncle, Mr. Tooey," he said. "This is your mother's brother, yes? He supports our Cause?"

"Well . . . ," Lucy said. "I don't know, for certain. But he wants what's best for me, and I want what's best for Pauline, so he must support the Cause, in a way. He never chews gum. And once —" Lucy glanced at the bolted door and went on in a whisper, "— and once I heard him call the tax collector 'a bucket of guts.' Not to his face, of course. He would never hurt someone."

"Lucy," said the printer. "Go to your uncle. Tell him all you have told me. Tell him, 'Lu Mingshu begs a word with you.' Say nothing to Miss Cant. Say nothing to no one!" He rose, and patted the sleeve that held the manifesto. "The kettle comes to a boil, Lucy Wickwright. The people shall know the truth. You have told me more than you know!"

"Thank you, sir!" Lucy said. She pulled on her jumper and followed Lu to the door. "Have you any message for Arden Gutz? I hope to visit him again, and tell him what has happened."

The printer opened the door, and the cat ran out and began to scratch the ground.

"You will not be allowed to see Arden Gutz, I think," said Lu.

"But, sir, why not?" Lucy asked. She had hoped to see the

prisoner that very night, if the gaoler would allow it, for she imagined Arden was anxious to see her, too.

"You are a wise child, but there are things you don't know," the printer said. "Your uncle, perhaps, will be able to enlighten you — tell him all. Go now, and take care, Lucy Wickwright!"

The printer bowed. Lucy bowed, and curtsied, then hurried down Stork Lane, jumping puddles in the sun.

Chapter 16

AT THE PERCH AND PILLOW

*T*he Wickwrights' cat had grown fat in his years at the Perch & Pillow. Hock Tooey's kitchen and stables provided Penrod a menu rich in rodents, and from the kitchen pail he stole the occasional morsel of mutton fat or fish guts. He had got so lazy, in fact, that he patrolled only the kitchen on most days, leaving the mousing of the stables to an irregular crew of alley cats. His chief duty, it seemed, was to lie on the hearth rug, or atop the hitching beam in front of the inn. Today the beam was wet with the earlier rain, and Lucy found him in the common room, his pink tongue busy at the methodical grooming of his kind.

She knelt beside him and pressed her face to his moist, friendly muzzle. The inn was full of customers this market day, and those nearest the fire pushed back their stools to give her room. One man gave Lucy a puzzled look — a man of the countryside, by his appearance, who doubtless had never seen such outrageous clothes, and who would enjoy a moment of celebrity at his native tavern when he told the story of the girl in breeches. Uncle Hock came in, just then, with a jug of beer in each hand.

"Lucy!" he cried, setting down the jugs. "Come to see your old uncle at last, eh? Where were you last week? I was beginning to think you'd forgot all about me in your grand castle."

Lucy jumped up and threw her arms around his neck. When the innkeeper had spun his niece twice around, and squeezed the air out of her, and kissed her cheek and been kissed in return, he set her down and held her at arm's length.

"Who's this pretty beanstalk, now?" he asked, looking her up and down. "Why, you're going to lose sight of your feet if you keep sprouting up like that. And look at you! Dressed up in new clothes and your hair all brushed — oh, there's many a lovelorn pup gnawing their hearts up in that castle, if I'm any judge of things!"

Her uncle's talk was all nonsense, of course, but it was a niece's privilege to hear such things. Lucy explained that she'd had to work in the laundry last week, then hugged her uncle again, for the sheer pleasure of breathing his malty, oaten, manly smell. If only bears had been as gentle as Uncle Hock, and less disposed to eating children, Lucy could have happily been a woodcutter in the forest, living among the bears, coming home every evening to a cottage full of bear-hugs.

"Penelope!" her uncle called to his maid-of-all-work. "Bring out a bowl of stew, and don't be a miser with the fat pieces! You let me finish my business," he told Lucy, "and then we'll have a good long visit. Tuck into that stew, now — it's a fine thing to be pretty, but you want to put some meat on your bones!"

It was Uncle Hock's opinion that Lucy was the skinniest slip of a girl that ever threaded a needle, and every time she came to the inn she was made to eat stew until she felt as fat and sleepy as Penrod the cat. But today she was hungry, and when Penelope brought out the stew — with a bottle of squash and a kiss of her own — Lucy sat cross-legged by the fire and ate it like breathing. It was said that people came from as far as Twee to taste the stews at the Perch & Pillow, and that you could mortar a wall with the gravy. A Perch & Pillow stew sat up in the bowl. It had red potatoes rich as truffles, and chunks of carrot that wanted cutting to eat, and onions and cabbage and herbs, and great cubes of mutton that melted in your mouth like candyfloss and stuck in your belly like a visiting aunt.

Penrod climbed on to Lucy's roomy new trousers, and she slipped him the fat pieces of the stew when Penelope wasn't looking. She had just finished the last bit of carrot when Uncle Hock returned and took off his apron. He beckoned Lucy from the back door, and when she had lifted Penrod off her lap, scraped her bowl over the kitchen pail, and returned to the hearthside for her squash, she followed him out to the stable yard. Clouds dotted the sky, but the day was warming, and steam rose from the thatched roof of the stable. Gil Blemesch, the stable boy, leaned on the handle of his pitchfork, watching sparrows pull worms from the rain-wet yard. He looked up as Lucy approached, and pushed the damp hair from his eyes.

"Hi, Lucy," he said.

"Hi, Gil," sighed Lucy.

"Where were you last week?"

If there was any drawback to visiting Uncle Hock it was that at some point Gil Blemesch would appear, and breathe through his mouth, and stare at Lucy as though she was a two-headed hen, and ask her silly questions. He was a lanky boy of twelve years, with raw knuckles and a forelock of chestnut hair.

"I had to work in the laundry."

"Up in the castle?"

Lucy nodded.

"Do you want a piggy-back ride?" Gil Blemesch asked.

"Gil!" said Uncle Hock. "When you've done pestering the poor girl, do you think you might find a piece of work to do? Or do I pay you to lean on a pitchfork in the May sunshine?"

"No, sir," the boy said. He looked around the yard, as though a piece of work might crawl like a worm from the ground, then shuffled glumly into the stable, the tines of his pitchfork plowing the mud behind him.

"Now," said Uncle Hock, sitting on a bench by the stable door, "tell me where you've been hiding this last fortnight. What's this business of working in the laundry? Did the little princess get you into trouble again?"

Lucy took a drink of squash, wiped her mouth, and, as she had so much to tell, and as it was all so terribly complicated, she decided to begin at the beginning.

"We were playing with a catapult on the flanking tower, a week ago yesterday," she began.

Lucy was a good storyteller. She had read many, many story-books, and she understood that you had to give an earful of details, because something that might not seem important at the beginning of a story often turned out to be very important later on. For example, she made sure to mention that Dr. Sauersop had lent her his handkerchief in Costive Gutz's office, or else she would have had to go back, later, and explain what it was doing in her pocket when she got to the point where she talked to Dr. Sauersop again.

Uncle Hock, fortunately, was a good listener — unlike those grown-ups who listened to children only to break in and correct their grammar, or deliver a lecture on the importance of washing behind their ears. Hock Tooey chuckled when Lucy described the flying bloomers, and frowned at her capture by Costive Gutz. He scratched his head at Mr. Lemonjello's riddling talk, and gave a low, wondering whistle at the words of Arden Gutz. But he never interrupted, until Lucy told what she had seen and heard in Vlad Orloff's office. Then, for the first time in Lucy's memory, he cursed. He rose and paced the muddy stable yard, muttering "The scoundrels! The scoundrels!" His thick hands clenched and shook with anger. He shouted for Gil Blemesch to fetch him a half pint, and he gulped it like medicine when he sat again by Lucy.

"The scoundrels!" he repeated. He brushed back Lucy's fringe and examined the knob left by her run at the office door. "I'll have their heads for this," he said. "Orloff will rue the day he was born, and Retsch too! The craven, bloodless, pigeon-hearted . . . scoundrels!"

He was ready to mount a horse, spur it to the castle, and demand an audience with the Baron. An honest, simple man, he believed that Lord Cant must surely put the scoundrels in irons the moment he learned of their misdeeds. Lucy waited till he had sputtered and fumed to a low boil, then put her hand on his.

"There's more, Uncle Hock," she said.

She told of being turned back at the gatehouse, that very morning, and how she had escaped the castle and taken the manifesto to Lu Mingshu. Her talk with the printer was fresh in her memory, and she gave it to her uncle word for word, for she guessed that Mr. Lu had gleaned something important from her story, something he had not shared with her. She finished by telling her uncle that the printer wished to speak to him. Hock Tooey stared at Lucy as though he hardly recognized his niece.

"You are a wonder, Lucy Wickwright," he said. His voice was low, and Lucy could tell he was still digesting her story. "Orloff said the *child* is not to leave the castle?" he asked. Lucy nodded. Mr. Lu had pressed her on this point, too.

"Do you suppose," she asked, "that they know I'm trying to help Pauline? Is that why they want to keep *me* in the castle, too?"

Hock Tooey shook his head.

"Lucy," he said, "what do you remember of the day that . . . the day Orloff came to the chandlery? Tell me what happened — everything that Lady Sweetbread said, everything you can remember. It's very important."

Lucy did not like to think about that day, much less talk about it. But she told her uncle all she could remember, though she had often to stop, and bite her lip, to put the events in their right order. When she finished, her uncle's face had gone pale. She feared he might do something rash — such as race to the

castle and pummel Orloff with one of his official stamps —
but he only stared at the muddy stable yard and asked a peculiar question.

"You're sure he wanted to look at your feet, Lucy?"

Had her uncle taken his ale too quickly? Lucy wondered. It
seemed a strange detail to fix upon at the end of so much story-
telling. But she had never known Uncle Hock to be confused
by ale, even on those rare occasions when he took as much as a
pint.

"Yes," she answered. Even now her toes curled to remember
it. "She said — Vlad Orloff, that is — that I had good, sound
feet . . . useful for sweeping, I believe he said. He'd asked if I
was handy with a broom — I forgot to mention that. Was that
important?"

"Lucy," said Uncle Hock, "there's something you must
know." He took up her hands and pressed them together between his own. "I meant to wait until you were older . . . your
mother meant to tell you, someday. She worried that she ought
to have told you when you were small, but you were such a
happy little girl, so bright and cheery . . . Why tell you at all?
was my thought, but your ma'am was afraid you'd hear it from
someone else. And after the tragedy . . . well, I couldn't tell you
then, Lucy. And since you've been at the castle, why, I've simply
put it out of my mind. I couldn't see any reason to hurry about
it. Until now."

Lucy waited patiently for her uncle to come to his point.

"Tell me, Lucy," he began again. "You're a big girl. . . . Do
you know where babies come from?"

"Oh, yes, Uncle Hock," Lucy said quickly. No wonder her
uncle was being timid — he meant to tell her the facts of life!

It seemed an odd time to bring them up, but she was happy to put his mind at ease. "We come from our mothers, like puppies."

Hock Tooey patted her hand.

"Good," he said. "That's it exactly. Now, what I have to tell you, Lucy . . . you see, sometimes a baby doesn't come from its mother. Well, it does, of course, but sometimes a mother can't rear her own child, or the parents die when the child is still quite young —"

He stopped abruptly.

"Lady Cant died when Pauline was a baby," Lucy said helpfully.

"Yes, I know," said Uncle Hock. "But she still had the Baron to look after her. The children at the Mission, now, they've lost both their parents. They have to hope that another man and woman will take them in and be their mother and father. Do you understand?"

"Yes, they want to be adopted."

"Exactly," her uncle said. "I knew you'd see that. Well, then. What I have to tell you, Lucy . . . oh, I wish I weren't such a stumble-tongue fool of an innkeeper! . . . what I have to tell you is that my sister was not your natural mother. The plain truth is, she and Lon found you on their doorstep, one fine morning, bawling your wee eyes out in a basket by the milk can. They took you in, and brought you up as their own, and they loved you so much it pricked my eyes to see it. And a grand girl you turned out to be, Lucy. I love you as much as ever your mother and father did, if such a thing is possible."

Lucy blinked her eyes. The sun had emerged from behind a cloud and glared from a puddle in the stable yard. Though she turned her head and pressed her face to her uncle's chest, she could not escape the light. Hock Tooey put his arm around her.

"But . . . ," Lucy said. "But . . ." A thousand questions wanted asking, but in her bewildered state she could not imagine which one came first. She opened her mouth and let one tumble out at random. "You . . . you mean I was already an orphan?"

"You were a foundling, Lucy," said Uncle Hock, "but I don't think you were an orphan."

"But what do you mean, Uncle Hock?" Lucy asked.

"It was your toes, Lucy," her uncle said. "That's why Lady Sweetbread wanted your shoe off . . . blast him! The scoundrel wanted to count your toes. To see if you were the child he was looking for."

"My toes?" Lucy asked.

"Think, Lucy. You're a busy-toed girl. Was your father busy-toed?"

"No, Uncle Hock. Daddy was tongue-toed."

"As was Casio. And your mother? You know as well as I that she was a plain-toed woman. Now, a tongue-toed man and a plain-toed woman may have a tongue-toed child — like Casio — or they may have a plain-toed child. But never did a tongue-toe and a plain-toe produce a girl with twelve piggies, Lucy. Lady Sweetbread was looking for a child, a girl with twelve toes, and he found her. He was afraid what might happen if her secret got out, and rightly so. And when he'd done his vile deed, he sent Guuzi to fetch you to the castle, where he thought he could hide the secret forever."

"He didn't want me to know I was a foundling?" Lucy asked. None of it made sense to her. Why would a man dress as a woman, and go about counting children's toes, and throwing their families from cliffs? How could it hurt Vlad Orloff, now that Lucy knew the truth?

"He didn't want you to know who your parents were, Lucy," her uncle said. "Or, rather, someone else didn't want you to know, for I'm sure Orloff didn't act alone."

"But *why?*" Lucy said, confused as ever. "Do *you* know, Uncle Hock? Do you know who my parents were?"

"I've no idea who your mother was," Hock Tooey said, "but I'd be twice a blind fool if I couldn't see who your father is, after what you've told me." He looked solemnly at his niece. "Lucy . . . what Orloff said about the Baron, about his getting a woman with child before he married Lady Cant . . . well, I'd heard it whispered, too, but I always put it down to idle gossip, for where was the child? Now I know. Lucy, when Vlad Orloff said the child must not leave the castle, he wasn't talking about Miss Cant. It was the Baron's first child he meant."

"Orloff has hidden the child in the castle?"

"She's not in the castle, sweetcheeks," said her uncle. "She's sitting here with me. Don't you see, Lucy? Orloff was talking about *you* when he said the child was not to leave the castle. That's why you weren't allowed to leave for your half-holiday this morning. *You* are the Baron's daughter, Lucy. You are the rightful heiress to the Barony of Cant."

The mud of the stable yard rushed up at Lucy. Had her uncle not been a nimble-handed man, her smart new clothes might have been ruined on the first day she wore them. But Hock Tooey caught his niece, and lifted her up, and carried her to a bed in the Perch & Pillow. Lucy had fainted dead away.

Chapter 17

*L*ucy had been lying awake for an hour when Mrs. Dingleberry, the sub-assistant chief of domestic staff, swung her bell the next morning. The girls groaned and wiped their eyes, but Mrs. Dingleberry only gave the bell another *clang!* and said, as she always did, that the kitchen floor gave no sign of sweeping itself. The coals, she might have added, gave no sign of hauling themselves, or the fires of lighting themselves — and her mistress, Lucy knew, gave no sign of waking up, much less of dressing herself.

Lucy rose, tidied her cot, and breasted the sluggish stream of girls making their way to the dressing room. She had washed out her t-shirt and stockings and drawers before going to bed, and, as there was no stove in the garret, had set them to dry on one of the ovens in the kitchen. Mr. Broom tolerated this practice, but he gave Lucy a cross look when she collected her things, and muttered about "maids padding about in night-shirts when a man's trying to work."

Lucy refused to believe she was the Baron's daughter — at least, as she had told her uncle, until there was certain proof. Moon-hammers she could accept, if a librarian vouched for them, and if Arden Gutz insisted that peasants had the means to buy chewing gum in other parts of the globe, well, she would have to take his word for it. But it was beyond her imag-ination to believe that she — a servant-girl and the daughter of chandlers — was the natural child of Adolphus, and the right-ful heiress to the Barony of Cant.

Uncle Hock's reasoning was sound, she had to admit, and Orloff evidently believed he had found the Baron's daughter when he ran his horrible finger over Lucy's toes. But there were many busy-toed girls in Cant — some of them foundlings, no doubt — and it was entirely possible that Orloff was mis-taken. She would continue as a plain servant-girl and spy, for now, and let others untangle the snags in the baronial line.

Her uncle had not wanted Lucy to return to the castle. He argued that Vlad Orloff had already proved himself capable of murder, and begged his niece to remain at the Perch & Pillow, where he could defend her from such scoundrels with a pitch-fork, if necessary. But Lucy had answered that Pauline was in peril, too, and that the Cause needed a competent spy within the castle walls. Her uncle finally agreed to let her go, but only after giving her his special charm (seven fennel seeds sewn up in a mouse's pelt, hung from a thong round her neck) and showing her how to topple a man in combat (with a maneuver he called "a swift knee to the progeny," which, he assured her, would "let the steam out of any man's kettle").

Hock Tooey did not intend to stand idle, however. Before Lucy left he filled a bag with bread and cheese, ordered Gil Blemesch to saddle a horse, and put Penelope in charge of the inn. He would first confer with Lu Mingshu, he told Lucy, then ride out on the East Road in search of Sir Henry Wallow. He would speak to Clara Swain, and learn the truth of Lucy's beginning.

"Unless I'm thrice a bat-blind fool," he said from his saddle, "when I return you'll have a claim that can't be denied."*

Lucy had walked to the castle at twilight, grateful for her new jumper in the cool air. Its drawstring hood was much more practical than a baronial cap, she thought. Besides, if she became the Baroness, what would become of Pauline? Her mistress was such an impossible girl — so willful and proud, yet at the same time so feckless and shilly-shallying — that being a ruler was really the only job that suited her. All in all, it would be best if Pauline rose to the barony, as she was always meant to do, and Lucy sank to the contented life of a chandler and retired spy.

From Tenesmus she had followed a footpath through the tall aspens of the Micklewood. Where it went round a boulder cloven like a deer's hoof Lucy turned south and hiked to the foot of the cliff on which the castle stood. She pushed back a

---

*A claim to the baronial cap. In Cant, the barony fell to the first-born child, whether the heir was the fruit of marriage or a natural child of the Baron regnant. (Decretal on the Baronial Succession, Article I, Clause I)

bramble and squeezed through a crack in the rock, then fumbled in the gloom for the candle and matches she had left in the small, dry cave. A stairway rose from the back of this cave, hewn from the rock of the cliff, its two hundred and sixty-six steps ending (or beginning) in the deepest cellar of the castle's south wing. Lucy and Pauline had discovered the stairway last summer while playing at archæology. No doubt it had served as an escape route, in the grim days of siege warfare, but it seemed now that even the captain of the guard had forgotten its existence.

It was a long, weary climb in the dark, the candle dripping on her fingers. At the top of the stairs she slid back a panel and climbed through a wardrobe that held the musty parkas and rotted mufflers of a bobsled team (for the crypt where the hidden stairway began was devoted, as it happened, to the relics of alpine sport — the cellars of Castle Cant entombed centuries of such moldy junk). Lucy climbed to the garret and washed out her things, then took them down to the kitchen, and finally climbed back to her cot and lay down. But it had been an eventful day, and she found it difficult to sleep. Even putting aside her uncle's surmise that she was the Baron's daughter, she had learned that she was a foundling, and this revelation, like an unfamiliar pillow, kept her tossing half the night. She longed to hear the morning bell and return to the familiar, workaday world of caring for Pauline.

After dressing in the morning Lucy went back to the kitchen, where she loaded a tray with tea things, jam, and freshly baked madeleines. With these incentives she would lure Pauline from her bed, and strengthen her for the ordeal of dressing. Rousing her mistress was often the hardest task of Lucy's day, for Pauline — who so closely resembled a whirlwind at other times — was a hopeless slugabed before taking her morning dose of tea. Lucy sometimes resorted to extreme measures to drive her from the bed, including wrestling away the blankets (a technique most effective in winter), blowing her mistress's bagpipes (Pauline generally excelled Lucy at music, but neither of them had got happy results from this instrument, which Pauline called "the infernal squid"), and probing under the blankets with a broomstick ("Quit it, Wickwright. Quit it! QUIT IT!"). Most mornings, though, she had merely to fan the aroma of madeleines toward the bed, and back away slowly as her mistress groped for the plate.

The door to Pauline's apartment stood open. This was unusual, and Lucy paused in the corridor. Was Pauline receiving her visiting cousins? If so, Mr. Vole had not marked it on the day's calendar. She peeked around the doorsill, then walked in and set her tray on a table by the fireplace. Pauline's bed was empty, the blankets thrown back as though she had fled a bad dream.

"Mistress?" Lucy called. She searched the dressing room, then the adjoining room where the copper bath hung from a peg on the wall. Why hadn't Helen filled the bath? She looked into Pauline's drawing room, then the music room, and finally her "toy closet" (which had once been a ballroom and was so large that the girls played badminton there in winter). Her mistress was nowhere to be found.

Lucy doubted that Orloff would attempt any mischief while

the Baron still lived, but she was troubled. Only a great calamity could have drawn Pauline from bed without the incentive of tea. She turned to go back to the bedchamber and collided with Blaise Delagraisse, the new under-footman, who stood blocking the doorway.

"Hullo, Lucy," he said.

"Good — *ouch!* — good morning, Delagraisse," said Lucy. She rubbed the knob on her forehead, still tender from her run at Orloff's door. "Have you seen my mistress?"

"No, ma'am. I've —"

"I must find her," Lucy interrupted. She tried to go around Delagraisse, but the under-footman stood squarely in the doorway, so like a stricken calf in its stall that Lucy would not have been surprised to hear him say *moo*.

"Your new haircut is pretty," he lowed instead.

Lucy tried to squeeze past the under-footman. She did not know what to do with compliments, unless they came from her Uncle Hock, so generally she pretended not to hear them. Delagraisse did not budge.

"Excuse me, please," she said. "I must find Miss Cant."

"She isn't here," said Delagraisse.

"I see that," Lucy said, growing exasperated. "Ergo, I must find her."

This puzzled the under-footman. He colored slightly, as during the confusion of pints and dozens.

"Ergo?" he asked.

"Delagraisse," said Lucy (very much in the tone of a senior staff member to her junior), "may I ask why you are here?"

"Mr. Vole sent me," the boy said. "What does that mean, *ergo*?"

"Don't slouch, Delagraisse. *Ergo* means that something follows another thing," Lucy explained. "My mistress isn't here, so it follows that I must look for her. I must look for her, *ergo* you are in the way. Please to step out of the doorway."

"I hadn't heard that word *ergo* before," Delagraisse confessed. "But it doesn't follow at all, begging your pardon."

"Doesn't it?"

"Not at all," said Delagraisse. "You needn't look for Miss Cant. I've come to take you to her."

"But why didn't you say so?"

"I meant to. But you interrupted me, begging your pardon."

Lucy had to admit the justice of that.

"I'm sorry," she said. "Where *is* my mistress?"

"Why, Miss Cant is with His Lordship," said Delagraisse. He seemed surprised by her question. "The Baron took ill yester-evening. Didn't you know?"

"Saturday is my half-holiday," Lucy said weakly. She was filled with an awful premonition. Her lungs felt like limp sacks of wool. "Is Lord Cant terribly ill?"

Delagraisse chewed his lip a moment, then took Lucy by the arm and led her across the drawing room. He leaned his head toward her, and spoke in a low, confidential tone.

"My aunt, Mrs. Bittertoast, does for Mr. Splint, His Lordship's own physician," he said. "She told me she was all night carrying water to the Baron's chamber and laying damp cloths on his brow. He's talking out of his head, she said. They've leeched him, and cupped him, and given a purge, but he's failing terribly. He called for Miss Cant not half an hour ago."

"Poor Pauline!" said Lucy. "It's to the point of leeches? Are you certain? When did you talk to your aunt?"

"Why, just now," said Delagraisse. "She was sent to fetch you."

"Well, why are we dawdling?" Lucy said. "Does my mistress wish me to bring her anything?"

"You're only to bring yourself, as I understand it," Delagraisse said. "It wasn't your mistress who called for you, though, begging your pardon. It was the Baron."

"I beg your pardon?"

"Aye, His Lordship!" said Delagraisse, his eyes wide. "He laid his hand on my aunt's like they was old friends, she told me — as well he might, for she's been doing for Mr. Splint these twenty years and more — and he says, 'Dear woman, fetch me the child they call Lucy Wickwright.' He called her 'dear woman,' my aunt says, which just goes to show His Lordship has the common touch. Are you well, Lucy?" the boy asked. "Perhaps I ought to fetch the doctor to you. You've gone awfully pale."

"I . . . I'm perfectly well," said Lucy, but her face was white, and she gripped the under-footman's arm as though she might otherwise topple over. "There is tea in the bedchamber. If I could just take a sip . . . I'm a little parched. Then we can go. Thank you, Delagraisse."

The tea had cooled enough to be drunk quickly. Lucy felt bad about taking the only teacup, but the under-footman poured tea and milk into the saucer and drank it that way. He pressed Lucy to eat a madeleine — "for your strength" — and put several into his pocket — "as they'll only go to waste." Lucy felt not at all hungry, but she dipped the madeleine into her tea and managed to take a few bites.

The Baron dwelt in a lavish suite of rooms on the third floor of the castle. Lucy had found it odd, when she first entered service, that Pauline and her father should live so far apart from one another. It was very grand, she supposed, that her mistress should have her own bedroom (Lucy had shared a bed with Casio in a curtained-off corner of their parents' room), to say nothing of the dressing room and drawing room and marvelous "toy closet." But if the Baron spoiled his daughter with rooms, he was remarkably stingy with time. Oh, Pauline sat with her father at ceremonies and banquets, surrounded by ministers and serving men and other ornaments of his power. She held his hand at festivals and fairs, while he reviewed the prize sheep or tasted some goodwife's partridge pie. But they were never alone together, that Lucy saw.

Once or twice a week the Baron summoned Pauline to his chambers, and for that half an hour her mistress was uncontainably happy. She told her father all she had done since they last met, pantomiming her adventures and lampooning various persons in the castle. Lord Cant quizzed her on her lessons, or sent for her theorbo, to hear what progress she had made with that instrument. But always a barber was present, or a tailor with a measuring tape, and the Baron would be shaved or fitted while he interviewed his daughter. Always some vital business of the Barony drew him away at the end of half an hour, and Pauline would be sent back to her world of toys and clothes and servants. And later that day, or early the next, she would break out in a terrible Whim.

At first Lucy had accompanied her mistress to these interviews, sitting quietly on a chair just inside the door. Adolphus had stared at her briefly when first she came, but in subsequent weeks he never glanced at his daughter's new maidservant. In time, Mr. Vole informed her that she need no longer attend Pauline on her visits to the Baron.

So it was years since Lucy had entered this part of the castle. A guardsman stood at the sickroom door, his face as expressionless as his dull bronze helmet. He grasped the hilt of his sword as Delagraisse approached.

"State your business!" he commanded.

"I'm fetching this lady to His Lordship," said Delagraisse. "Just like he asked for. Miss Lucy Wickwright."

The sentry narrowed his eyes at Lucy. Plainly he did not think she merited the title of "lady." He turned and knocked twice on the door, which opened the breadth of a hand, revealing another guardsman on the inside. They whispered together a moment, and the sentry turned to Delagraisse.

"You may leave now," he said. "You," he told Lucy, "may approach His Lordship. I trust you know how to make a curtsey to your betters. Do not speak until you're spoken to! Go on."

The room was heavily curtained, and lit by a solitary candle on the nightstand. Camphor steamed from an iron kettle upon a small stove. A music box plucked a tinny measure as Lucy entered, but it faltered and fell silent before reaching the final note. Lucy nearly cried out when her eyes had adapted to the dim light, for Vlad Orloff was there, talking in whispers to a man holding a wooden stethoscope.

Pauline sat on a chair at the bedside. Her eyes were red, her face as haggard as is possible on a young girl. She leaned against a bonneted woman — surely the under-footman's aunt, Mrs. Bittertoast — who held her in a comforting arm. The Baron lay under a crumpled blanket in a tall bed overarched by a velvet canopy. His hair was tangled and his eyes bloodshot, his nightshirt plastered to his heaving chest.

Orloff glanced up as Lucy approached. His face hardened, and his mouth turned down in a grimace that set her heart racing. But he could not know, Lucy assured herself, that she had stolen the manifesto. It could have been anyone hiding in the cupboard.

"My Lord," he said, turning to the sick man, "may I remind you of Mr. Splint's warning. This is no time to tax your strength."

"Begone, Vladimir," gasped the Baron. "We wish to — *gooh!* — speak to this child." He breathed heavily, his speech punctuated by wet, weak coughs — *gooh! gooh!* — like those of a sickly infant. His broad, heavy face was wan and unshaven.

"You mustn't allow this, Splint," Orloff said. "His Lordship is in no condition —"

"Peace!" The Baron struggled to prop himself on an elbow. He glared at the Commissioner of Posts.

"Vladimir Orloff," he wheezed, "we wish to — *gooh!* — speak to this child. You will leave this chamber. All of you! Leave us at once."

"My Lord —" Orloff began.

"Guard!" the Baron cried. "Empty this chamber! Orloff, out! Splint, out! Leave us — *gooh!* — good woman," he said, turning to Mrs. Bittertoast. "Everyone, out!"

The doctor and his assistant left the bedside, staring openly at Lucy as they left the room. Orloff lingered. When the guardsman approached, he went to Lucy and pulled her roughly to him by her jumper.

"If you breathe a word of what you hear! . . ." he whispered.

"Or — *gooh!* — loff! Out!" said the Baron. The guard, who seemed unwilling to anger the Postal Commissioner, gestured feebly toward the door.

"I must ask you to come with me, sir."

Lucy barely heard Orloff's whispered threat. Her eyes had fixed on the sickbed, where Lord Cant, in struggling to rise to his elbow, had kicked away the blanket from his feet. His toes were clenched in pain, but even by the dim light of a candle there was no mistaking their number. Adolphus, Lord Cant, matched Lucy toe for toe. The Baron was a busy-toed man.

Chapter 18

Morte d'Adolphus

$\mathscr{T}$he yellow tongue of the candle flickered when the guard
shut the door, leaving Lucy alone with the Baron and Pauline.
Lord Cant fell back on his pillows and gestured weakly to the
vacant chair by his daughter.

"Sit, child."

Pauline had put on a great quilted dressing gown over her
nightshirt. She looked as though she had not slept at all — as
though only its padded shell kept her from toppling over. A
coal stove by the bed gave her face the sheen of fever, and her
plain-toed feet, under the eaves of the dressing gown, hung
pale and vulnerable as newborn bats.

"Has Wickwright come to take me away?" she asked her father. "Please don't send me out, Papa. I want to stay with you!"

"No — *gooh!* — no, my dear daughter," he said. "You shan't

leave me. O, that I should forsake my flesh and blood! Come, give me your hand. Sit beside me. What a moldy ruin is man!"

"Do get well, Papa," Pauline said, when she had climbed on to the great bed and tucked her feet beneath her. She took her father's hand and kissed it. "Won't you try to sleep? Mr. Splint said you must rest."

Adolphus winced and clawed the blanket in a spasm of pain. Phlegm rattled in his lungs.

"I shall sleep, in time," he said. "A long sleep, and a cold one. But I must speak, now, with what breath remains to me. Dear — *gooh!* — dear child, I have left undone that which I should have done. Lucy Wickwright, are you listening?"

Lucy looked up.

"Yes, my Lord," she said.

"You must fetch a scribe," said the Baron, "and two persons of good character . . . to serve as witnesses. . . . Do not let that man enter this chamber . . . Orloff — *gooh!* — the man who was here. . . . He waits at the door, I am sure. Stay!" he gasped, as Lucy stood to carry out her orders.

"Yes, sir."

"His venom has felled me — *gooh!* — the foul serpent!" Adolphus wheezed. "The fault is mine, mine, all mine . . . I ask no forgiveness . . . I deserve none . . . but we may yet pull his fangs, my children. All may not be lost. *Gooh!*"

"Mistress," Lucy whispered, taking a cloth from a bowl of water on the nightstand. She wrung it out and gave it to Pauline, who would bear up better, Lucy thought, if given something to occupy her hands. The Baron's eyes fluttered open as Pauline pressed the cloth to his brow.

"Bless you, child," he said. He had fallen asleep the moment he stopped talking.

"Please rest, Papa," said Pauline.

"I shall, my dear daughter," the Baron said. "I shall — *gooh!* — I shall know a moment's peace, I hope, before I sleep. Have they fetched her, dear, your little maid? The girl called Lucy Wickwright?"

"But, Papa, she is here already," said Pauline. "Do you want her to bring the scribe?"

Adolphus lifted his head and looked at Lucy.

"So she is," he said, falling back on the pillow. "I thought I had dreamed it. So often I've dreamed of this moment. But I am poisoned — *gooh!* — the fang is in my heart. Hear me, Pauline, for this concerns you greatly. Come closer, Lucy. I wish to look at you — *gooh!* — at both of you."

Lucy moved to the chair that Pauline had vacated. Adolphus gazed at her a long moment, but it was to Pauline that he spoke.

"*Gooh!* Time is a friend to no man, my dear daughter. I shall speak plainly. I am greatly — aye, terribly to blame. I deceived your mother, and treachery has kenneled in my heart, and battened upon my soul. Sweet child — *gooh!* — do you know whence you came? Hast seen a new-born foal?"

"Yes, Papa," Pauline answered. Her face had lost its fevered tint, now she had moved away from the stove, and had gone pale as her nightshirt. The Baron spoke with great effort, wheezing and coughing, his lungs wetly rattling.

"A man lies with his mate," he said, "as do hounds and horses and all the beasts of the field. Well — *gooh!* — horses do not lie . . . nay . . . but you understand, I'm certain. Your lamented mother and I lay together — *gooh!* — and in due time she was delivered of a beautiful girl. That is plain, isn't it, daughter?"

Pauline nodded. Adolphus licked his dry lips.

"Ah, my tongue shrivels," he moaned. "Give me to drink, child."

Lucy filled a tumbler from a jug on the bedside table and gave it to Pauline, who held it to her father's mouth. Water trickled down his chin. The very act of swallowing seemed to cause him pain, and after scarcely wetting his tongue he coughed and pushed the tumbler away. Pauline handed it back to Lucy, and wiped her father's chin with the blanket.

"Bless you, daughter," he said. "It comes to this, child. I lay with another woman, before I wed your mother. *Gooh!* She, too, bore a child. And that horrid man, Orloff — fear him, daughter! He is bile! He is rot! — he compelled me to secrecy . . . O, I am weak, I am bottomless! Aye, and Orloff plotted an even greater infamy, but I thwarted that, at least. The child lives, and — *gooh!* — and I have done for it what my little strength, and my small courage, allowed. But my strength fails; it ebbs away. I rely on your courage now!"

"I . . . I don't understand, Papa," said Pauline. "You have another child? . . ."

"A daughter, Pauline!" said the Baron. "No longer a baby — *gooh!* — nay, she is your elder. Yet she needs your help. Orloff will destroy her! While I lived I contended with him . . . he dared not take the final step, though his hands are red . . . *Gooh!* . . . but I cannot live forever . . . indeed, my hours are numbered . . ."

"But, Papa, where is she?" Pauline asked. "How can it be?"

"Ah, that I kept you in ignorance!" Adolphus moaned. "Yet that is not my greatest trespass, for the child herself — *gooh!* — she knows not her father. What a feast of corruption awaits the worms! Aye, the last feast I hold shall be the greatest. But you, Lucy Wickwright," he said, lifting his watery eyes, "dost think we have no pages to fetch a scribe to us? Do you not wonder why we have called you?"

Pauline gazed upon her maidservant, as though surprised to find her still there. She held her father's hand in her lap. Lucy felt herself to be truly a spy, now, and horribly so — eavesdropping, and trespassing in matters beyond her station. She had wandered into a great tragedy without the benefit of a script or proper costume.

"Respectfully, my Lord," she said in a small, unsteady voice, "my uncle — Mr. Tooey, of the Perch & Pillow — has guessed what you mean to say."

"What is it, Papa?" asked Pauline. "Why did you bring Wickwright here?"

The Baron struggled to rise from his pillows.

"How long have you known, my child?" he asked Lucy.

"Only since yesterday, sir. Though I did not believe it till now, begging my Lord's pardon."

"Papa?" said Pauline. She looked from her father to Lucy. "Papa? I don't understand. What didn't Wickwright believe? How long has she known what?"

"My dear — *gooh!* — dear daughter," said the Baron, "she is the one of whom I speak. Do you not see? I kept you together, at least . . . flesh of my flesh. . . . Would that I had been a worthy father to you both, and not the prey of serpents! *Gooh!*

Wilt forgive me, Pauline? Your mother, rest her bones, never knew."

Pauline petted her father's hand, as though soothing a troubled child.

"But, Papa . . . it can't be," she said. "My maid is an orphan. Isn't that so, Wickwright? Her people were chandlers in Tenesmus. Surely you remember, Papa — she came here when her poor parents died."

"She is twice an orphan," Adolphus said, "and no orphan at all. That loathsome man, Orloff . . . he demanded I expose the child. But I could not. I bade the midwife carry her to Tenesmus — *gooh!* — where I trusted some good folk would care for a foundling child. When Orloff discovered my ruse . . . *Gooh! Gooh! Gooh!*"

A fit of coughing seized the Baron, and the great bed shook with his convulsions. Pauline watched helplessly until the episode passed, then held the tumbler to her father's mouth. When he had drunk he lay back on the pillows and gazed up at her.

"There is no time for talk," he said. "She is my daughter, Pauline, and I shall acknowledge her this hour, before witnesses — *gooh!* — in accordance with our customs. Wilt forgive me, and embrace a miserable wretch?"

He held open his arms, and Pauline threw herself on her father's neck. Adolphus stroked her hair tenderly, and turned his head away to suppress another fit of coughing: *Gmmph! Gmmph! Gmmph!* At last he looked at Lucy. His eyes watered, though whether from sickness or sorrow, she could not tell.

"My time approaches," he said. "Make haste to fetch the scribe . . . speak to no one else, save two trustworthy witnesses . . . *Gooh!* . . . I leave it to you to choose them . . . Yet stay!" he said, as Lucy stood up. He reached out his hand, with which he had been consoling Pauline. "Far greater is my offense to you, Lucy. Wilt forgive me, and kiss your father?"

The Baron's hand trembled. Pauline, her cheeks wet with tears, turned to look at her maid. Lucy had been staring at the candle, remembering that great day in the Guild Hall, when the people of Tenesmus had chosen the Candle of Cant as their Token to the Baron. Her father had reached down his hands to her, and spun her round and round, his eyes bright with happiness and love. Adolphus, from sheer exhaustion, let drop his hand, then lifted it again, feebly.

"Wilt kiss your father, Lucy?"

Lucy looked away. A great lump was in her throat.

"Forgive me, my Lord," she whispered. "I can't. My father is dead."

The Baron's hand fell to the coverlet. His voice was faint.

"Verily," he said, "he is dead, indeed. Go with my blessing, child. Fetch the scribe."

Lucy fled the sickroom. She hurried past the glaring Orloff and soon lost her way in the unfamiliar corridors of the Baron's suite. When she had twice passed the same suit of armor she stopped, hid behind a tapestry, and sobbed into her hands. Eventually she collected herself, wiped her nose on the back of the tapestry, and found a passage to the castle's north wing.

The printing press was long established in Cant, but the official documents of the land — proclamations, edicts, decrees, decretals, bulls, constitutions, and codes — were still committed to sheepskin by hand, for which task the Baron maintained a small scriptorium. Lucy ran there and explained her mission to the Master of Nibs, who, taking up a traveling desk, made haste to the Baron's chamber.

That left the matter of witnesses. Dr. Azziz — when Lucy had caught her breath and told the reason for her coming — readily agreed to serve, and Lucy raced off before the librarian could ask what, precisely, she was meant to witness. The Baron's time seemed short indeed to Lucy, and she was afraid of losing precious minutes, should she stop to tell the fantastic turn of events.

She ran from the library without a clear idea of whom else to ask. Arden Gutz was in the dungeon. Mr. Lemonjello did not like to come down from his tower, and Lu Mingshu was far away. As for Mr. Vole, he would certainly delay her with a thousand suspicious questions. At last she remembered Dr. Sauersop, who had always been kind to her, and she flew down the stairs to "Stores & Fabrication," where she found the Master Herald stooped over his worktable. His face fell when she told him of the Baron's condition.

"How fleeting is life!" he sighed. "I suspect His Lordship means to settle the matter of Miss Cant's regent, at long last. Let us hope he chooses well! Will you walk with me, Lucy?"

"I must see how Dr. Azziz is coming along," Lucy panted. "The Master of Nibs has gone ahead."

"I shall hasten to His Lordship, then," said Sauersop. But as they parted in the corridor he turned to Lucy, asking, "Who entrusted you with so grave an errand, child?"

"No time to explain!" Lucy called. Already she was running

down the corridor, for a great weight and urgency were on her heart. "Do hurry, sir!"

Dr. Azziz had just got into her sedan chair when Lucy returned to the library. Her assistant had recruited some of the less wrinkled scholars to bear her down the stairs and to the south wing, and on his word of command they hoisted up the poles and set off. The going was terribly slow, even before they got to the stairs, for the scholars were weak-armed and shallow-chested creatures, and as draught animals they were next to useless, stopping every ten yards or so to catch their breath and wipe the fog from their spectacles. Dr. Azziz endured the journey with quiet dignity, looking a queen of the Moors in the ponderously swaying chair, and offering encouragement to her black-robed bearers.

Lucy ran ahead of the librarian, and hurried back to her, and fretted when the scholars stopped on the landings to mop their lofty, deep-thinking brows. She was in a state near panic. She had done a terrible thing in refusing to kiss the Baron, she now believed. She felt grimed with treacle and ashes. Her only thought was to get back to the sickroom, kiss the dying man, and so lift the guilty burden from her heart. She begged the librarian's porters to hurry. When they at last reached the floor of the baronial suite, she abandoned them and flew ahead to the sickroom.

She thought at first she had made a wrong turning, for the corridor was deserted. Orloff, Mrs. Bittertoast, Mr. Splint, the sentries — all had vanished. The sickroom door stood open, and from inside came wet, whimpering, snuffling sounds. Lucy rounded the corner and walked timidly into the room.

The sentries flanked the foot of the bed, swords held before their stoic faces. Mrs. Bittertoast, standing behind the doctor, sobbed openly. Mr. Splint had been holding the Baron's wrist, but now, shaking his head, he let it fall to the coverlet. Orloff, Lucy saw with a shudder, stood beside the bed, stroking Pauline's hair with his bony yellow claw.

The Baron's eyes were open, but they stared sightlessly at the bed's lofty canopy, and a sticky film had already formed upon them. Pauline held her father's hand to her cheek and rubbed it tenderly, as though she could coax his spirit back to the lifeless flesh. The Exalted & Merciful Protector, Adolphus d'Urbano Laertes Thibaut, the twelfth Baron Cant, was dead.

Chapter 19
A UNIFORM MISUNDERSTANDING

*L*ucy did not see Pauline at all the next day. Her mistress shut herself up in her chambers, with guards posted at the doors, and only Mrs. Bittertoast was allowed to approach her bedside, bearing broth and dry biscuits for the grieving girl. Vlad Orloff appeared in the evening and ordered the guards to let him pass, but he retreated moments later in a hail of crockery. Pauline, who had a fearful aim with a teacup, did not wish to be disturbed.

The castle was eerily silent. By ancient custom its denizens daubed their cheeks with ashes and spoke only in whispers after the Baron's death. Lucy, relieved of her normal duties, was put to work hanging crêpe and turning pictures to the wall, and as the day wore on she noticed that whispers followed her about the castle. Yet when she approached the whisperers they fell silent, and averted their eyes, and suddenly found excuses to be somewhere else. No one wanted to talk to Lucy, it seemed, but everyone wanted to talk *about* her. She feared that rumors of the Baron's dying wish — murmured from mouth to ear and hissed in knowing huddles — had gone before her.

When an errand took her to the cellars she found a moment to weep quietly. Lucy could never think of the Baron as being truly her father, but it was hard to lose him on the very day he claimed her as his flesh and blood. She sat on a barrel and wetted her t-shirt with tears, feeling much as she had on the day, years ago, when Lady Sweetbread had rattled out of view, leaving her alone and helpless on Chandlers Lane. She was tempted to run to her uncle, but she knew that Pauline, sooner or later, must call for her. Already Lucy had applied twice to Mr. Vole to see her mistress. The steward had refused her requests.

"Miss Cant," he hissed, "is in no state to deal with servants."

"But sir, I only wish to —"

"Shhh! Need I remind you His Lordship is dead?"

Lucy lowered her voice.

"No, sir, you needn't. But I only wish —"

"Lucy! I'll have none of your cheek, on this of all days. And, may I add, I've exerted myself a good deal on your behalf recently. I should hope you feel some gratitude to the house of Cant and its officers when you go to your cot this night. Then perhaps you will remember who took you in, and helped you in your own hour of grief."

"Sir? I don't understand."

But Vole merely snapped his fingers, and bent again over the great chart on which he had been penciling the various duties of his staff for the coming days. Barons of Cant were interred with awful pomp, and the steward had but a little time in which to train his pages, footmen, maids, and other staff to their roles in the burial rites.

Lucy discovered his meaning when she returned that night to the garret, where a new maidservant's uniform lay on her cot. After all the months of paperwork and delay, Mr. Vole had been as good as his word. She held the brown woolen shift to her body, and admired the spotless white apron and lacework cap on her pillow. Brass-buckled shoes stood by the bed, with a rolled-up black stocking in each. The girls in the garret gathered round to congratulate her, and Lucy found herself wanting to cry again. They had never paid her any attention before.

Yet in the morning she dressed as usual in her jeans and GIZ-MOBOTS! shirt. Turning round pictures was dirty, dusty work, and Lucy hated to ruin her new outfit before Pauline had seen it. She felt she had terribly wronged Mr. Vole by grumping and grousing about him for almost a year, and when she had finished her porridge and crust she went to his pantry and knocked shyly on the open door.

"What is it?" Vole said sharply, glancing up.

"Sir," Lucy said, remembering to whisper. "Thank you for my uniform."

Vole did not seem as generous of spirit as Lucy had imagined him. He exhaled loudly and tapped the staff chart with his pencil. He looked frightfully severe.

"You remember that you *are* a servant, don't you, Lucy?"

"Why, yes, sir!" Lucy said, taken aback. "Shall I be turning pictures again today, sir?" she added.

"No. Cook has prepared a cauldron of salt water. You're to fetch a sprinkler and drown all the potted plants in the receiving rooms. They must be dead by the day of the interment. But first," he said, looking down at his chart, "you may wish your mistress a good morning. She has called for you."

"Yes sir good day sir!" Lucy said, turning on her heel. She hurried to the back stairs and took them two at a stride, not stopping until she reached the garret. There she draped her shift and apron over her arm and, after a moment's hesitation, took the cap as well. It might cheer Pauline to see that she had got a uniform at last. It would hardly do for the new Baroness of Cant to be served by a girl in sneakers.

Lord Cant had died without stating his intentions in the presence of witnesses, and that, to Lucy's thinking, settled that. Nothing counted in Cant that was not written down, so — officially speaking — Pauline remained the Baron's only child and must now become the Baroness. Vlad Orloff was a grave concern, but with Arden's help Lucy would expose his villainy. When his misdeeds were brought to light, the Commissioner of Posts would never be allowed to serve as Pauline's regent.

And how Arden would smile when Lucy told him all she had done! She had not visited the dungeon yet — between shock, grief, and the hanging of crêpe there had simply been no time — but today, as soon as she took leave of Pauline, she would go to him. As she raced down the stairs to her mistress she pictured Arden rising from his pallet, overwhelmed by her courage and devotion, and crushing her to his chest in a grateful embrace. He might well kiss her.

The sentries opened the door to Pauline's bedchamber. Heavy curtains covered the windows, and a low fire of apple wood provided the only light. The bed was piled with cuddly toys — Lucy could scarcely make Pauline out among the jumbled bears and other animals. Her mistress, in a plain white nightshirt, clutched the largest of the bears. She looked up blankly as Lucy approached the bed.

"Oh, there you are, Wickwright," she said.

"Good morning, mistress."

Pauline sat up. Her hair was flat on one side of her head, and her cheek wrinkled from long lying on the seam of a pillowcase. She had always been a fair-skinned girl, but now, in the dim light of the fire, she appeared almost ghostly white. She did not look at Lucy as she talked.

"I hadn't thought," she said, "that you would keep secrets from me, Wickwright."

"Mistress?"

"I deserve no better, I suppose. Everyone says I'm spoiled and willful."

She let go the bear, now, as though it, too, had been gossiping about her. The beast's glass eyes gazed at Lucy.

"Begging your pardon, mistress — they do not. They adore you."

"No, it's only fair," Pauline said. She turned to her side and rested her head on a pillow. "Why, little more than a week ago, I let you take the blame for that trifling affair of the catapult."

"But mistress —"

"So one can hardly blame you for sneaking about, and keeping secrets, and plotting and skullduggery and so forth, even though I brought you a bite of supper in the laundry, which I wasn't supposed to do, as you were being punished."

Lucy stepped closer to the bed. Pauline's lip trembled.

"But I haven't sneaked about . . . that is, I have, but —"

"I suppose it's the Stone of Justice for me!" Pauline cried suddenly, choking on the words. A tear fell to the pillow. "Just like Marie-Antoinette!" she sobbed.

"Mistress! No! I —"

"You knew all about it, Wickwright! And you kept it secret!"

"But I never! I'd just found out, from my Uncle Hock. It was only because I overheard Tybold Retsch and . . . and . . ."

Lucy hesitated, for Pauline had reached under her cuddly bears and pillows and brought out a piece of paper. She sat up in the bed and shook it under Lucy's nose.

"How do you explain *this*?" she asked, then paused to snuffle and wipe her nose on the sleeve of her nightshirt. "I found this note on my pillow this morning. Apparently he quarreled with Papa, but Commissioner Orloff —"

Lucy gasped.

"— says he has evidence that you've been spying, and plotting against me. I suppose a servant-girl *would* want to be a baroness, but I should have thought you'd have the courtesy to say so to my face. I'd . . . I'd . . . thought of you as a *friend*, Wickwright."

Lucy opened her mouth to protest, to warn her mistress that she must not under any circumstances trust Orloff, but she found she could not speak. Pauline had called her a *friend*. She could only gape at her mistress, more stunned, if possible, than she had been when Uncle Hock guessed the secret of her birth. The Adored & Honorable Pauline, the Exalted & Merciful Baroness of Cant, thought of her, Lucy, as a friend. A log popped and whistled in the fireplace.

Overcome, Lucy reached out for the corner post of the bed, and in doing so let fall the uniform she carried on her arm. Pauline now noticed it for the first time. She reached out and held by its collar the woolen shift, then lifted wondering eyes to Lucy.

"Wickwright, what's this?" she asked.

"A maidservant's uniform," Lucy said weakly. "Isn't it grand?"

"*You* would think so, wouldn't you?" Pauline said. She reached for a small bear and clutched it to her chest. "I suppose you're very happy, aren't you, Wickwright?"

Lucy could not understand her mistress's reaction.

"Well, I've waited such a long time . . ."

"Oh, yes, years and years!" Pauline cried.

"Mistress? What do you mean?"

Pauline stood on the bed, clutching the bear round its neck. Tears started in her eyes, and Lucy felt herself quite unable to breathe as her mistress pointed an accusing finger at the uniform.

"My . . . my . . . *gooh!* . . . my poor father's not even in his tomb," Pauline sobbed, "but you simply couldn't wait to see me on my knees in a uniform, scrubbing fireplaces! You're heartless, Lucy Wickwright!"

"Mistress, no!" Lucy cried. "You don't understand!"

"Guard! Guard!" Pauline wailed. The doors burst open and

sandals slapped across the marble floor. "Take this creature away from me!" she demanded.

"Please, mistress, let me explain!" Lucy implored, but strong hands were already dragging her away from the bed. "It isn't what you think!"

"You'll look very grand in your baronial cap!" said Pauline, falling to her knees. She picked up the uniform's lacework bonnet and threw it at Lucy. "I hope it gives you a headache!"

"No!" Lucy said, but in vain — already the sentries had slammed shut the doors behind her. Lucy broke away and grabbed the latch, but she was no match for guardsmen twice her size. They peeled free her fingers and pushed her down the corridor, making her stumble and fall. When she had resettled her glasses she stood and, in a heartsick fury, stamped her foot at them. Then she turned and fled down the corridor. At the first turning she collided with Vlad Orloff, who cried *"Oof!"* and fell back against a clattering suit of armor. Not having the heart to beg his pardon, Lucy ran on.

Wanting air and solitude, she raced up to the parapet walk, where her eye fell on the guardhouse. She remembered Arden, languishing in the dungeon, still unaware of her triumphant rescue of the manifesto. She would go pour out her heart to him, and he would tell her what to do.

She raced to the flanking tower, down its winding steps, and across the ward. A lone sentry sat in the guardhouse, with a caged squirrel and a sack of filberts, with which he fed the beast.

"I've come to visit one of the prisoners," Lucy whispered breathlessly when the man looked up. "Mr. Arden Gutz."

"Prisoners?" the guard asked.

"Yes," said Lucy, "one of them. Mr. Gutz."

"There's no prisoners here, unless you count this little fellow," the guard said. He offered a filbert to the squirrel, who looked curiously at Lucy as he nibbled it. "They were all let out when His Late Lordship passed away. On account of the amnesty."*

"Mr. Gutz is not here?" Lucy asked.

The guard looked quizzically at the squirrel.

"Your name's not Gutz, is it?" he asked.

The guard could not tell Lucy where Arden Gutz had gone. Most of the prisoners had lit out for Tenesmus, he believed. A few of the longer-serving ones had been dragged unwillingly from their cells, he said, for they could no longer imagine a life without chains. They had knocked off their gaolers' helmets in hopes of being locked up again, but the guards were having none of it. They welcomed a holiday from hauling up the prisoners' slops.

Crestfallen, Lucy walked back to the carriageway that led out of the castle. The area generally bustled with guards, but now they were all at drill in the ward, rehearsing their parts in the Baron's funeral. She wandered toward the portcullis. The

---

*All prisoners were freed upon the death of a ruling baron. The practice was established by Honoré, whose predecessor, Gustaf I ("the Fey"), had filled the dungeons with so many men whose "treasons" amounted to little more than wearing the wrong fashion in hats that the new Baron despaired of ever sorting the true criminals from the merely hapless. "Therefore let All be set Free," he wrote [in the Proclamation of Merciful Amnesty], "for We may trust that the Innocent shall continue Blameless, & the Wicked perpetrate such Crimes as will commend them again to Chains."

drawbridge was down, and a lone sentry sat at the gate, whittling with his penknife. His back was to Lucy, for he had positioned himself to enjoy the view down to the plains. Lucy looked around. No one else seemed to be watching, and when she had crept past the sentry only half a league of road — and all of it downhill — stood between her and Tenesmus. She took it running.

Chapter 20

THE TIDINGS OF CLARA SWAIN

*C*onsidering it sensibly, Lucy understood why Arden had not sought her out as soon as he was released from his cell. Eager as he must have been to see her, and to learn the outcome of her mission, he would not have wished to compromise her. Orloff, as yet, did not know who had taken the manifesto, and if its author had raced to Lucy as soon as he was let out of the dungeon the Commissioner would surely have grown suspicious of her. Arden's bolting for Tenesmus appeared quite gallant, in that light. It showed his concern for her welfare.

When Lucy got to Tenesmus she found its wags out in numbers, for the Baron's death provided wonderful exercise for their tongues — even if they had to speak in whispers. His subjects were saddened, of course, but the great man's death, while regrettable, certainly relieved the tedium of day-to-day. There were mourning clothes to be aired and pressed, and mourning cakes to be baked. And while most shops were shut until after the interment, the townsfolk could hardly mourn their Baron without a consoling pint. So the public houses were open and did a thriving business.

The whispers seemed to have followed Lucy from the castle. She heard someone hiss "Gizmobots!" as she passed a huddle of tradesmen who stared from the door of a pub. On Fenway Road, near the Mission, she was approached by one of the orphan girls, who was dressed like her in jetsam from the charity bin. The girl carried an armful of pamphlets, which she had been hawking to passers-by, for it was one of the burdens of orphanage life that, in addition to having no parents and being entertained by clowns, the children had to earn their bread and salt by passing out tracts such as "Dancing: Too Close for Comfort?" and "Soap for the Soul."

Lucy hurried her steps, hoping to get by without having to take a pamphlet, but the girl was older and faster than she and cut her off, waving the pamphlet high in the air.

"Learn about the scourge of chewing gum, miss?" she asked.

"No, thank you, I'm — What did you say?"

"Chewing gum," the girl said. "Bad for the teeth, bad for the Barony. Read all about it. And if you could spare a little something to advance the work of the Mission . . ."

Lucy, fortunately, had two ha'pennies in a pocket of her new trousers. She handed them to the girl and took the pamphlet, which, as she had suspected, began with the words "Comrades! Cantlings!" Lu Mingshu had printed the manifesto.

To the manifesto as Arden Gutz had written it, however, Mr. Lu had added an appendix — entitled "Concerning the Hereditary Barony" — in which he plainly hinted that the "presumptive heiress" (he meant Pauline) had no true claim to the baronial cap. He went so far, indeed, as to say, "the wise shall know her [the true heiress] by this sign: before her go *Gizmobots!*"

And here was Lucy, not wearing her jumper, walking about Tenesmus with GIZMOBOTS! blazing from her chest! She crossed her arms, and held the pamphlet in front of her t-shirt, and hurried down narrow lanes and alleyways to the Perch & Pillow, where a great crowd had gathered. If the taverns generally were busy during this time of mourning, Uncle Hock's house was openly buzzing. Lucy, skinny as she was, could barely squeeze in at the door. The common room was packed with folk, the likes of which she had never before seen. At the fireside men with swords and muddy boots whispered so loudly that it scarcely counted as whispering, and laughed openly at crude jokes. A matron eating rashers with her brood shushed them, but if the Baron's passing touched these swordsmen they bore their grief easily.

Lucy pushed through the crowd, looking for her uncle. Gil Blemesch, the stable boy, had evidently been recruited to help in the tavern. He passed a few yards from Lucy, holding flagons of ale overhead, but though she whispered herself hoarse Lucy could not attract his attention. She dodged men's elbows and ladies' bosoms and finally made her way to the kitchen, where a great quantity of stew simmered on the stove. An old woman sat on a stool by the back stairs. Though the kitchen was hot she wore a shawl over her shoulders. She held a glass of wine, which dribbled from her toothless mouth when she drank.

"Hallo," she said, wiping her chin. She wore a country woman's bonnet, and as she leaned forward one of its untied laces fell into the wine. The woman fished it out and sucked the spirits from it.

"Good morning, missus," Lucy said, taking a cautious step toward her. Both of the bonnet's laces were stained red at the ends, she saw. The woman squinted and licked her lips with a pale tongue.

"Who are ye, now?" she said. "Do ye belong here?"

"I'm looking for my uncle, missus. Mr. Tooey."

The woman let out a high, unnerving giggle, and choked on a draught of wine. Red drops dangled from the hairs of a mole on her chin, but her questing tongue found them and lapped them up.

"You're looking for your uncle!" she said. "Mr. Tooey!"

"Yes, missus," Lucy replied, for she had said exactly that. Stepping closer, she saw that the woman's shawl was stained the same red as her bonnet laces, and even the frilly cuffs of her gown had turned crimson with wine. She reminded Lucy of the castle cooks on a day when they had been slaughtering chickens. The woman beckoned Lucy closer.

"Let us have a look at you," she wheedled. To Lucy's horror she reached out a gnarled hand and clutched the neck of her t-shirt, pulling Lucy's face to within inches of her own.

"Please, missus!" Lucy said, struggling to keep her feet.

"Look at her now — sweet as new peas!" the woman crowed. "Have ye been kissed yet, my darling? Have ye?"

"No!" said Lucy. She turned her face from the woman's foul breath.

"'Tis pity you wear spectacles," the old winebibber went on. "Ye've got lovely peepers. Oh, and pretty, pretty toes! Ye've a shoeful, haven't ye? Are ye my little busy-toed baby girl, are ye, my doll?"

"Let me *go!*" Lucy cried. She broke free and staggered back across the floor, her glasses slipping to the end of her nose. She meant to turn heel and run away from the old woman — who cackled now like a mad, triumphant hen — but she bumped into something solid and unmoving, and strong hands grasped her arms. Lucy screamed.

"Lucy!" said Uncle Hock.

Lucy threw her arms around his neck, and he lifted her up and embraced her.

"How is it you're not at the castle?" Hock Tooey asked when he'd kissed his niece. "What are they saying up there?" He tried to put Lucy down, but she clung to his neck as a drowning girl clutches a log.

"I don't know what to *do!*" she wailed. "Pauline thinks I want her to be my maid, and the guards carried me off before I could explain. Arden Gutz has disappeared. And I found a girl from the orphanage handing out *these!*"

She reached for her pocket. Hock Tooey let her down, and she opened the manifesto to Mr. Lu's appendix. Her uncle nodded grimly when she pointed to the mention of *Gizmobots!*

"I've seen it," he said. "We're all at a loss what to do in these times, Lucy. But come, let's talk in my parlor. I've someone I want you to meet." He led her back to the old woman, who had drunk off her wine and leered at Lucy, now, as though she was an uncorked jug. "This is my sister's girl, missus, as I told you about. Lucy, this is Clara Swain."

Hock Tooey, after a night's hard riding, had found Henry Wallow and his men encamped some miles east of Twee. Sir Henry reacted coldly when the innkeeper asked to talk with Clara Swain. Undoubtedly he believed the castle had sent out a spy. But when Hock Tooey mentioned his niece, and how she'd arrived in a basket on Chandlers Lane at the time of the Baron's betrothal, Sir Henry started up and called for the old midwife to be brought to him. She was cold and weary with the camping, and refused to speak until given a draught of wine, but with her throat thus warmed she gave her story gladly. She repeated it now to Lucy, in the small parlor behind the pantry, after Uncle Hock had refilled her glass.

"I've slapped the breath into many a baby," she boasted, "and many a times I was called to the castle, for in those days my cousin was a mighty one on the staff. Now, the last time ever I went up there it was all hush-hush. A little maidservant was in a bad way, and not married at all, and I was told if I kept quiet about the matter I'd be pleased with my reward. And one feller, who I didn't like the look of, told me if I breathed a word of it, it'd be the dungeon for me!"

"That was Orloff," Uncle Hock put in. "You see, the Baron wasn't yet married, Lucy. He had his eye on Esmeralda, the daughter of Lord Simone-Thierry — or I should say he had his eye on her dowry, for her old fellow was terrible rich. At that time Orloff worked for Simone-Thierry, and he'd come with a party from La Provence to negotiate the terms of marriage.* Well, when he found Adolphus had got a servant-girl with child, he saw his advantage. Blackmail, it's called in plain speech."

"Aye, he was a black-hearted one," said Clara Swain. "There were guards at the door, where the poor thing was confined in her birth throes, and he stood there with 'em like a fox guarding a henhouse.

"It went poorly with the girl," she continued. "She was a wee thing, pretty as a pigeon's tongue, which I suppose caught the Baron's eye, for they did say he liked to tickle the chambermaids, begging your pardon, little miss. And a poor girl might well have her head turned by Adolphus, for wasn't he mighty and rich?"

"It's not fit matter for a child's ears," said Uncle Hock, looking at the floor. "But you have a right to hear it, Lucy, of all people."

Lucy had heard some of it already, from Lord Cant himself, but she felt a long way from understanding it. You were supposed to celebrate when a baby was born, and pass it from arm to arm, not lock up the mother with guards at the door. She drew her feet up, and put her arms around her knees. Clara Swain, sitting next to her, sighed.

"No, 'tis not a fit tale at all. The dear, poor creature was confined three days — 'twas as if the wee baby had peeked out and didn't care for the look of things. And no wonder. When the child came at last — a two-fisted, twelve-toed, bawling baby

*La Provence: a region in the east of Cant, ancestral home of the house of Simone-Thierry.

girl — its dear poor mother was not long for this world. The Baron's own physics came to care for her, but it was no good. She hadn't the strength to carry on."

Lucy looked up at the old woman.

"What was her name?" she whispered.

"Why," the midwife said, "there was no talk of giving the child a name. For the nonce we found it a wet-nurse from among the maidservants, but —"

"No," Lucy said. "Not the baby, the . . . her . . . my mother."

Clara Swain put down her wineglass. She put a hand to Lucy's cheek.

"Oh, forgive me, child. The wine does go to my head. Jocasta was the poor dear's name. Worn out as she was, she had a smile and a kiss for her little one, when you came along at last. May she rest in peace."

Lucy wiped her cheek. From the public room came dimly the sounds of chairs and cutlery, and the faint shush of the patrons' whispers, like wind blowing over a field of dead rye. Hock Tooey cleared his throat.

"I suppose Orloff had risen as far in corruption as he could in La Provence," he said, "and wanted to be nearer the fat purses of the castle. Of course, his master would never give Esmeralda to Lord Cant if he knew of a child. Orloff's price for keeping his tongue was a position at Castle Cant. Already the noble persons of La Provence were slaves to his blighted gum, and as Commissioner of Posts he could profit from every piece of gum shipped on the post roads. You see how it stands today. The nobles must have their cud, and to pay for it they've raised the tithes and duties until the common folk can scarcely afford to butter their bread."

Lucy hardly heard him. Tithes were a great problem, no doubt, but her mind was far away, with Jocasta. A servant-girl — like Lucy herself — she had been locked up to bring her troublesome baby into the world, and had died without so much as giving it a name. Esmeralda, too, had faded after giving birth, though she lingered a year and more before leaving Pauline without a mother. It was a perilous business, it seemed, bearing the children of men. Clara Swain reached for her wine.

"But he meant to do right by his old master, too," she said. "It was Orloff as said the child must be exposed. Left out in the wind and rain for the wolves to get at, I mean to say. Well, His Lordship may ha' been a weak man, but he wasn't no murderer. His maid's death grieved him, I suppose. So he calls for me, late at night, and he says to me, 'Take the child to the Micklewood, good woman, as like you're a-going to expose the poor wee thing, but then carry it over to Tenesmus in secret, and leave it at the door of some honest Cantling folk.' And so I did, and I took ye to Chandlers Lane especial, having in mind to leave you with tradesfolk, as might have means to care for a little one."

"Thank you, missus," Lucy said faintly.

"Somehow Orloff found that you survived," said Uncle Hock. "Why he didn't then kill you outright I can only guess. He may have felt his position was not so secure, with Esmeralda dead, and her dowry safely in the Baron's coffers. Or perhaps he didn't see you as such a problem, then — provided you didn't learn the secret of your birth. The fiend! I have no doubt he slew your parents and poor Casio. He wanted to have you at the castle, where he could keep you under his eye."

How much of life went on before we were born! Lucy

reflected. A girl might spend half her mortal years simply coping with the accidents of her birth — and now even Pauline was in danger, who was born to the pomp and riches of Castle Cant. She looked at her uncle.

"We must stop Orloff, Uncle Hock."

"Aye, we must do that," he agreed. "And fortune may be with us, Lucy. After you were safely in Chandlers Lane, Adolphus bought this woman's silence with a pension, and she returned to her family in Haslet March. But in time Henry Wallow got wind of her story."

"I never could keep a secret," the old woman confessed.

"Sir Henry, it seems," Hock Tooey went on, "is no great friend of Gaspard Simone-Thierry —"

"Pauline's grandfather," Lucy said.

"The same. Wallow would sooner salute a pig than a granddaughter of Gaspard, with whom he has a long dispute. Now he learns from this good woman that there's another claim to the baronial cap. Well, it's one thing to have a claim; it's quite another to press it. So Henry Wallow finds himself in need of allies, and for that he's turned to the followers of the Cause. He left here some time ago to parley with your Mr. Gutz."

"Arden?" Lucy said, letting go her knees.

"Aye, the young firebrand," her uncle said, frowning. "The guard have been looking for him under every rug in Tenesmus, which I'll warrant is Orloff's doing. He's hiding himself at the American Mission, and has been stirring up trouble these past days, sending round the orphans to peddle that manifesto until half Tenesmus is ready to march on the castle and turn the lot of gum chewers on their ears."

"Come with me to the Mission, Uncle Hock," Lucy begged. "Pauline is in a terrible state. She thinks I want her to be my servant, when really I don't even want to be the Baroness at all. We had a frightful row. So we mustn't allow Ard — that is, Mr. Gutz, to go about making trouble. Pauline has suffered a great loss, after all. She's an orphan."

"And aren't you an orphan, Lucy?" asked Hock Tooey. He leaned forward and gazed tenderly at his niece. "And shouldn't you have a taste of fine clothes, and no work to do, after all you've been through — and you an orphan twice over?"

"But I'm not fit to be a baroness, Uncle Hock," Lucy protested.

"And who is fit for that?" asked her uncle. "Why, them that's born to it, that's who. Gustaf the Fey wasn't fit to be a baron, if you want to talk about fitness, but he was born to it, and there you go. Rules is rules, as they say round my dartboard. You're the first-born child of the Baron, as this honest woman can attest, so —"

"And you're a *good* girl," Clara Swain broke in. "One as will remember a poor old woman who saw you into this world, and laid you at a loving doorstep when others might have left you to the wolves. You won't get all high and mighty, and forget a poor old woman, when she wants a peck of coal for her grate, I dare say."

"So why shouldn't you be the Baroness, Lucy?" Hock Tooey concluded.

"But Uncle Hock, Pauline is —"

Lucy's speech was cut off by a clatter in the kitchen. The source of the tumult became evident when Blaise Delagraisse appeared, banging shoulders with a swordsman who was determined to enter the parlor before him. They reached the narrow doorway together and fought for place, but the swordsman's greater size and strength won out. He strode up to Hock Tooey, Delagraisse following close behind.

"My master sends his regards, sir, and this message from Mr. Gutz," he said, handing a note to Lucy's uncle. Hock Tooey looked at it, then passed it to Lucy, who saw it was addressed to her.

Miss Wickwright, in care of
Mr. Tooey, at the Perch & Pillow

"And my mistress sends *hers*, Lucy," said Blaise Delagraisse, with a sidelong, none-too-friendly glance at the swordsman. He, too, had been charged with delivering a note.

L. Wickwright

it was addressed, in Pauline's looping, undisciplined hand. Lucy stared at the two notes.

"How did Miss Cant know I was here?" she asked the underfootman.

"Begging your pardon, she didn't," Delagraisse said. "But when you couldn't be found at the castle I asked among the other girls, and Jane Cedilla told me as you had kin in Tenesmus."

But how had Arden Gutz known her whereabouts? Lucy wondered. Impulsively, she broke the seal on his note. It was written, she saw, on the back of a torn-off cover of "Soap for the Soul."

To the Valued & Heroic Lucy! [it began]

Report has reached our ears, relayed by one of the little foot-soldiers of our Cause — I mean the young pamphleteers of the Mission, where I have now taken sanctuary; they have been pressed into service, despite their tender years; such is our urgent need! — that you have been spied this very morning on the streets of Tenesmus. Fly to us, Lucy! For we have learnt the unguessed secret of your birth, inferred by Lu Mingshu and confirmed to us by Sir Henry Wallow. Fortune smiles on our Cause, little one! for we have now within our grasp . . .

Lucy's heart — when she read *Fly to us!* — fluttered like a bird shaking out its wings. Arden needed her — his Valued & Heroic Lucy! She skimmed the rest of the note — which filled the page in tiny cursive script, barely leaving room for his initials *A.G.* in a corner — but the rest was mostly gum and politics and subordinate clauses. Arden certainly was windy, Lucy had to admit. And why did he persist in calling her "little"?

She broke the red wax seal of Pauline's note, with its impress of the baronial arms. Her mistress, too, had sent an urgent message, but it was expressed with a poet's economy of words.

Wickwright,
    Come here at once. I need you.
            P. E. S.-J. von Cant

Her mistress had chosen the smallest notepaper from her drawer of stationery. Lucy rested the note on top of Arden Gutz's unfolded letter, and his close, wordy script made a dark frame around Pauline's spare rectangle with its two short sentences.

The swordsman spoke to Hock Tooey.

"I was told to escort the little lady back to the Mission if I found her here," he said. "And Sir Henry begs the favor of your company as well. I may add that Mr. Gutz has come to terms with my master, and a course of action has been agreed upon."

Clara Swain clapped her hands.

"Oh, there'll be a row and a ruckus!" she said to Lucy. In her gown stained with wine, the old midwife might have just attended some awful and bloody birth. "And isn't it always so, when a mighty one dies? Remember me, little thing, when you come into your own!"

Hock Tooey stood up.

"Shall I saddle a horse, Lucy?" he asked. "Or would you walk?"

Lucy folded the notes and put them in her pocket. She embraced her uncle and kissed his cheek, then crossed the parlor and stood beside Blaise Delagraisse.

"Will you give my regards to Mr. Gutz, Uncle Hock?" she said. "I have to go back to the castle."

"But Lucy! —"

"Now, see here," said the swordsman. "You're to come with me, I said. My master wants to have a word with you. *Sir* Henry Wallow, mind! When he calls for a body, he expects 'em to hop!"

Had Lucy seen herself, then, in the cracked mirror of the servants' garret, she might not have recognized the person reflected back to her. She gave him such a look that the swordsman — six feet tall if he was an inch — unconsciously stepped away from her.

"I beg your pardon," she said — though she hardly sounded sorry — "but my *mistress* wants to have a word with me. Pauline Esmeralda Simone-Thierry — *Lady* Cant, mind you! Your master will simply have to wait. Come, Delagraisse."

She spun on her sneaker and left the room. Blaise Delagraisse — perhaps five feet and two inches tall, when he remembered not to slouch — turned to Sir Henry's swordsman and stuck out his tongue triumphantly before running out of the parlor after her.

Chapter 21

POST MORTEM

*L*ucy raced back to the castle, expecting fire, swords, and treason, and found instead a needlework lamb. Pauline sat in bed among heaped pillows and cuddly toys, a book resting on her knees, and gazed forlornly out the high windows of her bedchamber. A tray of food — apples, biscuits, toffees, tea — sat untouched beside the bed.

"Ah, there you are, Wickwright," she said. The sentry pulled shut the door as Lucy walked to her mistress's bedside, and the latch fell with a muted, respectful *clank.* The maidservant's uniform was gone.

"Forgive me, mistress," said Lucy. "I'd gone to visit my uncle in town."

"You were at Tenesmus? Is it your holiday?"

"No, mistress. I'm afraid I've been truant."

"I see." Pauline put aside her book. "Well, I shouldn't wonder you'd want to play the loafer, considering all the work you're made to do. It must be very tiresome."

"I like to work, mistress," Lucy said truthfully, for she did find a measure of satisfaction in completing her duties. She found considerably less amusement in starting them, but she saw no reason to mention that to Pauline.

"I think I should like work, too," her mistress said, "except for all the stooping and fetching and hauling and scrubbing and so forth, which strike me as perfectly dull. I've been giving a good deal of thought to the question of an occupation, Wickwright," she went on, again looking out the window, "and I've come to the conclusion that I'm best suited to being a poetess. The only labor is dipping a quill, and one spends a great deal of time outdoors among the flowers and zephyrs, seeking inspiration. Do you know what a zephyr is, Wickwright?"

"I believe it's a type of wind, mistress," Lucy said, and added — because Pauline was a musical girl and always said the most wonderful nonsense — "I think you'd make a very good poetess."

"Thank you. You're right about the zephyr, which is the west wind. I used to confuse it with the zither, which as you may know is a stringed instrument. But really it's quite an understandable misunderstanding, because the zither produces a light and airy — indeed, a zephyry — tone, and both words begin with a zed."

"Yes, mistress," said Lucy. Pauline's confusion was itself poetical, she reflected, for it arose from a kind of simile. Her mistress had grasped wonderfully the likeness of a zither and a zephyr. She considered pointing this out, but Pauline's thoughts, it seemed, had moved on. Her mistress stared at the coverlet, at the molehills made by her upturned feet, and bit pensively on a corner of her lip. When a long moment had passed in silence, Lucy coughed quietly. "You wanted to speak to me, mistress?"

"Yes. You see, I've done the most wretched thing." She reached across the bed for an embroidery frame, stretched with webbing on which a scene had been sketched in charcoal. As usual, Pauline had begun by stitching the figures in the foreground — the "fun parts" — rather than the broad background of grass and sky, as Lucy would have done. "I had the drawing master make this scene for me," she explained, "but the light was poor this morning, and I chose the wrong color yarn for the sheep. I want you to pull out the stitches, so I can begin again."

"Yes, mistress."

Lucy dragged a chair to the bedside and began to pull out the yarn. The picture showed a stout, dark-haired shepherd — a figure very like Pauline's father — standing with his crook beside a solitary lamb, which her mistress had begun to stitch in yellow yarn, rather than white. An eagle hovered in the sky. Pauline had got all the other colors right — the crook was brown, the eagle black, the flowers pink and white — and Lucy wondered that she had gone wrong with the sheep, as the light in her room ought to have been stronger by the time she began stitching it.

"Wickwright," Pauline said, when Lucy had pulled out a good length of yarn, "Mr. Vole explained to me about your uniform." She looked away, and twisted a corner of the bed linen in her hands.

"Yes, mistress?"

"Yes. And . . . well, I mean to say, one behaved badly. You see . . . it's absurd, of course, but . . . one supposed you meant to demote me, and make me your maidservant, because of what Papa said."

"Think nothing of it, please, mistress," said Lucy. She had stopped pulling yarn. "You couldn't have known. It was an understandable misunderstanding."

"No. It was ill-mannered and rude, and one . . . I mean to say . . . I apologize."

"Yes, mistress," said Lucy. She could not remember Pauline's ever saying such a thing in the past, and she hardly knew how to respond. "Thank you," she added.

"You're welcome, I'm sure."

Lucy began to pull another stitch, but Pauline threw off the coverlet and took hold of the embroidery frame.

"Here, I'll do that," she said. "It was my mistake, after all."

"It's no bother, mistress."

"No," Pauline said firmly. "I want to learn to do for myself."

That, Lucy thought, would require a great deal of study, but she let go the frame and said nothing as Pauline struggled with the stitches. Her mistress had used the wrong color on purpose, Lucy realized, as an excuse to send for her and offer an apology. She decided not to tell Pauline, just now, the story she'd heard from Clara Swain, though her heart was filled with it, and indeed she'd repeated it to Blaise Delagraisse on the road back to the castle.

"It was good of Mr. Vole to give me a uniform, at long last," she said instead, when, after painstaking effort, her mistress had managed to pull three or four stitches. "Shall I try it on?"

"What, that thing?" Pauline said. "I had Vole take it away."

She picked at an especially tight stitch, her tongue protruding with the effort.

"I could fetch it," Lucy said. "Anyway, the shoes and stockings are still under my cot, so I should have to fetch them, as well. I should like to see it all together."

"I'm afraid you can't. I instructed Vole to burn it."

"But . . . but . . . mistress!" Lucy said.

Pauline let go the embroidery.

"Do you honestly believe," she said, "that I would consent to have you waiting upon me, after what I learned from Papa?"

Lucy's heart beat wildly in her chest. Pauline was sending her away!

"Mistress, please, don't say that. I promise I won't tell anyone!"

Pauline looked at her curiously.

"Tell anyone what?" she asked.

"Why, what His Lordship said, about my coming first. There were no witnesses, so it doesn't count! Please, I've waited forever to have a uniform. Don't sack me!"

Pauline put aside the embroidery frame. She swung her legs over the edge of the bed and took Lucy by the hand. Her hair fell over her face, partly hiding a shy, tender smile.

"Sometimes you really are a dolt, Lucy Wickwright," she began.

After much talking they agreed that, at least until after the interment, Lucy should keep up the appearance of being Pauline's servant. For better or worse, the grown-ups would decide who wore the baronial cap. If it was to be Pauline, she would appoint

Lucy to some grand-sounding office, such as Minister of Firefly Preservation, or Inspectress of Seesaws and Sandpits, in which she could wear a dress and be a proper court lady. In the meantime, Pauline enlisted Lucy as a spy.

"I'm not saying you need snoop about Orloff's office again," she said (after Lucy had told her of that adventure), "but, as you've already learned the trade, you may as well keep a finger in the wind, and see if you can discover his plans. I never liked the man. I can't understand why Papa kept him on."

Lucy was not long in discovering the method, if not the plan, of Vladimir Orloff. As she belatedly salted the plants that afternoon, Delagraisse brought her a message from Dr. Sauersop, begging Lucy to meet him and the librarian, Dr. Azziz, in the latter's parlor at midnight. The Baron's physician, Mr. Splint, was to be there as well, according to the under-footman.

Lucy barefooted out of the garret when the castle clocks struck the third quarter. She wore her nightshirt and cap, hoping that the ghostly raiment would scare away any guardsman who might see her. The guard were a superstitious lot, as a rule, being mostly country boys nurtured on grisly tales of Gustaf the Fey, whose victims were said to haunt the castle in terrific numbers.

The moon was halfway to full, and after the utter darkness of the back stairs the library's windows shone like lamps. Scrolls and folios lay open under velvet bookweights on the long tables. Lucy spun the great globe as she passed it, and the rusty sound of its axles — *ah-wicked!-ah-wicked!-ah-wicked!-ah-wicked!* — brought an anxious face to the parlor door. Dr. Sauersop's monocle glinted in the moonlight.

"Ah, Miss Wickwright," he whispered to Lucy. "Please to come in."

Dr. Azziz sat near the fire, a rug covering her legs. Mr. Splint had brought a hard chair from the reading room, and he stroked his moustaches as Dr. Sauersop led Lucy to a settee on the farther side of the fire. The herald drew his robe around him as he sat down beside her.

"I am an old man," he said, "and had not hoped to follow another baron to his grave before being borne to my own. Surely these are grievous days for Cant. But heavy as my heart lies within me, it weighs still heavier when I imagine the days ahead. We have heard strange tidings, Miss Wickwright."

Lucy shivered. A goodly fire burned upon the grate, but her nightshirt was thin with laundering, and goose bumps had risen on her arms and legs. The librarian, Mr. Splint, and Dr. Sauersop regarded her closely. Dr. Azziz now spoke.

"I found it exceeding queer," she said, "that Commissioner Orloff's first action following His Lordship's death was to have Miss Cant taken away. The poor child was dumb with grief, of course, but I could almost imagine that he feared, for some reason, that anyone should speak to her. My suspicions were further aroused when I asked the Commissioner why His Lordship had called for the scribe and ourselves."

Lucy had been dragged by guards from the Baron's death chamber within seconds of running in ahead of the witnesses. When she saw Delagraisse's aunt leading Pauline away she had chosen to follow her mistress rather than stay behind and make explanations. She had not since spoken to the librarian or Dr. Sauersop.

"What did Mr. Orloff say?" she asked.

"He told us that His Lordship, knowing his hour was at hand, had meant to settle the question of his daughter's regent," said Dr. Azziz. "Naturally one believed Adolphus would wish to make his desires known on such a matter. This regent will effectively rule the Barony for the next decade and more, until Miss Cant arrives at her majority."

"But, ma'am —"

"And we learned," the librarian continued gravely, "that for this important office Adolphus had chosen no other person than Vladimir Orloff himself."

"No!" Lucy said, starting up. "He's wicked! He murdered —"

"Peace, Lucy!" Sauersop said. He grasped Lucy's hand, and she sat again beside him. "We are well aware of that man's wickedness, though I had not believed he would resort to killing. I confess I'm surprised to hear you level that charge, for only today did Mr. Splint suggest to me that such a thing might be true."

"Murder is a strong word," the physician said. Like Mr. Vole, he wore a high, starched collar, but unlike the steward he had no chin. He thus appeared to have poked his head up through a funnel, his lips barely rising above its narrow rim. "A strong word," he repeated. "But I believe that the Commissioner at least exercised a baleful influence on Lord Cant.

"Some months ago," Splint explained, "His Lordship consulted me on what then seemed a trivial matter. He had decided to give up the habit of gum chewing, believing it to be responsible for the poor condition of his teeth, and his bad stomach. But he found it rough going. He craved the calming effect of the cud. He had no appetite, and found it impossible to sleep. I prescribed beer and exercise to stimulate the appetite, wine as an aid to sleep, and thought little more about it until a month later, when the Baron summoned me again. He complained now of being tired and fat. I discovered that His Lordship was drinking enormous quantities of wine in his effort to quit chewing gum, yet he still reverted to the cud at least twice a week.

"We all witnessed his decline these past months. Of course I have railed against chewing gum since it was first introduced to the Barony — by Commissioner Orloff, I may add in passing — but never did I imagine its effects to be so evil. In the outlands the stuff is chewed even by children, I'm told, with little bad effect except to their teeth and diction. I undertook to make inquiries, writing to a number of outlandish medical authorities, and learned that none had observed this powerful hold of the cud upon its users. Yet we have seen its effect on His Lordship. Despite my best efforts, I believe his intense craving for gum resulted ultimately in his death."

It seemed far-fetched to Lucy. Arden had said that the peasant children of Oxford chewed gum continually, and she could not believe that a great strong man like the Baron had been felled by a childish treat.

"I chewed a gum once," she said, remembering the rubbery sweet Minister Guuzi had offered her when she first arrived at the castle. "I don't recall any harm in it."

"Ah," said Splint. "Here we come to the nub of it. I believe it is the habitual use of the stuff that creates the dependence. Just over a fortnight ago, as the Baron declined, I put this theory to the test."

The physician paused, his face grave. Dr. Sauersop, who it seemed had already heard the tale, shook his head and muttered, "Shocking! Shocking!" The coal fire cast a macabre light in the little parlor, and a rising wind whistled and moaned round the castle's towers and battlements.

"With the help of a stableman," Splint said, "I trapped a pair of rats for my experiment. To one of the vermin I fed a single dose of gum, and to the other three doses daily for a period of one week. The first rat indeed showed no ill effects — as in your own experience of gum chewing, Miss Wickwright — but when, after a week, I withheld gum from the second rat, the result was nothing short of grotesque. It threw itself at the wires of its cage and gnawed them. I restrained the beast with a leathern strap and observed that, in this extremity, the desperate rodent chewed upon its own forepaws.

"I then gave the poor animal a saucer of wine. It had shown no appetite for food to this point, but it lapped the wine greedily — indeed, it drank itself into a stupor. Upon waking it was again agitated, and now chewed so furiously upon the wire cage that its muzzle bled freely. I gave it no more wine, but provided ample cheese, crusts, and water. The beast grew more desperate, yet weaker, in the days following, neither eating nor drinking, and so damaged its jaw that, out of pity, I provided it a ball of gutta-percha to chew upon. On the third day the rat lay exhausted. Its breathing had become labored, and I observed acute spasms in the limbs. By day's end its spirit had returned to the earth."

"Appalling!" said Dr. Azziz.

"Put plainly," Splint concluded, "His Lordship was drugged.

I'm convinced that the gum imported to our Barony is treated with some manner of physic, so that its users are condemned to chew the stuff regularly, lest they suffer those pangs and cravings that brought Adolphus to his grave."

"We must stop him," Lucy said, horrified by this account. "Arden says — that is, my acquaintance, Mr. Gutz, says that Vlad Orloff will stop at nothing. Miss Cant's very life may be in danger."

Mr. Splint looked at Dr. Sauersop, but the herald now deferred to Dr. Azziz.

"We all agree that Commissioner Orloff would make a most unsuitable regent," said the librarian. "I may add, Lucy, that neither do we believe Lord Cant desired such an outcome. We wondered, then, why His Lordship called for witnesses in his last hour. And why did he entrust the task of fetching them to his daughter's maidservant, a young girl and a commoner? We hoped you could enlighten us on this matter."

She gazed at Lucy, who squirmed uncomfortably on the settee.

"Well," she said elusively, "His Lordship . . . I believe . . . wanted to make his wishes known."

"And might those wishes have had something to do with you, Lucy?" asked Sauersop. "Is that why you were summoned to His Lordship's deathbed? For that is a most curious circumstance, you must agree."

"Yes, sir. Most curious. Yes, I do agree."

"Perhaps I can jog the girl's memory," said Splint. "After I had composed His Lordship's body and signed the proclamation of death, my thoughts turned to Miss Cant. The girl was quite mad with grief, and indeed my aide, Mrs. Bittertoast, could scarcely keep her from pulling out her hair. Hurrying to her chambers, I first turned out several well-meaning staff members" — here he glanced at Lucy — "and then gave Miss Cant a dose of laudanum, after which I settled in to keep watch.

"The Baron's daughter is a strong-willed girl," he went on. "I have heard her described as impetuous. Headstrong, I think, puts it mildly. She fought the influence of the sedative, and though I increased the dosage she remained fitfully awake, and talked at great length in a rambling fashion. The tale I pieced together from her speech was so fantastic that at first I put it down to the influence of the laudanum. For in addition to confessing to certain crimes involving garden slugs and baskets of laundry, she claimed that her maidservant, an orphan and a commoner, was the rightful heiress to the Barony of Cant. Time and again she cried out *Fetch the witnesses.* I was led to the astonishing conclusion that His Lordship had intended to claim the paternity of another child."

He stopped, and gazed intently at Lucy. She in turn glanced at Dr. Sauersop and the librarian, but their faces expressed the same unspoken question. Lucy heaved a deep sigh, and shrugged.

"It seems rather far-fetched," she mumbled.

"So it seemed to me," said Sauersop, reaching up his sleeve, "until this was brought me, this very morning, with other news from Tenesmus." He held a copy of the manifesto. "Here's a jolly thing, Miss Wickwright! Have you seen it? The Causists, as they are called, openly question Miss Cant's claim to the barony. And they hint quite strongly that the true heiress is the adored Pauline's maidservant. I've further learned that this maidservant's uncle, an innkeeper in Tenesmus, is even now hosting Sir Henry Wallow and an armed party from Haslet March. It seems Costive Gutz was right, eh? Your volley of bloomers at the recent execution really was a revolutionary gesture!"

"No, sir! That was Pauline's idea, as Mr. Splint said. You said you heard her confess to it, didn't you, sir?" Lucy appealed to the physician, who made no reply. Dr. Azziz then wheeled her chair close to Lucy.

"Lucy," she demanded, "are you Lord Cant's daughter?"

Lucy hung her head.

"Mr. Wickwright was a chandler, ma'am."

"Don't play that game with me, Lucy Wickwright," said the librarian. "I know you too well. Drunken guardsmen, indeed! I'm asking you whether Lord Cant was your natural father. Is that why he called you to his deathbed? Why he called for witnesses? Don't mumble, child!"

Lucy shrugged glumly. "Yes, ma'am," she said. "But I'd much rather Pauline became the Baroness."

The fire of heaped coals collapsed in a cloud of ashes. Lucy had closed her eyes, to rest them, for the hour was very late. She felt the librarian pick up her hand and hold it between her own. She looked up. Dr. Azziz gazed at her fondly, yet with a great depth of worry in her eyes.

"You poor child," she whispered.

Dr. Sauersop walked to the fire and dropped the manifesto upon it. The paper flared up, throwing the parlor's shadows into stark relief, and was quickly consumed. Sauersop turned to face Lucy, but before speaking he bowed his head, as though addressing a noble lady.

"As to Pauline's assuming the barony," he said, "I'm afraid

it's not a question of what you or she or any of us may wish. Ah, no. Ours is a land of tradition and of law. Plainly, Sir Henry intends to press your claim — for reasons of his own, I'm sure — and evidently he's enlisted the help of the Causists. This can't be swept under a rug, Miss Cant . . . er, excuse me, Miss Wickwright. We face perilous times. Am I to understand that you're in league with young Gutz? Where is he now?"

"I . . . I shouldn't say I'm in league with him, exactly," Lucy said. "I was able to do him a good turn. I'm told he's hiding at the American Mission, in Tenesmus. I hope to see him soon."

Sauersop returned again to the settee. He spoke solemnly.

"Lucy," he said, "I've known you only a short time, but from the first you struck me as a good girl. Dr. Azziz has since confirmed me in that opinion. We want to help you — it's for that reason we asked you to come here tonight. I beg you to place no great faith in Henry Wallow. He may be on the right side of tradition, but these provincial noblemen have always their own interests at heart. Nor, if you ask my counsel, should you become too entangled with young Mr. Gutz." He glanced at the fireplace, at the manifesto's ashes. "I support his Cause in its opposition to chewing gum, certainly. But Arden Gutz expresses himself rather too . . . er . . . *warmly* for my taste."

"But who *am* I to trust?" Lucy asked.

"Ah," said the old herald, "in the end, we mortals may have no one to trust but ourselves. Yet that brings more troubles than any trust in others. Orloff, now, is a man who believes in himself utterly, but I should be very sad to see you become like him."

"I . . . I don't know what to do, sir."

Sauersop looked at her tenderly, but said nothing. Dr. Azziz still held Lucy's hand in hers. She squeezed it now, as though to press her own store of courage into the faltering Maid of Cant.

"Lucy," she said, "your whole concern since you entered this chamber has been for your mistress. Other girls would have had themselves fitted for gowns and jewels by now, if anyone had offered them the barony. They would want a host of counselors, too, because those who care only for themselves should never trust their own judgment. But when you first care for others, your heart won't often mislead you, child. Trust that."

The castle's clocks struck one as Lucy walked down the tower stairs. At each landing a torch burned, and she stopped beneath one to rub and blow on her feet, which were frozen right through. Spring had brought warm days to the mountains and meadows of Cant, but the castle's stones thawed as slowly as blocks of ice, and the steps still held a winter chill.

Lucy was eager for a holiday from spy work, so Mr. Splint had accepted the duty of keeping their little conspiracy informed. As a respected physician he was ideally suited to take the pulse of the castle. His task was to discover which of the high officials and Privy Councilors stood with Orloff, and which might be counted upon to oppose him when the story of a maidservant's noble lineage became widely known.

To Dr. Azziz fell the task of unearthing all the edicts, decrees, and proclamations that dealt with the succession to the barony. Early in its history Cant had settled all such disputes with the sword, but in later times even its noble persons had seen the advantage of fighting with words rather than cutlery. The librarian would gather from her archives every document that touched upon the question of who should become the next Baroness of Cant.

As for Dr. Sauersop, he would go to Tenesmus and confer with Hock Tooey, Henry Wallow, and Arden Gutz. Lucy had assured him that her uncle was not a rash man, but Sauersop greatly feared that Sir Henry would get up to some kind of mischief. He offered no further opinion of Arden Gutz, but Lucy could not forget his dropping the manifesto on to the fire. The herald cautioned her to speak of their meeting to no one but Pauline and Blaise Delagraisse. The under-footman would be enlisted as a go-between.

"Master Delagraisse is fond of you, I think," Sauersop had added. "There is no harm in that. He may find me in my workshop, most days. We must consider the matter of your coat of arms, Miss Wickwright. I shall endeavor to sketch an agreeable design."

Like Dr. Sauersop, Lucy had had something up her sleeve at the meeting, but unlike him she had kept it hidden. Now she took out and unfolded Arden's note, which she had kept with her all day, and read countless times. It praised her "heroic and inestimable service" in retrieving the manifesto, and denounced Orloff in grand, difficult words. The political arguments she had skimmed over, but she had its concluding paragraphs almost by heart:

Undoubtedly you are anxious, little one, as to what further rôle you will play in our Cause, and indeed in our Barony. You may well imagine my surprise when Lu told me his belief that you are in fact the natural daughter of Adolphus! For my part, I believe that Fate led you to my prison, so that one who stands to inherit so great a power should not be without a Protector & Guide. 'I am but a common girl!' you will no doubt protest, 'How shall I lead a people?' Fear not, young Wickwright! If indeed you don the baronial cap (as is devoutly to be hoped), a wiser head than yours shall order the affairs of Cant, and a stronger arm rid it of Orloff and his corruptions! All I shall require of you is to cut ribbons, and preside at banquets, and comport yourself in a manner befitting a sovereign lady (and Miss Poke assures me that she can teach manners and grooming even to such an humble girl as yourself).

But I must bring this letter to its close, sweet Lucy, for time is of the essence. I urgently desire to see you at first opportunity. This will be difficult, for I dare not show my face in the castle. I beg you to come to the Mission if that be possible, but if you cannot I shall endeavor to steal into the castle. The Reverend Mr. Frodd possesses of a quantity of greasepaint (it being his custom, yearly on the Baron's anniversary, to entertain the orphans by dressing as a clown), and with it I can perhaps concoct a disguise, and so speak to you before the Baron's entombment.

Until I see you, little one, be brave! The sun is behind us!

Earnestly,
A.G.

Lucy had meant to show the note to Dr. Sauersop, but had changed her mind when he spoke slightingly of Arden. She did not think he would be pleased to know that Arden Gutz had proposed to serve as her regent, should she indeed assume the barony.

But was that what Arden had actually proposed? She read again, by torchlight, the words that caused her to doubt. *Sweet Lucy!* Could it be that Arden did not propose to serve as her regent, but had in mind a different proposal altogether? A personal, rather than a political, alliance? If life resembled a storybook, she thought, the beautiful young sovereign would be served not by a counselor, but by a wedded consort.

Sweet Lucy! She pictured Arden on his knee, asking for her hand, and the glitter and pomp of a court wedding, and the wonder and jealousy of those who had teased her, in her t-shirt and jeans, while they flaunted their fine uniforms and admired their bumpy figures in the glass. Of course it was silly, for she meant to let Pauline rule the Barony, and anyway Arden may have used those words in a strictly brotherly sense . . . but for a moment, as she pictured the fireworks and the sumptuous wedding feast, she forgot her frozen feet, and the blight of chewing gum, and her and Pauline's peril and the uncertain days ahead. She refolded the note and put it up her sleeve, then hurried back to her cot, flitting silent as a ghost through the halls of Castle Cant.

Sweet Lucy!

Chapter 22

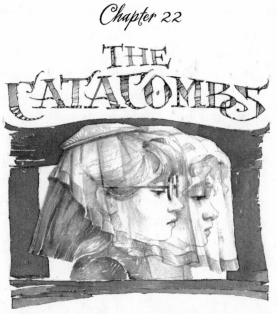

THE CATACOMBS

Castle Cant rose above a forest — a cold, sweating forest of
stonework. Dark groves of granite filled its cellars and vaults:
great hewn trunks that four men standing fingertip to fingertip
could scarcely encompass.

Among grown-ups only the wine stewards and coal-porters
often entered the catacombs, but they were not unknown to
others. For amidst the junk of twelve generations there were
treasures to be found — rat-scrabbled, dusty, forgotten things
that needed a child's eye to be seen. It seemed to Lucy that she
had spent as much time down there as in the upper floors of
the castle — playing hide-and-go-seek with Pauline, or sliding
in chain mail down the coal-chute, or digging curios from the
cellars' great seams of bric-a-brac. Both their lamps had run
dry together once, when they were playing there, and they had

found their way to the light by memory, hand in hand, twice blind but doubly determined.

Now Lucy's shoes pinched as she walked through the catacombs in a slow procession of torch-bearing guardsmen, snuffling mourners, and heavily perfumed courtiers. Before her went the bier of Adolphus, Lord Cant, borne by six struggling ministers in sweeping gray robes.* The air was thick with smoke and toilet water and the fumes of a censer that went before the bier. Behind Lucy and Pauline straggled a cortège of ministers and nobles, courtiers and commissioners, ladies, knights, squires and squirrels. All were daubed with ashes and dressed in gray, and somewhere among them walked Vladimir Orloff. Lucy felt his eyes on the back of her neck.

With Lord Cant dead there was no one, strictly speaking, in *charge* of Pauline. The Privy Council would convene to appoint a regent, who would govern the Barony in her name, and govern *her* in her father's memory. But by ancient custom the regency began only after the late Baron was entombed, and in the present interval (called the *interregnum*) Pauline was, in theory, the supreme authority of Castle and Barony. By her word of command she might have outlawed muffins, or declared war upon Indiana. But only this morning had she exercised her power — when, to general astonishment, she insisted that Lucy walk beside her in the funeral procession. Mr. Vole had been summoned by the flustered Minister of Ceremonies, who begged him to reason with the girl. Pauline sat up in bed, her chin resting on the head of a large bear whose button eyes

---

*Gray, rather than black, indicated mourning in Cant.

glared sullenly at an audience of maids, ministers, and men-servants.

"Your affection for this girl is entirely understandable, mistress," Vole had said (with a sidelong glance at Lucy in which she saw anything but understanding). "Indeed, it is becoming in a prince to love his subjects, as the Wise Teachers declare. But in matters of decorum, surely, we should take our direction from Sir Plinth."

Sir Plinth Paget-Plinth, the Minister of Ceremonies, stood a little apart from Mr. Vole. He had come to the bedchamber to instruct Pauline on the details of the funeral, and as the house-steward spoke he arranged and smoothed his gown with nervous, well-manicured hands. He now stepped forward and smiled weakly at Vole.

"Truly well spoken," he said. "But say rather that we should take our direction from the immemorial practices of the House of Cant, of which I am but the humblest steward. To me falls the keeping of its rituals, rubrics, and observances. Now, the order of the funeral cortège is of great antiquity, being indeed unchanged since the time of Gustaf I, popularly termed 'the Fey.' Immediately behind the bier walk, in order, the widow, the children, and the near kinsmen of His Late Lordship. Lady Cant having preceded His Lordship in death, however . . ."

"Lucy shall walk with me," Pauline said stubbornly. Since the arrival of Vole she had refused to meet any eye, though her bedchamber was so crowded that a face stared back at her almost anywhere she looked. In addition to Vole and Paget-Plinth there were two seamstresses waiting to fit Pauline into her mourning dress (which, like a third member of their party, stood between them on a dressmaker's dummy). The Misses Prunella and Estrella Guuzi, who held the title "Ladies-in-Waiting," slumped on a settee by the fireplace, wearing the bored, stoic expressions they always adopted when forced to attend Pauline. The hairdresser chewed his fingers in a corner, eyes darting anxiously from the mantel clock to Pauline's matted, unwashed hair, while his assistant attempted to soothe him by massaging his neck. Two members of the Privy Council had arrived with Paget-Plinth, for reasons unexplained, and the maid Helen, having hauled up water for Pauline's bath, stood with her empty pails in the middle of the room, too timid to ask the noble folk to make a path for her. And then there was Lucy, the stumbling-block, who sat on a hard chair at the bedside and stared at the floor.

"With all respect, mistress," Vole said, unable now to keep the starch from his voice, "it will hardly serve His Lordship's memory to be followed to his tomb by a common maid-servant!"

Pauline glared at him.

"You speak to me about servants!" she said. "May I remind you that *you* are a servant, Vole? To say nothing of 'common'!"

"If I may interject . . . ," began Sir Plinth.

"I humbly beg your pardon, mistress," said Vole. "But —"

"Don't *mistress* me!" Pauline's voice rose to a shriek, and Lucy recognized the beginnings of a tantrum. "If you insist on believing I am the Baroness of Cant, MISTER Vole, you will address me as 'my Lady' or 'Ma'am'!"

"Indeed that is fitting, my Lady!" Plinth said, stepping between Vole and Pauline and raising his hands, as though to keep them from each other's throats. "But if I may put forward a modest suggestion? I had already recruited a lad to carry the censer before His Lordship's bier, but I know of no injunction against a girl-child filling that office. In this way —"

"*No!*" Pauline stood on the bed and heaved her bear at the startled Minister of Ceremonies, who had just wits enough about him to catch it by a forepaw. "She will *not* carry the stupid censer! Lucy walks with me, or I shan't *be* in your stupid parade!"

"*Cortège,* my Lady," corrected Plinth.

"*Stupid!*" said Pauline. She began to run in circles on the bed-clothes. "Stupid stupid stupid stupid stupid STUPID!"

Everyone — even the jaded Misses Guuzi — gaped at this performance, and Lucy took the opportunity to slide beneath the bed a platter of crumbs, which had been sitting on the bed-side table. Pauline's appetite had returned with a vengeance that morning, and Lucy had watched with mounting anxiety as her mistress consumed half a dozen sticky buns and a pot of strong black tea. It had been only a matter of time before the sugar took effect. Lucy almost felt sorry for Sir Plinth and Mr. Vole. The house-steward now stepped forward.

"My Lady," he said, in a voice so sharply creased it could have sliced fresh crumpets, "as steward of this house I have a responsibility to uphold its dignity. I cannot allow a raga-muffin upstart to tramp behind His Lordship's bier . . . in that ridiculous . . . *vest!*"

By "vest" Vole meant the GIZMOBOTS! shirt (for he was an old-fashioned man and never uttered what he called "outlandish barbarianisms," such as *t-shirt*). By "ragamuffin upstart," Lucy knew, he could only mean *her*. Pauline stopped her galloping around the bed and, clinging to a bedpost, lifted her head.

"Guard!" she cried. "Fire! Treason! Impertinence! Guard! Guard!"

A hurried *patter-flop* of sandals came from the doorway, followed by two bewildered guardsmen clutching the hilts of their swords. Pauline picked up one of the many pillows on her bed and threw it at Vole.

"Behead that man!" she demanded.

The guards looked anxiously toward the Privy Councilors, who seemed to be the highest-ranking grown-ups present (and who had frowned when Pauline said, *If you insist on believing I am the Baroness of Cant . . .*). Sir Plinth Paget-Plinth tut-tutted, and lifted an indulgent smile to Pauline.

"Surely that is unreasonably harsh, my Lady?" he said.

FLOOF! A pillow struck him in the face.

"Off with his head!" shouted Pauline. She leapt up and down on the bed, her bare feet making craters in the feather mattress. "Heads shall roll! Heads shall roll!"

Lucy stood up, afraid that Pauline might fall and hurt herself. At the same time Mr. Vole approached the bed, livid with rage. He grabbed Pauline by the wrist and shook her.

"You will stop this nonsense at once!" he said.

Scarcely had the words left his lips when sharp steel flashed from the guardsmen's scabbards. In a single bound they were at Vole's side. A hand seized his neck, and the keen point of a sword hovered an inch from his throat. Vole blanched. A gasp went up from the seamstresses, the hairdresser, and his assistant. One of the Misses Guuzi frankly squeaked.

"Please to unhand the Lady, sir," the senior guardsman calmly said.

Vole loosed his grip, and Pauline fell to the mattress. Lucy helped her mistress to sit up, glaring at Vole when she saw the red marks on Pauline's wrist. Pauline, her lip trembling, pressed her cheek to Lucy's t-shirt. A Privy Councilor stepped forward and laid a hand on Sir Plinth's arm.

"Surely an exception can be made to the protocols of the funeral cortège," he said.

"P-p-perhaps," stammered Mr. Vole, before Sir Plinth could answer, "if the girl were suitably costumed . . ."

"A-herm!" coughed Paget-Plinth. "Well, certainly the desires of a sitting Baroness must come before the dictates of . . . of . . ."

He gulped.

". . . mere *tradition*."

"Splendid," said the Councilor. "We mustn't become hidebound, after all. Have you a suitable dress, little girl?" he asked Lucy.

"I shall give her a dress," said Pauline. She looked up at the house-steward, her voice breaking. "That was perfectly beastly, Vole."

"My Lady, forgive me!" Vole said, making such a bow as the nearness of the guardsman's sword allowed. He blushed deeply. "His Lordship's passing, you understand, has caused a great strain upon my nerves . . ."

"What would you have us do with him, Ma'am?" the elder guardsman asked.

Pauline began to snuffle. Lucy smoothed her mistress's hair, and looked crossly at the Minister of Ceremonies.

"I think all of you should go, and let my mistress have her

bath," she said. "I should think you'd have some consideration for a poor orphaned girl."

Paget-Plinth exchanged a glance with the Privy Councilor. The latter nodded to the guardsmen. Mr. Vole was released and, bowing deeply to Pauline, he hurried from the room. The hairdresser and his assistant, the seamstresses, the Misses Guuzi, and Helen followed. The guardsmen returned to their posts, and finally the noble persons bowed and made their exits. When the door had closed behind them, Pauline looked up at Lucy.

"Whatever are we going to do?" she asked.

It was a simple question, Lucy thought — or a very complicated one. When Pauline had learned of Orloff's vile influence upon her father, and his cold-blooded murder of Lucy's family, she had decided that he must at all costs be kept from the regency. Lucy should be the Baroness of Cant, she now declared — it was only fair, as she was the elder — and, for her part, Pauline should like to be Poet Laureate. But how they were to bring this about — with no evidence of her father's last wishes, and with most of the Privy Council dependent upon Orloff's gum and under his influence — this they had not discussed. Having no answer for the complicated question, Lucy very sensibly dealt with the simple one.

"I think," she said, "we should get you into your bath."

So it was that, some hours later, Lucy walked beside Pauline in the funeral cortège, her twelve toes crammed into shoes that were meant for ten. She and Pauline were much the same size, so the purple dress fitted tolerably well, but Pauline's feet were shorter than hers as well as one toe narrower, and the slow procession to the crypt was a pinching agony to Lucy. The bier pitched and yawed before her, the ministers who bore it unused to lifting anything heavier than a bribe or a piece of gum. Adolphus seemed even larger in death than in life. The plain sheet that covered him rose like a pillowy mountain above the bier.

The cortège wound through the gloomy underneath of the castle, coming at last to the ancestral crypt of the House of Cant. Beneath the fell runes graven on its doors stood images of the Wolves of Rotwood, here depicted as the Guardians of the Pockets of the Dead. Tybold Retsch, who had marched ahead of the incense-bearer with a number of swordsmen, now went forward and turned the iron key. He pulled open the great bronze doors, then faced about and addressed himself to the shrouded figure upon the bier.

"Enter, my Lord, the House of Never-Leaving!" he cried.

"And Sleep with the Dust of Thy Fathers!" came the response (from those mourners who had followed Adolphus's father to his tomb, and remembered the ancient ritual).

The swordsmen now took charge of the bier. Beyond the doors two galleries stretched ahead, their marble façades hewn with every flower of the stone-carver's imagination: volutes and dentils, triglyphs and acroteria, rosettes and astragals — all the tongue-numbing terms of the classical orders, as sweet to the eye as they were clumsy in the mouth. Here, behind epitaphs in Greek and Latin, slept ten generations of the House of Cant. To Lucy, glimpsing the curlicues of marble by the light of torches, the necropolis seemed a city made of sugar-icing. She trembled to imagine the fat flies feasting in the tombs.

Between these galleries a stair led to a deeper excavation, to which the swordsmen now carried the listing bier. Here lay Lord Urbano and his wife, and Pauline's mother, Esmeralda. Adolphus's tomb, begun some fifteen years before, was still unfinished, and except for it and the Doric façade of his father's sepulcher the walls were of living granite, and sweated. Six more generations of the house must rise and fall to fill them, and then they would become galleries in their turn, overlooking still deeper tombs.

At the bottom of the stairs the noble pallbearers took the bier back from the swordsmen and carried it to a pair of wooden horses. Lucy took Pauline's arm as they went down, for she could barely see through her stifling, itchy veil (behind which her glasses had fogged), and she was unused to walking in anything but sneakers. They took their places beside the bier and waited for the rest of the cortège. Vlad Orloff, walking at the rear, stared so intently and with such malice at Lucy that he nearly lost his footing on the steps.

Those who carried torches put them in brackets on the walls. The crypt was close and airless, and soon became hot. Though there seemed to be ample room in the lower crypt, several of the mourners had stationed themselves on the galleries overhead. They wore loose, flowing cloaks, and one of them, Lucy noticed, kept a hood over his face, despite the great heat. His features seemed strangely pale, though it was hard to see in the shadows.

Now an old man mounted a dais. This was Sir Virgil Fallow, Minister of Dead Tongues, to whose office fell, by immemorial custom, the honor of speaking the funeral oration. Lucy steeled herself for the ordeal. How she hated speeches! One would think a funeral a sufficiently depressing occasion without the added torment of oratory. A bead of sweat fell on a lens of her glasses.

The speech was even worse than she feared. It was given entirely in ancient Greek, and — to add insult to injury — Sir Virgil delivered it in a murmury mumble like the buzzing of numberless bees. He spoke from notes, and Lucy was dismayed to see several pages of them trembling in his hands.

When the first tendril of sweat inched down her ribs she thought of snow, and mint, and other cool things. She grew terribly sleepy. She gazed at the marble of the upper tombs and imagined pressing her cheeks to the crisp white stone. The men up there seemed as bored as she was by the eulogy. They signaled to one another, and moved about in the shadows thrown by the torches. One man's cloak came partly open as he walked, and Lucy had the absurd notion that she glimpsed an archer's bow beneath it.

She took a sharp breath, and suddenly was no longer drowsy. Why had none of the men in the galleries thrown back their heavy cloaks in this terrible heat? She looked at Tybold Retsch. The captain of the guard was struggling to keep his eyes open, and his swordsmen drowsed where they stood. Lucy lifted her veil and peered intently at the cloaked men. It was hard to see through her fogged glasses, but they seemed malshapen, like a troupe of hunchbacks. With a sudden chill she realized they carried quivers beneath their cloaks. Bowmen!

Lucy tried to catch Tybold Retsch's eye by waving her hand in desperate little circles (so as not to distract Sir Virgil from his oratory). The captain of the guard, staring blankly into space, stifled a yawn. But, glancing toward the stairs, Lucy saw Vladimir Orloff moving toward Retsch — he, too, had spotted the intruders. One of the bowmen marked him, and hissed a warning at the hooded man, evidently their leader. The latter lifted his arm.

"Now!" he shouted, bringing down his hand with a flourish.

BOOM! The bronze doors of the crypt crashed shut. The intruders threw off their cloaks and fitted arrows to their bowstrings, sighting down their shafts at the astonished swordsmen of the guard. A pair of bowmen took the stairs, cutting off the only means of escape. The collective gasp of the crowd gave way to a frantic babble peppered with snatches of ancient Greek. Lucy, her heart pounding, stepped closer to Pauline. The hooded man stood at the edge of the gallery.

"The tyranny of cud is ended!" he cried, lifting his arms in triumph. Lucy's heart sank. She recognized that voice.

"Gutz!" shouted Vlad Orloff.

Arden Gutz threw back the hood of his cloak, and Lucy felt she must surely be sick. Her champion had covered his face in greasepaint, clown-wise, to throw off the sentries at the gatehouse. The paint had melted in the terrible heat, and now his eyes were black wilted flowers, his mouth a grinning wound. His voice, so earnestly appealing in the dungeon, had become a lunatic caw. Such is the fate of revolutionists. Arden Gutz, so handsome in defeat, had become horribly ugly in victory.

"Like rats in a trap!" he crowed, pacing the verge of the gallery. "You are at my mercy, Orloff! The people have thrown off their yokes! No longer will they buy the contentment of nobles with their labor and sweat! Nor shall they allow a *pretender* . . . your *puppet!* . . . to inherit the Barony of Cant!"

He drew a sword and pointed it squarely at Pauline, but Lucy felt he had thrust it through her own heart. She opened her mouth — to scream, to protest, to denounce the Cause — but no word came out. Pauline stepped back, bewildered by the venom of this furious clown. Lucy caught her arm.

"Guards!" said Tybold Retsch, rousing himself at last. His swordsmen made a half-circle of flashing steel to protect Pauline and Lucy, who stood with their backs to the bier. Pauline's face had gone white behind her veil. She gaped at her former maid, and spoke in a tremulous whisper.

"Have you tricked me, Lucy?"

"Mistress, no! Forgive me! I didn't . . ."

"Order your men to lay down their weapons, Gutz!" said Tybold Retsch. "You may yet escape with your life if you surrender now. Can you be so mad as to believe that the people of Cant will support your . . . your . . . vile *effrontery?*"

"He is not mad," came another voice. All heads swung round to the other gallery, where an ill-favored man with a squint to his eye had emerged from the shadows. "He is not mad, nor is he alone. We have already taken the gatehouse — indeed, by now our supporters have filled the bailey. It is you who will be lucky to escape alive, Captain Lickspittle!"

Retsch drew his sword, but he had to choke his wrath. A dry voice cut off his reply.

"Ah, I heard that you had trotted our way, Henry Wallow," said Vlad Orloff. The Postal Commissioner stood at his ease in the frightened crowd, gazing up at the renegades, a wattle of flesh quivering from his stubborn jaw. "Have you come all this way, Sir Henry," he asked, "to fall under the spell of a lunatic? Or merely to enjoy the hospitality of our dungeons?"

"I shall escort you and that vile moppet to the dungeons, Orloff," Wallow said, "for conspiring to usurp the privileges of the rightful Baroness of Cant."

Tybold Retsch found his voice.

"Who lays a hand on Miss Cant will never lift his hand again!" he warned.

"Seize the pretender!" cried Arden Gutz. Retsch's swordsmen tensed, expecting the rebels to charge the stairs, but the attack came from behind. Lucy saw it first, and screamed — for Lord Cant seemed to be rising from the dead. The white pall flew from the bier, and in a shower of pillows a man leapt down from it. The renegades had stolen Adolphus's body, and put one of their own in its place. The counterfeit baron seized Pauline bodily, pinning her arms to her sides, and held to her neck a dagger with a terrible shining blade. Strong men squealed, and ladies uttered black oaths. Retsch's swordsmen faced about and held their blades to the ready.

"Make way!" the rebel said. "I'll slit her throat as pretty as you please!"

"Let me go!" cried Pauline. She kicked furiously at the man's shins, but he wore stout leather gaiters, as though he had anticipated such a strategy. The renegades had, in fact, planned everything perfectly, and this fact was not lost on Tybold Retsch. He considered the situation — his swords outmanned by a superior force of bowmen on higher ground; Pauline held hostage; the enemy holding the only means of escape — and he grimly sheathed his sword.

"Fall back!" he ordered. "Let them go."

"No!" Pauline screamed, wiggling and kicking desperately. "Fight them, Retsch!"

Lucy had been scanning the galleries, on the hopeless chance her Uncle Hock might be among the bowmen. He would put a stop to this. But of course he was not there — he would never have consented to the use of arms in the first place. The guardsmen fell back, and Pauline's captor ran with her to the stairs, the crowd parting before him. A confederate pushed open the door, and the rebel escaped with Pauline. Lucy, pushing between two guardsmen, ran after them.

"Unhand her!" she called. "Unhand her! I command it!" For it had occurred to her that Wallow's forces meant to win *her* the rule of the Barony. Surely his men must obey her!

But Lucy was unused to wearing dresses and running in shoes with heels, and before she had gone a dozen paces she fell. She skidded across the stone floor and came to rest at Orloff's feet. The Postal Commissioner stooped and seized her arm in his bony claw. He pulled her face to within inches of his, so that she saw the pink-veined yellow of his eyes above his ashen cheeks. A tendril of saliva swung from his lip.

"You were hiding in my cupboard, weren't you, little rat-girl?" he hissed. "I was twice a fool not to have dealt with you then — but you'll not escape me again!"

He raised his hand to slap her, but before Lucy could even close her eyes against the blow something astonishing happened: Vladimir Orloff sprouted an arrow. The fletched end branched from his nape like a twig that had budded feathers. The pointed end protruded from his throat, and where it met his skin a sap of blue-red blood oozed. Lucy looked up to the gallery. One of Wallow's men gazed back at her, his drawing fingers pointed at Orloff's neck, his string still quivering between the nocks of his bow.

"Oh!" said Orloff. Even that small word bubbled in his throat. He sat down heavily, and Lucy, breaking free, raced up the stairs after Pauline. Riot had broken out in the crypt. The captains shouted orders above the melee as the swordsmen pushed their way through the panicked horde. Lucy had almost reached the doors when another hand seized her and swung her round. It was Arden Gutz. His clown face dripped with exultation.

"We've won, my puppet! . . . I mean, we've won, my poppet!" he cried.

"Let me go!" said Lucy. "What have you done with Pauline?"

"Never mind her!" said Gutz. "She'll find the dungeon no less hospitable than I did. She can't —"

Lucy tried to pull free, but Gutz had got both her arms in his hands.

"She can't be allowed to rally her forces, my little soldier!" he said, shaking her. "Listen to me, Lucy! You've served the Cause well, and you shall be our Baroness. But you mustn't meddle in things above you!"

Lucy clamped her eyes shut. She felt they must burst with tears otherwise, and she would not have Gutz see her cry. She mastered herself, breathed deeply, and glared at her former comrade.

"I *hate* you!" she cried.

Her uncle's charm had fallen out in her struggle to get free, and swung from her neck on its leather thong. She remembered his words of advice, and his trick for "letting the steam out of any man's kettle." Lucy was not ordinarily a girl for fighting, but there was a saying in Cant that *tough meat calls for sharp knives.* So she brought her knee up swiftly between Arden Gutz's legs and, just as Uncle Hock had promised, he dropped to his knees with a sharp *phwee!* of escaping breath.

Lucy stepped away. She barely heard the twang of bow-strings and the clash of swords all about her. Her lip trembled, for she knew she had been used by Gutz, who looked up at her in pain and bewilderment. The hideous greasepaint, she saw, was the true complexion of his Cause. The handsome face of the prisoner had been its disguise.

"You're just another grown-up," she said, choking on the words. "You're just like all the rest!"

She turned on her heel, left him there, and went running after Pauline.

Chapter 23

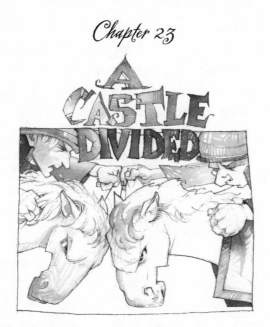

𝒯he "Lucine" party held most of the castle, under the general-ship and standard of Sir Henry Wallow.* His forces, drawn largely from the disgruntled townsfolk of Tenesmus, had grown by way of defections from the "Paulinine," or Loyalist, party. Among the turncoats were some who simply wanted to be on the winning side — such is the loyalty of a prince's court — but there were others who, though they perhaps despised Wallow and Arden Gutz, had accepted the facts of Lucy's birth.

The Loyalists held only the baronial residence and one tower, and their leader lay abed with an arrow through his neck. Orloff had survived, but with the dart lodged so close to

---

*His arms were vert an orle sable a sow and suckling piglets or (a gold pig and piglets on a green and black ground).

various arteries, nerves, and vertebræ that the doctors dared not remove it. His captain, Tybold Retsch, was hard-pressed to hold even the residence, for he lacked enough troops to guard the countless corridors, passageways, and stairs that afforded points of attack to the Renegades (as the Loyalists termed the Lucine party). Some corridors he had blocked with piles of furniture, while others had sulking servant-girls as sentries, pressed into duty under threat of going without their suppers.

Criers on horseback had sped word of the uprising to the far reaches of Cant, sometimes overtaking those earlier riders who bore news of Adolphus's death. The denizens of Haslet March and Trans-Poltroon mourned Lord Cant with loud wailing and ashes — and calculated the benefit to themselves of a change in régime. For years the tithes on their cornfields, pastures, and fisheries had supported the gum-chewing of nobles. Now plain self-interest — aided, no doubt, by provincial resentment of "those fancy folk away in the castle" — argued powerfully for throwing in their lot with the Renegades.

Doomsayers predicted civil war. With the exception of Tenesmus, the lands along the North Road from the castle to the frontier at Fort Gustaf remained loyal to the House of Cant. Away over on the other side of the Barony, La Provence, too, scorned the Cause, because Pauline was a Provençale by blood, and the region would surely prosper should the grandchild of Gaspard Simone-Thierry inherit the baronial cap.

But Pauline had been tried — and found guilty — of Treason, Despotism, and Fraud. Arden Gutz (who now called himself the "August Provisional Regent to Lucy, Lady Wickwright") had signed a Decree of Banishment. It condemned "that most foul and pernicious Pretender" (Pauline) to be exiled, nevermore to return to the Barony of Cant.

For the present, however, she remained in the dungeon. She could not be exiled save by way of the North Road, which ran through Loyalist territory, and Sir Henry dared not withdraw troops from the occupation of the castle to escort the prisoner. There would be time for that later, when the castle was secured and the new Baroness capitalized.*

Indeed, the Lucine cause seemed destined to triumph but for one troubling fact — its Baroness was nowhere to be found. An ongoing search had failed to flush Lucy out, and Arden Gutz had grown desperate. On the evening of the fourth day he climbed to Lemonjello's aerie.

"It seems Commissioner Orloff's days are numbered," the astronomer said, after the old conspirators had exchanged greetings and news. "But I'm frankly troubled, Arden, by the . . . ah . . . er . . . severity of your measures. Our goal, I thought, was to rid the Barony of the plague of chewing gum. Can we not accomplish that without sending a poor girl into exile?"

Gutz was resolute. He had taken to wearing a guardsman's tunic, and a scabbard hung from a belt round his waist.

"The diseased plant must be torn up root, bole, and branch," he said. "The new Baroness could never be secure with a pretender at liberty in her realm."

"But but but you've not *got* a new Baroness," said Lemonjello, plucking nervously at his robe. "She's gone missing, I heard."

---

*That is, invested with the baronial cap (as in the coronation of crowned heads of state).

Arden Gutz rose from his seat on the desk and joined the astronomer on his narrow, untidy bed. He laid his hand on Lemonjello's, and spoke in an intimate, beseeching voice.

"That's where I need your help, old friend," he said. "These girls were playmates of a sort, I gather, despite the difference in their ranks. Indeed, I'm told they at least once came here together, and looked through your telescope. You were friendly with the prisoner . . . that is, with Miss Cant, were you not?"

"She was not responsible for her father's crimes, or those of Orloff," Lemonjello said. "Miss Cant was a good and charming young lady, if rather too . . . um . . . energetic for some tastes. Yes, I was friendly with her, draining though her visits were." He looked in Gutz's eye. "And Miss Wickwright — or Lady Wickwright, if you like — she was very fond of her, too."

"I must find her, Luigi," said Gutz. "I must find Lucy. They were a regular pair of rats, according to what her uncle told me, always nosing about in the cellars and attics, playing hide-and-go-seek and such games. Miss Cant surely knows her secret places. I want you to visit our prisoner, Luigi. She'll trust you. Find out where Lucy may be hiding."

Lemonjello stood. He opened a door of the wardrobe, peered into it through his thick glasses, then took down a nightcap from the upper shelf and closed the door. He tugged the cap over his black curls and smiled apologetically at Gutz.

"Bit of a nip in the air," he explained. He walked to his parrot's cage and wagged a finger through its bars.

"*Hok!*" cried the bird.

"What of this uncle, by the way?" Lemonjello asked, peering at the parrot. "Miss Wickwright's uncle. Is he one of us?"

"What, Tooey?" said Gutz. "No — well, yes, in a sense, but

I've had to dismiss him, and Lu as well. Neither of them had much fiber. Naïve, of course, like so many Cantlings. No sense of politics. I was telling Apryl just the other day, we could learn a good deal from the Americans, here in Cant. They are a progressive, practical race. But will you help me, Luigi? Will you see the girl?"

"Americans?" said Lemonjello. "I hope you're not developing . . . er . . . ah . . . republican sympathies, Arden. I've no objection to Lucy Wickwright donning the cap, but I won't bow my knee to a president!"

"Trust me, Luigi! Will you do as I ask?"

"Why, certainly," the astronomer said. "I should welcome a chance to talk to Miss Cant."

"Excellent," said Arden Gutz, rising from the bed. "I'll leave you to your planets, then. Be sure to find where Lucy may be hiding, old friend. Victory is in our grasp!"

Lemonjello lifted the door for his guest.

"Indeed. That's all to the good, I suppose. Good night, Arden."

"It is what we have worked for," Gutz said, climbing down. "The sun is behind us!"

"*Rawt!*" cried the parrot.

The astronomer closed the door.

"It is behind us indeed," he murmured, "but does it rise, or set?" In a louder voice he added, "Well, he's gone. You may come out now."

The door of the wardrobe swung open. A pair of sneakers emerged, followed by the stiffly stretching body of the girl who wore them. Lucy stood and rubbed her backside, a wounded expression on her face.

"You certainly have a great muddle of boots in your wardrobe!" she said.

Lemonjello looked down at his stockinged feet.

"Ah. Well. You see, it's because I never wear them," he explained. "I've nowhere else to put them. You, um, heard everything, I take it?"

Lucy sat on the bed and nodded.

"Dr. Sauersop is right," she said. "Pauline must be got to La Provence. She'll be safe with her grandfather. It's the only solution."

Lemonjello took a coin bank from the dresser. He opened the parrot's cage and poured birdseed from the bank into its feeding cup.

"There is an alternative," he said. "Should you accept the baronial cap, that is. You would not strictly *rule*, of course, until your twenty-first birthday . . . but . . . you would surely have some influence upon your regent, I should think. You might have Miss Cant's sentence reduced."

Lucy shook her head. "That horrid *Gutz* calls himself the 'provisional regent,'" she said. "And if it's not he, it may well be Wallow, or Guuzi, or someone even worse. No. I won't be Baroness if it means taking orders from a regent. And who is Apryl?"

"Eh?" said Lemonjello. "What's that?"

"That horrid Gutz mentioned someone named Apryl."

"Oh!" The astronomer blushed. "Ha! Er, well now. Yes. Erm. I believe the lady in question is Arden's consort, frankly speaking. The American woman. From the Mission."

Lucy's mouth fell open.

"Miss *Poke?*" she squealed.

"Er, yes, Apryl Poke is the name, I believe."

Lucy flew from the bed. She stamped her foot on the dusty floorboards.

"I will *not* have a consort I mean a regent!" she said. "I *won't!* I am taking Pauline to her family in La Provence. The people will have to get along without a baroness!"

Ptolemy fluttered in his cage. The astronomer giggled nervously and cleared his throat.

"Miss Cant remains behind bars," he reminded her. "That that that presents a difficulty."

"I've been considering that," Lucy said, pacing the cramped apartment. "I shall want a knapsack. And traveling clothes for Pauline. Candles would be helpful. Have you a roomy cape, Luigi? Or can you obtain one?"

"Why why yes, I believe I can," said the astonished astronomer. "But what do you propose? How —"

"I've a plan," said Lucy, with an appraising glance at the timid scientist. "How much weight can you carry?"

Lemonjello looked doubtfully at his skinny ankles, round which his stockings had fallen.

"*Och!*" cried the parrot.

Lucy had chased Pauline's captor through the catacombs and cellars, falling twice from her borrowed heels before kicking them off and continuing barefoot. That proved a mistake, for her quarry soon climbed the steps of a flanking tower and set off across the rock-strewn ward. Lucy clenched her jaw and charged on, the sharp flints biting and tearing her feet, but in the end her courage was in vain. The gatehouse was surrounded by Wallow's men, who sent up a great glad shout when the struggling Pauline was carried inside. Lucy veered away and climbed halfway up a corner tower before sitting to catch her breath, her trail marked in blood on the steps below.

She took off her dress, when she had recovered, tearing it with her teeth and hands to make bandages for her mangled feet. Then, wearing only her (that is, Pauline's) slip, she climbed to the parapet walk. Crouching low, so as not to be seen from the courtyard, she hobbled back to the castle keep and up to the servant's garret. This was risky, but she could not go about without clothes and proper shoes. By good fortune no one came to look for her until she had gone.

Since then she had been a ghost in Castle Cant — imagined in the corners of eyes, heard behind walls, scented but unseen. A woman would rise from her tea, close a shutter, and return to discover the biscuits gone from her plate. Jars of milk seemed to walk out of kitchens, pies to take wing from window-sills. *She's holed up in the old armory,* swore one old footman, and *She's disguised as a milliner in Great Pillow,* claimed a young maid. But no one saw Lucy save her trusted allies, who took it in turns to harbor the fugitive.

She might have lived thus a long time, for at Pauline's side she had discovered all the castle's deep and secret ways. They had explored them in their games and hijinks, on bored rainy days and stifling sunny ones, running from trouble or racing toward it, giggling or sober, speaking or silent, together or . . . well, always together. She noticed it only now that she was alone. They had always been together, from the moment Mr.

Vole had presented Lucy to her mistress and Pauline asked what on Earth a "rick-wight" was. And if her mistress must go into exile, Lucy would not stay behind. They would leave the castle together.

She worked out the details of a plan as she lay curled under the stars that night, beside the astronomer's telescope. Blaise Delagraisse could find a knapsack, and Jane Cedilla some clothes for Pauline — Lucy would provide the key to her wardrobes. Lemonjello had assured her he could acquire a cape, and even overcome his fear of descending the staircase. Lucy would have to measure the astronomer's stride, and her own, and find grease for the bobsled, and candles, and a stout pair of braces. . . .

When she had gone twice over all the details she took off her glasses and pulled her blanket up to her chin. There would be all the leagues of Cant to cross after she rescued Pauline, but that problem could be dealt with later. Oh, but she wanted a map! Ask Dr. Azziz to find a map, she thought. She put it on the list in her head, between "Delagraisse: knapsack," and "Pantry: grease." Ask Dr. Azziz for a map, she repeated, engraving it on her memory. Ask Azziz for map. Ask Azziz for map.

The stars wheeled slowly overhead. Wolves trotted from the eaves of Rotwood to hunt for sheep on the hillsides, pastures, and plains. Owls scoured the meadows for mice, hungry foxes sniffed the air, and Wallow's sentries patrolled the ward and the parapet walks. The moon rose and threw its light on all these things and on the pale, determined face of a spy, asleep on a tower of Castle Cant.

$\mathscr{T}$he candles had been lit, the runners greased, the sums checked and rechecked. The plan stood every chance of success, if only Mr. Lemonjello could persevere to the dungeon. He leaned heavily on his cane and wiped his brow with the back of his hand. The day had been hot, and even now, with the sun fallen beyond the western mountains, the air was close and sticky. His breathing was labored as he approached the gatehouse, outside which two sentries were playing at a game of mumblety-peg. The man about to throw glanced up, the knife's blade pinched between his fingers.

"Here, what are you about?" he demanded. His rustic accent marked him as one of Wallow's men, but he had somewhere acquired the flat, broad helmet of the Baronial Guard.

"I've come to see Miss Cant," said the astronomer. "I am Luigi Lemonjello."

"Go on, fatty," the man sneered. "No visitors. Off with you!"

"No, that's right," said the other man. He was older, and evidently the superior officer. "Lemonjello, aye. Gutz approved it. Put away that toy, Tim, and take the gentleman down."

"Here, why don't you take him down?" Tim asked. "I'm throwing, Tom."

"'Cause I'm the boss, you weeping bedsore!" growled Tom. "Move!"

Grumbling, Tim led the astronomer into the gatehouse, where he lit one candle and put a second, unlighted, into his pocket. He squinted at Lemonjello, then pulled back the astronomer's heavy cape. He scowled at the black robe underneath.

"A great lot of clothes for a hot day," he said.

"I've been ill," Lemonjello explained. "Er . . . gout, you know."

"Well, come on, then."

Lemonjello lumbered down the stairs with difficulty, supported by his cane and a hand on the wall. The sentry waited impatiently at the bottom. The astronomer made better progress in the level passage, but when he came to the low granite lintel — the beloved device of Lucy's first guide to the dungeons — he was forced to one knee, and he nearly toppled as he passed beneath it. The sentry pulled him to his feet.

"You ought to lay off the heavy sauces, mate," he said. "My grandda turned blue and croaked, carrying that kind of lardage."

"I hope to lose this weight very soon!" the astronomer gasped.

A few minutes later they came to the cell. When Lemonjello had mopped his streaming face with a handkerchief, Tim lighted the second candle and handed it to him.

"I'll wait outside," he said, turning the key. "Give out a holler when you've done."

The door swung open. Lemonjello tottered in, and the sentry shut the door behind him. The keys jangled and the bolt shot *clank!* Pauline sat on a pallet against the far wall, her knees drawn up, her head resting on her arms. She still wore her mourning dress (now a mass of wrinkles), and her hair hung in lank, unwashed tendrils. At the sound of the bolt she looked up, blinking at the candle's light.

"Why, Lemonjello," she said in a weary voice. "You've gone all fat. How good of you to come."

"The August Provisional Regent was kind enough to grant his leave," said the astronomer. He held a *shush*-ing finger to his lips, and rolled his eyes toward the cell door. Pauline nodded. Lemonjello then stepped beside the door, where he could not be seen through the grate, and rested his cane against the wall. "I thought," he said, opening his cape, "that you might welcome some company."

"Yes, I've been awfully dull." Pauline got up from her pallet, for her visitor had held out his candle and nodded meaningly at it. She crossed the cell and took it from him, though obviously baffled by the astronomer's behavior.

"I brought a book," said Lemonjello. He began to pull up his robe, scrunching it in his hands as he lifted it. He wore a long nightshirt underneath. "A story, I thought, might take Miss Cant's mind off her present misfortunes."

"A story," the prisoner echoed. The astronomer pulled his robe higher and higher, and Pauline, her jaw falling, discovered how he had put on so much weight so quickly. He had strapped a girl to himself. She hung from a sort of holster made from an old pair of braces, her limbs wrapped round the skinny scientist, her head buried in his concave chest. Lemonjello unhooked the straps and Lucy climbed gingerly down, stretching a cramp from her leg. She held a book — its dust jacket promised *Tales to Terrify Tots* — but when she opened it there was only plain handwriting on the first page. She held it out to Pauline.

I've come to rescue you!

it said. She turned the page.

Lemonjello will tell a story while I explain the plan.

Pauline nodded. Her chin trembled. Her eyes glittered in the candlelight, and Lucy was afraid she would blubber (and start her to blubbering, too). Lucy took a pencil from behind her ear and wrote furiously.

Don't! The guard will hear! Time to cry later.

Pauline bit her lip. She shook her head up and down, and snatched the pencil from Lucy.

I thought you had betrayed me!

she wrote. Lucy took the pencil back, and almost broke its point with the force of her punctuation.

Never!

"Er, very well then," said Lemonjello, as Pauline threw her arms around Lucy and kissed her many times. "A story. Well. Once upon a time, it appears, there were two little . . . er . . . what do you call them . . . ah . . . marionettes! Little puppet things, you understand. Now, they were terribly fond of marshmallows, the two of them, and . . ."

He prattled on, and, because Lucy and Pauline often turned the pages of the book, it must have sounded to Tim as though he was reading a story to Pauline. But the guard surely thought it the strangest story ever written, because the astronomer was not reading at all, but making it up willy-nilly off the top of his head. His marionettes escaped their wicked string-masters and went searching for the Great Marshmallow Forest, but they encountered fantastic difficulties along the way. The story grew more and more complicated, sprouting subplots and parallel plots and ambiguities until it seemed impossible they should ever be resolved. Lucy and Pauline, meanwhile, traded the pencil back and forth. The latter nodded, or looked puzzled and wrote questions, until all the details of the plan were clear, whereupon Lucy gave a signal to Lemonjello. He nodded.

"Then the Good Fairy arrived and waved his magic wand," he said, "and the two little marionettes were carried off to the Marshmallow Forest and lived happily ever after, dancing and singing and consuming marshmallows daily. The end."

"What a charming story, Lemonjello!" said Pauline. "How good of you to visit me."

"It was my pleasure, I'm sure," said the astronomer. "By the way," he added loudly, "Arden Gutz wonders if you might have an idea where Miss Wickwright is hiding. She's gone missing, you know."

"What, my old maid?" Pauline asked. "*That* Wickwright? Hmm. I fancy she's made a burrow down in the vegetable cellars. She was always fond of beets."

"Ah! I'll relay that information to Mr. Gutz, then. Guard!"

Lucy had flattened herself against the wall by the door, holding Lemonjello's cape in her hands. The astronomer held the candle, Pauline his cane. The lock creaked, the cell door opened, and Tim stood in the doorway.

"That was the daftest story I ever heard!" he complained. "Where did the Good Fairy —"

His question was swallowed by darkness, for Lucy had jumped from her hiding place and blown out his candle. Pauline extinguished the astronomer's at the same time, and before the guard had time even to gasp Lucy had thrown the cape over his head. A second later she felt Pauline poking her belly with the cane. She took her end, knelt, and made a *Pssst!* sound to alert Lemonjello.

"Help!" the astronomer cried. "She has a vegetable parer! Save me!"

Tim charged into the cell. Unable to see, he tripped over the cane and fell with a grunted *Oof!* to the floor. Lucy bolted, pulling Pauline behind her at the end of the cane. She misjudged her turning and bounced off the stone wall of the corridor, but she ignored the pain and pressed on — already she was counting her steps. The guard cursed. There was a brief scuffle and a squeal from Lemonjello, followed by the heavy pounding of Tim's boots chasing after them. Lucy reached for Pauline's hand and squeezed it to urge her on.

Now everything depended on her calculations! Yesterday, using chalk and tape, she had determined that her running strides were precisely eleven-eighths the length of Lemonjello's walking strides when the astronomer carried her piggyback. Tonight, while suffocating under his cloak, she had counted the astronomer's steps from the granite lintel to the cell door. Before explaining the plan to Pauline she had worked out the grueling problem on a blank page of the book, scratching out two absurd results before arriving at a figure of ninety-seven strides. There had been some worrisome numbers left over at the end, but that was to be expected when dealing with fractions, she told herself. She would count on ninety-seven strides to the lintel.

She guided them with the cane, screeching it along the stone wall while the numbers mounted in her head. Seventy-two . . . seventy-three . . . seventy-four . . . seventy-five . . . The pounding boots drew closer — she could almost feel Tim's breath on her neck. If only the other guard had come, who was older and fatter and might still be wrestling with Lemonjello! Eighty-seven . . . eighty-eight . . . eighty-nine . . . ninety . . . Lucy closed her eyes (she could see nothing, anyway), terrified of running headlong into the cold black stone. Tim seemed to be almost upon them, but it was impossible to tell in the close, echoing corridor. Ninety-three . . . ninety-four . . . ninety-five . . . ninety-six . . .

"Now!" she cried, and she and Pauline stooped together and

ran hunched like orangutans into the void. Lucy thought she felt something brush her hair. But the boots pounded on after them, and she was beginning to think she must have miscalculated — dividing when she should have multiplied — when

PRANNNNNG!

she heard a helmet crash against the stone, and the heavy *thwump!* of a falling body.

"Sorry!" she called out — but tough meat called for sharp knives. Besides, Tim had called the astronomer "fatty," so it served him right for being rude. It was a shame her first guide to the dungeon hadn't seen it!

Lucy went more slowly now, for they would soon be at the stairs. She pushed the cane along the floor in front of them, holding back Pauline when she found the first step.

"Twenty-seven steps up," she whispered, "then through the door, past the sentry, and on to the corner tower."

"The sentry?" Pauline asked. "You didn't mention that in the plan! Won't he try to stop us?"

"I'll let the steam out of his kettle, if need be," Lucy assured her. "Just head for the tower!"

They ran up the steps toward the dim light issuing from the gatehouse. There was a kind of barracks at the top of the stairs, where the guards made tea and took shelter on rainy nights. It had *felt* empty when Lucy passed through it under the astronomer's cape. It must be got past in any case, and they could not turn back, so she saw no sense in sneaking up to reconnoiter it. She charged up the steps, crossed her fingers for luck, and ran through the barracks at full gallop.

It was deserted. She glanced at Pauline running a few paces behind, and her heart beat a joyful anthem. She had done it! She had got her mistress out of the dungeon! Together they could hurdle any obstacle — they had only to get back to the castle keep to make their final escape!

With these exulting thoughts she ran to the carriageway that led from the drawbridge to the ward. The portcullis had been lowered and heavily guarded since the day of the uprising, so she would have to follow the tunnel to the ward, sprint to the corner tower, and lead Pauline through the labyrinth of passage-ways, catacombs, and crypts to the castle keep. She charged tri-umphantly down the carriageway, but where it issued into the courtyard she encountered something for which she had no clear plan — a dozen of Henry Wallow's soldiers, standing squarely in her path.

She had rescued her mistress at the hour of the changing of the guard.

"Lucy!" cried Pauline.

It was a blow on the magnitude of losing the skeleton key, and Lucy had only a second to devise a plan for dealing with these twelve armed men. She had no weapons, no path of re-treat, and no hope of escape. Her only asset was her momen-tum — but that she had in abundance, and she let it determine her career.

"*Aya-a-a-a-a-a-gh!*" she cried. She threw herself at Wallow's men, swinging the cane at their necks as though she wielded the deadliest sword ever forged.

The soldiers — who had been gossiping, or boasting, or rubbing sleep from their eyes — bolted in frank terror from this juggernaut of girlish fury. To a man they leapt from her path, scattering swords and helmets, covering their ears as from the dire omen of a banshee's cry. At Lucy's heels Pauline ran unmolested through the scattered ranks, and as she passed them she stuck out her tongue. She caught up with Lucy at the corner tower.

"You bowled them down like duckpins!" she panted.

"The prisoner!" Wallow's sergeant cried, brushing dirt from his tunic. "After them!"

"No time!" said Lucy. "Run!"

They flew down the stairs. Lucy had placed candles along her route, at the greatest possible intervals, so that by steering from one to the next she might safely pass through the dark bowels of the castle. She gave the first candle a *whack!* with her cane as she passed it, leaving the way dark behind them. But already the chase was joined! Behind her she heard the clatter and curses of tumbling soldiers (for she had put the candles on low boxes that she and Pauline could easily hurdle, but which brought down their pursuers in the dark). *Whack!* She struck another candle, and urged Pauline to hurry. *Whack!* They ran through a cellar ripe with mushrooms and along a dark passage toward the flanking tower. The sound of pursuit grew dim.

"Might we rest a moment?" Pauline gasped, when it seemed all of Wallow's men had turned back, or fallen, or lost their way.

"Not just yet!" said Lucy. She was winded too, but unless the sergeant was an utter fool he had sent men to intercept them at the flanking tower. When she had got Pauline beyond that they might rest a moment, and from there they had only to rush to the secret stairs, where Delagraisse waited — she hoped! — with a knapsack and supplies.

It proved well that they pressed on. The tower was not yet held against them, but two men came flying down the stairs from the courtyard as the girls raced to the passage beyond.

"Halt!" one shouted. "Halt, or taste steel!"

"Catch us!" Pauline taunted.

They ran into a cellar heaped with barrels, crates, and boxes. Here, against her every instinct, Lucy had to slow down, for Pauline had fallen back and they must be together when she sprung her final trap. She pulled her mistress's arm. Behind them she saw the dark shapes of the gaining soldiers.

"Hurry!" she cried.

Lucy and Delagraisse had piled a teetering mountain of empty barrels at the far end of the cellar. It was an avalanche-in-waiting. Lucy had only to knock loose a wooden wedge beneath it to bring the barrels tumbling down. But Pauline was hampered in her running by the long skirts of her mourning dress, and Lucy had almost to carry her the last several yards to the booby trap. She pushed her mistress into the passage beyond. The men were not five yards behind her when she brought down the barrels with a *whack!* of her cane.

"Look out!" yelled one of the soldiers.

The thunder was deafening. The empty barrels crashed and rumbled down, and Lucy nearly fell when a skittering bung rolled under her foot. Pauline caught her and dragged her away from the splintering chaos. Curses rose above the booming casks. The girls ran on to the next candle, where, without a word spoken, they both stopped.

"Oh Lucy!" Pauline panted. She was bent nearly double, hands propped on her knees, a tremendous grin on her face.

"This is *beyond* a madcap caper! This is *legendary*! I shall compose a poem in heroic couplets . . . with choruses for singing along!"

Lucy looked back down the corridor. She heard footsteps and a strife of tongues. A barked order was followed by the ominous *boom!* of a barrel striking stone. Already the soldiers were dismantling her roadblock.

"I hope you needn't write it in prison," she said. "They've sent reinforcements, I'm afraid. Have you got your wind? One last sprint, and we'll be free!"

"I'll race you!"

The girls were veteran runners — Pauline was forever chasing Lucy with warty toads or muck at the end of a stick — but Wallow's men were dogged in their pursuit. Lucy flew down the stairs to the deepest catacombs at such a pace that she stumbled at the bottom, falling headlong on the stones. Thudding boots echoed down the passage behind them.

"No time to rest!" said Pauline, helping her up. (She was having a delightful time.) "They're behind us again. Come on! We're almost there!"

They ran on, rounding a corner and flying down another passage. The last candle shone like a beacon at the crypt of alpine sporting tackle. They reached it together, and when Lucy had blown out the flame she tossed aside her cane and followed Pauline inside. Blaise Delagraisse was there. He stood beside the wardrobe to the secret stairs, clutching a knapsack in one hand and a dark lantern in the other. The wardrobe's doors gaped open, and between them, like an audacious tongue, protruded the back half of a bobsled.

"You did it!" the under-footman cried. "I knew you would!"

"You need to hide!" Lucy said, taking the knapsack from him and hoisting it to her back. "They're just behind us! Did you get a map?"

"I think Dr. Sauersop put one in," said Delagraisse. "You'll take care, Lucy, won't you?"

"May I steer, Lucy?" said Pauline. She had already clambered on to the bobsled.

"I don't think there will be much steering involved," Lucy said. Pauline gave the ropes an experimental tug, and Lucy turned to Delagraisse. "Thank you, Blaise! Now run, quickly, or you'll be caught!"

The under-footman seemed untroubled by the approaching boots and shouts of *This way!* and *Get her!* He shone the dark lantern on Lucy's face.

"I'll just see you off, Lucy," he said. "I've brought you these as well!"

He showed her an old helm that he had pilfered from one of the castle's many armories. When he had helped her to climb aboard the bobsled he fitted the helm snugly on Lucy's head, then produced another one and put it on Pauline.

"In case you take a tumble," he explained.

"This is *such* fun!" said Pauline, settling her helm. "Off we go!"

"Halt!" a man shouted.

Lucy looked round in terror. An archer stood at the entrance of the crypt, an arrow already fitted to his bowstring. Delagraisse leaned close to Lucy, his face only inches from hers.

"Good luck!" he said, and before he launched the bobsled he dared to kiss her. Lucy gasped, and her eyes lit up with brilliant stars and fireworks — for the archer had let his arrow fly, and it had ricocheted — *ping!* — off her helm and knocked her head against Pauline's. The bobsled fell forward on its greased runners, and Lucy had just wits enough to hold on to Pauline, who gave a mighty *whoop* as they hurled into the abyss.

Chapter 25

UN-TITLED

$\mathcal{L}$ucy woke with a tremendous pain in her noggin. In the feeble light she could just make out Pauline bending over her — two Paulines, actually, until Lucy had blinked several times and brought her eyes into focus. She sat up, wincing, and saw the splintered remains of the bobsled scattered across the floor of the cave.

"I don't think we should rest," Pauline said anxiously. "Can you walk at all?" She looked toward the stairs, down which echoed the grunts and thumps of men heaving furniture about.

Lucy thought she could walk. Her limbs, anyway, were not bent at peculiar angles. She stood, staggered, and clutched at Pauline, who held her till the wooziness passed. A great shout came down the stairs, and a crash, followed by the rumbling of boots.

"I must have swooned when the arrow struck me," Lucy said. Her helm, creased by the bowman's shot, lay at her feet. "I don't remember coming down the stairs."

Pauline kicked aside the debris of the bobsled as she led Lucy across the cave. A lamp, lighted by Delagraisse hours earlier, burned on a rock near the entrance.

"I'm glad your fellow thought of those helms," Pauline said. "But I must say, they didn't used to make bobsleds like they do today. One go down the stairs turned that one to kindling!"

She crawled under the bramble at the cave's mouth. Lucy followed her through the crack in the stone cliff, but when she stood up on the other side of the bramble everything went black. She woke a moment later, with Pauline gazing down at her and softly patting her cheek.

"You mustn't do that," Pauline said. From the cave's mouth, Lucy heard the rumbling of boots and a rattling of scabbards. Their pursuers were coming down the stairs.

"I'm sorry," she said. "I took quite a knock on my head, I think." She lifted her hand and found a great goose-egg pushing up her hair. Spy work, she reflected, was certainly hard on the skull! She had only just recovered from the bruise she suffered in Orloff's office, and now here was another one.

"That was great fun, Lucy," Pauline said, "but I'm afraid they're after us. Can you hobble a bit? I'll stand and fight if need be, but I don't like to draw blood if there's a way around it."

Lucy sat up.

"We must slow them down," she said, rubbing her head. "Suppose we pile up the bits of bobsled at the bottom of the stairs, and pour the lamp oil over them?"

"That will do the trick!" Pauline said. "You rest here. I won't be a second!"

She crawled into the cave. Lucy desperately wanted to lie down, but she was afraid of having another black spell if she closed her eyes. She stood up — slowly — and walked back and forth, letting the night air clear the mustiness from her head. The moon had not yet risen, but the stars gave a good light. Soon a red-orange glow flickered at the mouth of the cave, and a moment later Pauline crawled out, stood, and briskly rubbed her hands together.

"That's burning nicely!" she said. "Can you walk a bit now?"

Lucy nodded — and immediately regretted it, for it made her goose-egg throb horribly.

"I feel better," she said. "Come, we must hurry!"

The guards' cries as they raced down the stairs now seemed dangerously close, and if the old bobsled had caught fire quickly it would burn out quickly, too. But they had marched only a few steps when Lucy wheeled around and stared in anguish at the cave.

"The knapsack!" she cried. Only now did she miss its weight on her back. If she had dropped it on the stairs they would never get it back, and would have to cross all the leagues of the Barony without a map or any supplies. She had packed her beloved new jumper in it, as well. Pauline tugged impatiently on her t-shirt.

"You silly dolt!" she said. "I've had it all along!"

She turned and showed Lucy the knapsack on her back, then led her toward the fringes of the Micklewood, some three hundred yards away. Lucy could not run — it jogged her head awfully — but with Pauline's encouragement she made a brisk pace, and they had covered perhaps half the distance when faint barked orders sounded from atop the cliff, where the towers of Castle Cant hid the stars. An ominous creaking of timbers followed the word of command, and Pauline and Lucy exchanged an incredulous glance.

"That couldn't *possibly* be a catapult?" Pauline asked.

"*Pull!*" came the answer from above.

"*Run!*" Lucy cried.

They dashed for the Micklewood, but drew up short when a great rain of stones threw up the earth ahead of them. The projectiles struck sparks from the flinty soil and hurled great clumps of dirt and grass. Pauline pulled Lucy to the ground, then leapt up and dragged her back toward the cave, both of them spitting pebbles. But from the cave's mouth there now came a clamor of voices and the sound of swords striking the burning bobsled. Lucy clutched at Pauline's dress.

"No!" she said. "The fire won't stop them!"

"They're not playing fair!" Pauline protested.

Lucy had no choice, now, but to run with Pauline over the cratered ground — headache or no headache. They raced for the wood, but whoever directed the barrage from the towers must have had the eyes of an eagle. Scarcely had they regained their original position when the order came again.

"*Pull!*"

They ran on. When the missiles fell Lucy covered her face and charged blindly through the hurled-up dirt and stones, shrieking when a frightened bird flapped past her ear, its nest destroyed. Henry Wallow must have armed the catapults after the siege began, she realized, for the weapons were not normally supplied with ammunition, and indeed had thrown nothing but a pair of bloomers since the reign of Gustaf the Fey.

When the volley had ended she looked over her shoulder for Pauline. Hampered by the long skirts of her mourning dress, and burdened by the knapsack, her mistress had again fallen behind.

"Hurry!" Lucy called. Her head throbbed horribly, but she took heart in the knowledge that only three catapults stood on the castle's north wall. If they could survive one more barrage they would easily reach the wood before Wallow's men could reload the first weapon.

"*Pull!*" came the order from above.

Lucy redoubled her pace, and had gone perhaps ten more yards when an ominous whistling heralded the impact of an enormous projectile. A great, thudding *WHOOMP!* shook the ground, and she was engulfed in an almost solid wave of soil and stones. In the midst of the debris Pauline flew by, fully six feet off the ground and flipped upside down by the force of the explosion. She passed Lucy with her arms flapping wildly and a look on her face of profound indignation. Ten yards farther she came to Earth, bouncing twice on the springy turf before skidding to a halt in the shallow bowl of a fresh crater. By the time Lucy reached her she had already scrambled to her feet and was shaking a grass-stained fist at the unseen artillerymen.

"You great, ugly, cocoanut-eating *baboons!*" she cried.

Lucy had to hold her mistress back from charging the enemy single-handedly. When Pauline called someone a "baboon," you knew her dander was up. When she added "cocoanut-eating," it was prudent to hide the sharp objects and duck behind a stout piece of furniture. Lucy dragged and pushed her the last few yards to the outlying brush of the Micklewood, from which point Pauline went on with only an occasional blood-curdling oath.

Their pursuers had now got past the burning wreckage of the bobsled, and with manly cries and unsheathed swords they charged from the cave in search of their quarry. Lucy pulled Pauline into a thicket and put a hand over her mouth. The men passed within twenty yards of them, and Lucy thought they must surely be caught, but after an anxious moment the swords-men crashed away through the brush in the wrong direction. When their cries faded, Lucy thought she and Pauline might rest a moment, but then she heard a tumult of barking up in the castle. Someone had set loose the hounds.

The wood was full of owls' hootings and unseen rustlings, and when they had passed Micklewood Pond the brush grew thicker and began to trespass on the path, forcing them to walk single file. Thorns snagged their clothes, and luminous eyes, it seemed, watched in the dark.

"Will the moon come up soon?" Pauline asked presently, stopping to pull her dress loose from a bramble. It had got thoroughly snagged, and she huffed pettishly as she ripped it free. Pauline had carried the knapsack since they left the cave, Lucy remembered, and was no doubt exhausted. Lucy was used to late hours, having lived as a ghost these last days, but Pauline had probably been sleeping fourteen hours a day in the dun-geon, with no one to talk to and nothing to do but make up rhymes in her head.

"The moon won't rise for an hour, at least," Lucy told her. "Perhaps we'd better rest. The hounds don't seem to have picked up our scent, thank goodness."

"Yes, rest!" Pauline said, promptly sitting down on the path. "A splendid proposal. I'm starving and my feet hurt. Is there any food in this bag?"

"Oh mistress, I'm sorry — I asked Jane to find walking clothes for you. There may be more comfortable shoes in the bag, as well as food."

"If there's no food, I'll eat the shoes!" Pauline declared, untying the knapsack's drawstring.

They emptied the bag and found that Jane had packed jodhpurs and a white woolen shirt for Pauline, along with a pair of supple, calf-high riding boots. There was flatbread, and cheese, and water in a flask of embossed leather. Someone among Lucy's grown-up allies had thought to include a magnetic compass. Pauline shrieked to discover several tablets of chocolate, which Lucy promptly insisted must be rationed (for she imagined Pauline running wild under the influence of a large dose). There was a medical tin with a little bottle of iodine, and a pocket edition of that invaluable guide, *Flora & Fauna of Cant.* The bag also held dried fruits, a knife, matches, a small saucepan, and a parchment bound tightly with string.

"Oh, Dr. Azziz put in a map," said Lucy. Pauline had taken off her fancy shoes, and stood up now to pull on the jodhpurs. "We must try not to eat too much," Lucy told her. "Or we may very well have to eat the boots before we get to La Provence."

"I do love wearing trousers," said Pauline, tugging the mourning dress over her head. "I always envied you that, Lucy."

"Envied *me?*" Lucy took the dress from Pauline, folded it,

and stuffed it into the bottom of the knapsack. Pauline put on the woolen shirt and pushed its tails into the jodhpurs.

"If I so much as smudged my hands I was plonked into a bath," she said. "I *so* hated bathing and dressing, bathing and dressing, a dozen times a day. No one ever minded that you were dirty, or not properly dressed."

"No, I suppose they didn't," said Lucy. She took up the knife and sliced the cheese as thinly as possible, then tore off a piece of bread. "Though Mr. Vole didn't like us to stink. Here you are, mistress."

She gave Pauline the bread and cheese.

"You know," Pauline said, "you needn't serve me, Lucy."

Lucy blushed.

"Of course not," she said. "I only —"

"And that's three times tonight you've called me 'mistress,' by my count," Pauline went on.

"I'm sorry," said Lucy, "only I —"

"It's certainly queer," Pauline said. "I shan't deny it's a queer situation we find ourselves in. I should think it makes you dizzy! One day you're a maidservant, laying out clothes and carrying up the teapot, and the next day you're the heiress to a whole great barony, and people are shooting arrows at you!"

"I think the arrow was meant for you," Lucy objected.

"I suppose that's so. But do you know what's truly queer?"

"What's that, miss — oh, there I've done it again! What's that, Pauline?"

Pauline swallowed a bit of cheese, then sipped from the flask and gave it to Lucy.

"I was so distraught about Papa — and you were so kind to

bear with me, Lucy, when you knew the truth by then, and might have gone to Henry Wallow and waged war on me instead . . . I was so upset that I couldn't think properly. And then there was the funeral and all that riot, and I was clapped in the dungeon and found guilty of treason, and sentenced to be banished . . . Did you know I was to be banished?"

"Mr. Lemonjello told me," Lucy said.

"I'm out of *that* pickle, thanks to you. But I was so *dreadfully* dull in the dungeon that I had time to think, at least. And it struck me — do you promise not to laugh?"

"Of course not! I mean, yes, I promise!"

"One knew, of course," Pauline said, "that you were the rightful heiress, because you were Papa's natural child, and you were born first. Those are the rules. And I'd *much* rather be Poet Laureate, and wear trousers every day. But in the dungeon it occurred to me, that if Papa was your father, and he was my father, then we are sisters, you and I! Isn't that absurd? I didn't think of it till then!"

Lucy coughed, and sipped from the flask. In all the time since she had learned the secret of her birth she had never dared to think of Pauline as her sister. That she should be the Baroness was somehow easier to grasp, for that was merely a title, something of concern to grown-ups, and of no more real consequence than an outfit of clothes, or a new way of wearing her hair. But to find that she had a sister was a great matter indeed. It meant that her family was not wholly taken from her, though Lon and Hester Wickwright and little Casio slept forever in the graveyard of Tenesmus. It meant that though she was still an orphan — twice an orphan, now Lord Cant was dead — Lucy was no longer alone in the world. She had a sister. She put down the flask and wiped her mouth, and, when Pauline was not looking, brushed a tear from her cheek. She vowed that, though Orloff or Wallow should hound them both to Boondock and back, no one would ever part them again. Then she said *"OOF!"* — for Pauline had squeezed her so tightly that her glasses went awry.

"So you mustn't *mistress* me, Lucy," she said. "It simply won't do. Besides, I much prefer a sister to a maid!"

"But you've lost your title, as well as all your servants!"

"Oh, I shouldn't know how to rule a barony," said Pauline. "There are those ghastly executions. And one has to give speeches! You're welcome to the title."

"But I've renounced it, too," said Lucy. "I'm a traitor, you know. I helped you escape."

"Why, that's true! We're two fugitives, Lucy! Isn't it grand?"

"It's certainly a madcap caper. Whatever will they do without a baroness?"

"Oh, they'll hunt up a cousin, I suppose. Eugenia Martlet would be only too happy to play baroness, the horrid girl, with her coat of arms and her silly mussel shells or."

"Or *what*?" Lucy asked. Pauline giggled.

"Or *not*," she said. "Would you care for a slice of cheese?"

The moon rose above Mount Quisling just as they gained the East Road, which ran from Tenesmus to the far reaches of Cant. The moonlight was as cheering as dawn after the earlier darkness, and at the edge of the road they stopped. Pauline turned expectantly to Lucy.

"Which way do we go?" she asked.

"Why, to La Provence," Lucy said. "To your grandfather. You'll be safe there."

"I know *that*. I meant, do you know how we get there?"

"Well," Lucy said, "this is the East Road. It goes direct to La Provence, only I'm afraid we oughtn't take it. They'll search for us on the main roads, surely. And the East Road goes through Haslet March, which is Henry Wallow's country, and I don't like to go there at all."

A breeze shook the treetops. Lucy heard the far-off clanging of a bellwether.

"Then what shall we do?" asked Pauline.

Lucy had been mulling that very question. She had never traveled beyond the familiar poles of Tenesmus and Castle Cant. Now she must lead Pauline across the countless leagues to La Provence, on foot, without money, probably pursued by both Wallow's supporters and the forces of Vlad Orloff. The entire journey would be through hostile territory, for any town that supported Pauline must consider Lucy an upstart, while Lucy's partisans would condemn Pauline as a pretender. Her Uncle Hock might have advised her, but Tenesmus was already a Wallovian stronghold, and Lucy dared not take Pauline there. They would have to find the way together.

"I think," she said, "that we may safely follow the East Road tonight. We'll try to reach the end of the Micklewood, and then find a road north, toward Great Pillow. We can rest when we're out of the wood."

"Find a road?" said Pauline. "You don't know where it is?"

"No," Lucy admitted. "At least not yet. Let's have a look at the map."

She shrugged off the knapsack — they had taken turns

carrying it — and dug out the rolled-up parchment. The knotted string came loose with a tug, and Lucy held the corners while Pauline unrolled it.

The sheet was blank.

"Wrong side," said Pauline.

Lucy turned the parchment over.

"But I asked for a map!" she cried, "not a coat of arms!"

They held the parchment between them. It was indeed a coat of arms, though drawn in the shape of a lozenge and topped with a true-lovers' knot. Dr. Sauersop must have sent it, Lucy realized. He had mentioned something about arms at their midnight meeting, but in the anxiety of the past few days she had forgotten all about it.

"Why, they're *your* arms, Lucy!" Pauline said. "It could only be that!"

Lucy, though greatly troubled by the absent map, looked curiously at Sauersop's sketch. The Master Herald had debruised the arms of Cant with a baton sinister, and had charged the baton with emblems that could apply only to her. Though she had an hour ago renounced any ambition to title, Lucy felt her heart swell within her. A great lump filled her throat when she thought of the shop on Chandlers Lane. If her parents could see her now!

She put aside, for a moment, her thoughts of the road ahead. The arms belonged to her as the Baron's child, but Lucy would bear them, if she ever bore them, as the humble daughter of chandlers — as a servant who sought to combat Evil and bring forth Good.

"C-can you blazon it, Pauline?" she asked. The drawing swam in the moonlight, however much she blinked her eyes.

"Oh Lucy, it's perfect!"

She might play ignorant to tease her cousin Eugenia, but Pauline Esmeralda Simone-Thierry von Cant was no novice of the heraldic arts.

"Per chevron gules and argent, three wolves sable," she sang out — and thus far her sister's arms were the same as her own. It was with the devices on the baton that Dr. Sauersop had shown his sense of humor.

"A baton sinister sable, three Gizmobots or!"

They laughed, but this time Lucy did not ask "Or what?" A dozen other questions crowded her mind, to which a map would have provided better answers. When they had admired the scroll a little longer, Pauline put it away and lifted the knapsack to her shoulders. Lucy wiped her cheeks, and took her sister's hand, and together they set out to find where their road would lead.

~End~

Appendix

Concerning Heraldry

*C*oats of arms (or simply "arms") have their origin in the Middle Ages, when warring knights wore suits of armor into battle. Because it was hard to tell one armor-suited knight from another, the shields they carried came to be decorated (or *charged*) with emblems of the lord for whom they fought (so that they might avoid the embarrassment of chopping off the heads of their allies). Over time these shields came to represent the noble families associated with them, giving rise to the art of *heraldry*, or the study of coats of arms.

The arms of Cant may described, or *blazoned*, in terms of the field (or *ground*) of the shield and the emblems with which it is charged.

Per chevron indicates the line that separates the red *(gules)* and silver *(argent)* parts of the shield. *Three wolves sable* means the shield is "charged" with three black wolves. Thus the arms of Cant are blazoned *Per chevron gules and argent three wolves sable.*

In the case of an unmarried woman who holds a title in her own right, the arms are represented on a lozenge rather than a shield, and the helmet is replaced by a true-lovers' knot. The example shows the arms of Lady Lamprey, Baronette of Boondock, blazoned *Purpure a lamprey argent.*

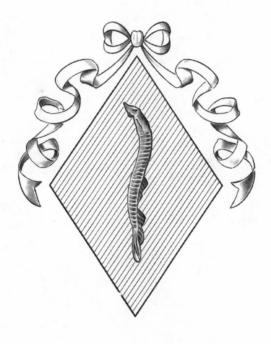

Acknowledgments

The author is grateful to Mike Street, Mary Jack Wald, and Andrea Spooner for their heroic efforts in bringing this book to publication, and to the Baronial Library of Cant for kind permission to reprint material from its archives.